T

n   en
to the hea
and the excited
that rippled ou
myriad fans.

Then he saw her. His blue gaze meshed with hers, steely and quietly intent. Its expression sent a frisson down her spine. In that look she read many things, none of them in the least bit reassuring. He had found her and there would be a reckoning. There was no way of knowing what form it might take, but suddenly it was much harder to breathe and a rabble of butterflies took wing in her stomach.

For a moment she stood transfixed as he made his way unhurriedly but inexorably through the throng towards her. It was effortless too: a word here, a touch there and the company parted to allow his advance. Claudia swallowed hard. Then, recovering some of her wits, she excused herself from the group and moved a few paces away, waiting.

And then he was in front of her, his gaze coolly appraising, taking in every last detail of her costume. In heart-thumping silence she watched him bow, then possess himself of her hand and lift it to his lips. The touch seemed to scorch.

'I believe the next dance is mine, my lady.'

Anthony Brudenell was a minor character who played a small but significant role in events. An unwilling participant in an arranged marriage, estranged from his wife, he raised some interesting questions, and it struck me then that his personal situation had the potential to become a novel in its own right. My editor agreed.

This book picks up the story three years later, but it appears Anthony has become a different man. After sustaining horrific injuries at Vittoria he is forced to resign his commission in the army. Cast out from everything he knows and values, he continues to serve his country by taking up a posting in the intelligence service.

This was a shadowy world which featured some fascinating characters—like the English spymaster William Wickham and Napoleon's Minister of Police, Joseph Fouché. The latter seems to have wielded enormous power, to the point where even Napoleon feared him. Although Fouché was out of office for a short time during the Emperor's exile on Elba, I have bent the facts slightly and brought him back a couple of months early to suit the events in my story.

As it turns out, Fouché's agents are only the beginning of Anthony's problems—because fate is about to reunite him with the beautiful and angry wife he abandoned eight years earlier.

Trapped in a marriage of convenience, Claudia has found fulfilment elsewhere and made a new life for herself—a life she conceals from fashionable London society. She has learned to enjoy freedom and independence, and has no intention of giving them up just because her absent husband has inconveniently returned. Claudia is determined to outwit him, but she has reckoned without the dangerously charismatic and powerful man who is equally determined to make her his wife in fact as well as name.

THE CAGED COUNTESS

Joanna Fulford

MILLS & BOON

the imagination … bearing the … d by any … to the author, and all the incidents are

… including … of reproduction in whole or … form. This edition is published by arrangement with … The text of this publication or … in any form … electronic or mechanical, including photocopying, … storage in an information retrieval system … or otherwise, … permission of the publisher …

First published in Great Britain 2013
by Mills & Boon, an imprint of Harlequin (UK) Limited.
Harlequin (UK) Limited, Eton House, 18-24 Paradise Road,
Richmond, Surrey TW9 1SR

© Joanna Fulford 2013

ISBN: 978 0 263 89801 9

Printed and bound in Spain
by Blackprint CPI, Barcelona

Joanna Fulford is a compulsive scribbler with a passion for literature and history, both of which she has studied to postgraduate level. Other countries and cultures have always exerted a fascination, and she has travelled widely, living and working abroad for many years. However, her roots are in England, and are now firmly established in the Peak District, where she lives with her husband, Brian. When not pressing a hot keyboard she likes to be out on the hills, either walking or on horseback. However, these days equestrian activity is confined to sedate hacking rather than riding at high speed towards solid obstacles. Visit Joanna's website at www.joannafulford.co.uk

Recent titles by the same author:

THE VIKING'S DEFIANT BRIDE
  (part of the *Mills & Boon Presents…* anthology,
  featuring talented new authors)
THE WAYWARD GOVERNESS
THE LAIRD'S CAPTIVE WIFE
THE COUNTERFEIT CONDESA
THE VIKING'S TOUCH

THE CAGED COUNTESS
features characters you will have already met in
THE COUNTERFEIT CONDESA

Look for
REDEMPTION OF A FALLEN WOMAN
part of *Castonbury Park* Regency mini-series
available February 2013

Did you know that some of these novels
are also available as eBooks?
Visit www.millsandboon.co.uk

For Barbara Smock and the Tally-Ho Arabians

Chapter One

Claudine settled back against the worn leather upholstery, letting her body relax into the swaying rhythm of the vehicle. Once or twice she glanced out of the window. Although it was still only early evening, the February rain had discouraged people from venturing abroad so the streets were quieter than usual. In truth she had no great desire to be out of doors either, but, on this occasion, it was unavoidable. Besides, it had been her choice to come to Paris and her choice to take up this post. One took the rough with the smooth. The risk had been part of the attraction. At the start of her career, this had been minimal. Since then it had increased significantly; not foolish dare-devilry but calculated risk taken for a good cause. What better cause than the service of one's country?

If her London acquaintance could see her now… She smiled wryly. It wasn't hard to envisage their shocked reactions. Her relatives would probably disown her. Most of them already viewed her actions with disapproval. The knowledge ought to have been disturbing but, instead, all she felt was a curious sense of detachment. She had been a pawn in their game for long enough. Independence had been hard won and she intended to keep it. For better or for worse it was she now who made the choices that affected the course of her life.

The fiacre turned off the main thoroughfare and into a quiet side street, eventually pulling up outside a house on the left-hand side. A lamp illuminated the number on the pillar by the door. With its stone frontage and shuttered windows there was little to distinguish this building from the others round it but, for the clientele who visited the establishment, its discreet appearance was part of its attraction. Discretion was the watchword of its proprietress too, and that made the premises useful for very different reasons. Even so, it wasn't a venue Claudine would have chosen. Her smile grew mocking. In her old life it would have been unthinkable to have gone there at all. 'But that was in another country,' she murmured, 'and, besides, the wench is dead.' She was someone else now.

Her hand moved involuntarily to the reticule in her lap, feeling the familiar shape of the pistol hidden there. It was a precaution only. Thus far she had never needed it but its presence was always reassuring. Drawing up the hood of her cloak she stepped out of the fiacre and paid the driver. He grunted an acknowledgement and then urged the horse on. As the vehicle rumbled away, Claudine hurried up the steps to the front door and reached for the bell pull.

The door was opened by a manservant whose appearance suggested that he had been hired on the grounds of size and strength rather than physical beauty. The broken and flattened nose was indicative of its owner having once been a prize fighter. He scrutinised the visitor closely for a moment and then, recognising her, greeted her with a nod and permitted her to enter. Claudine stepped into the lighted hallway and heard the door shut behind her.

'Who is it, Raoul?' The voice came from the staircase opposite. It was followed by a soft laugh. 'Well, well. Who'd have thought it?'

The speaker was a woman who stood on the upper landing surveying the scene below. Gown and coiffeur were elegant and the face carefully made up. In the subtle lighting that softened the hard lines about her mouth Madame Renaud passed for less than her forty-two years. However, despite the dulcet tone of voice, there was nothing soft about the eyes surveying her visitor. Even more disconcerting was the glint of private amusement visible there.

Claudine ignored it. 'I am here on business, Madame.'

'Aren't we all, my dear?' Madame Renaud jerked her head towards the landing. 'You'd better come up.'

Claudine joined her a few moments later. Ap-

praising eyes took in every detail of her attire from
the fine cloak to the gown just visible beneath it,
estimating their value to the last centime. The total
was quietly impressive, a fact which only served
to increase Madame Renaud's curiosity.

'I thought maybe you'd reconsidered my offer,'
she said.

'I told you, I'm here on other business.'

'Pity. With your looks you'd earn a fortune.' Madame glanced through the doorway into the room
behind them where half a dozen girls in gauzy and
semi-transparent gowns were laughing and talking
among themselves. However, it was early yet: the
clock on the mantel showed ten minutes to eight.

'You mean I'd earn you a fortune,' replied Claudine. The words were spoken without rancour and
merely stated as a matter of fact.

Madame nodded. 'You'd get a fair share of the
profits, I swear it.'

'If ever I decide to go down that road you'll be
the first to know. In the meantime I suggest we
stick to the present arrangement.' Claudine handed
over the purse concealed in the pocket of her gown.
'Is he here yet?'

Madame palmed the purse, mentally weighing
the contents, and then smiled faintly. 'This way.'

They passed along the landing and down a passageway with doors on either side. From behind
some of them Claudine could hear muffled voices,
male and female, and other more disturbing sounds

too, sounds that sent an unwonted shiver along her skin. She had often wondered what it must be like to lie with a man but, hitherto, her imagination had always explored that thought in the context of marriage. Her governess had left her in no doubt of a woman's duty in that regard, and, being a widow, Mrs Failsworth was qualified to speak.

'Intimacy is an unavoidable aspect of matrimony, my dear, and while no woman of good breeding could possibly find pleasure in it, she must be obedient to her husband's will in all things.' She proceeded to explain, with as much delicacy as she could, what that obedience involved. 'The procreation of children is the entire point of matrimony, and it is the duty of a wife to give her husband heirs to continue his line. Of course, childbirth is a painful and hazardous business. Many women die in travail or else suffer a fatal haemorrhage. Others die of childbed fever afterwards...'

Claudine listened wide-eyed and with increasing disquiet. She had sometimes wondered what happened after marriage but her imagination had never gone further than holding hands and kissing and then, after an interval, the birth of a child. Never in a million years could she have envisaged the awful possibilities that Mrs Failsworth had described, yet it seemed to be an inescapable fate.

Society regarded marriage as the only career open to women, or women of good birth at any rate. It was essentially a business arrangement, as

Claudine knew very well, and one that took no heed of personal inclination or feelings.

Certainly she'd been given no say in the matter. In her father's house his will was absolute. She'd only been informed of her forthcoming marriage when everything had been signed and sealed. Of course it was a long time ago and she had been a mere child then. In any case the marriage was dead—in all but name. In the years since, she had seen married women who seemed content enough with their lot, some even happy. Were they happy or were they pretending to be and putting a brave face on things?

That a woman might actually choose to yield herself nightly to the will of different men was something Claudine had never considered until circumstances had confronted her with the reality. Did Madame Renaud's girls find pleasure in what they did or were they driven by economic necessity? Claudine knew about the unsuspecting country girls who came to the city to seek their fortunes and whose innocence made them easy prey for the unscrupulous. Yet that didn't quite seem to fit here. Mrs Failsworth said that only women of a certain kind enjoyed intimacy with men. Was it possible to enjoy carnal union at all, never mind outside of marriage? Could any woman enjoy it, knowing she might conceive a child? Surely no woman wanted to endure childbirth, especially not an unmarried woman for whom the consequences were shame and disgrace. All the social conventions said not. It was confusing.

Madame Renaud's sphere of operations was a world completely removed from anything Claudine had ever experienced before. She hadn't known what manner of premises she was visiting that first time; all she had been given was the address and the name of the person she was to meet. It wasn't until she was inside that she realised the truth. While she hadn't baulked at being sent to seedy inns and gaming houses or masked balls held in distinctly disreputable surroundings, this was beyond all bounds. She had expressed her indignation to her employer when next they met.

Paul Genet had surveyed her with amused surprise. 'I did not think you squeamish, Claudine.'

'I'm not squeamish. I merely thought you might have told me beforehand what to expect.'

'Perhaps I should have. At all events you'll be prepared next time.'

'Next time!'

'Yes.' Seeing her expression he hurried on. 'You need not let it concern you, my dear. You will be there for a few minutes only; just long enough to meet your contact and retrieve the information we need.'

'Why there when there must be a dozen other places?'

'Because Madame Renaud can be relied upon to keep her mouth shut.'

'Even so, I cannot like it.'

'You are not required to like it.'

'Just as well, isn't it?'

He sighed. 'All right, I admit it's not the most reputable establishment in Paris, but it's safe and the information that we obtain is vital to the British war effort. Besides, you're an experienced and trusted operative.'

She shook her head. 'Save your flattery for someone who will appreciate it.'

'It wasn't flattery. I employ you because you're good at what you do.'

Claudine eyed her companion steadily. She guessed him to be in his mid-forties. Soberly clad, he was a short man with a form tending towards corpulence and a head that was almost bald. What hair remained was light brown and close-cropped. The round, clean-shaven face was unremarkable save for those small and piercing grey eyes. In a crowd of people he would have gone unnoticed. Yet she knew he had originally been recruited and trained by William Wickham, and the old spymaster had only ever chosen the best. The fact that Genet held her in regard was flattering whether she cared to admit it or not.

'All right, I'll go.'

'I knew you wouldn't let me down.'

'I have never let you down.'

'That's why I employ you,' he replied.

* * *

A series of ecstatic male cries recalled her attention abruptly. Claudine darted a glance towards the closed room that was the source of the sounds and then looked quickly away. Madame Renaud smiled.

'Estelle always knows how to please a man,' she observed. Then, seeing the look of embarrassment on her companion's face, the older woman raised an eyebrow. 'You can hardly be shocked. You're a married woman after all.' She nodded towards the wedding ring on Claudine's hand. 'The only difference is that we get paid for what we do.'

Claudine made no reply. She might be a married woman but she had no notion of what it meant to please a man in that way. What subtle arts could elicit the kind of pleasure she had heard from behind that door? Likely she would never know. With an effort she dragged her mind back to the task at hand, annoyed that she had allowed herself to be side-tracked in that way. Respectable women did not think about such things, much less discuss them. But then respectable women weren't found in bordellos either. The knowledge did nothing for her peace of mind.

They reached the end of the passageway and Madame Renaud gestured to the door on the right. 'In there.'

The room smelled of stale perfume and sweat. It was simply furnished with a large curtained bed, a wash stand with a mirror hung above, and a chair.

Two wall lamps provided soft light but its range was limited and the edges of the room were in shadow. The window opposite was closed and shuttered. The silence felt charged. Claudine frowned.

'Alain?'

The shadows stirred and a man moved into her line of vision. Claudine's heart leapt towards her throat. It was certainly not Alain. For a start he was a head taller than the person she had come to meet and the lithe, powerful figure bore not the least resemblance to the stocky frame she had been expecting to see. As he turned she drew in a sharp breath. The face with its almost sculptural lines must once have been handsome. However, two jagged scars marred the left side of his brow. Below it the eye and the cheek were concealed by a patch of dark leather. He seemed to emanate a dangerous virile power whose effect was both striking and unnerving.

With an effort she gathered her wits. 'Forgive me, monsieur. I must have mistaken the room.'

Her expression and the indrawn breath had come as no surprise to the man opposite. He was accustomed now to the way others regarded him; in fairness his appearance was hardly calculated to reassure.

'I think not, madame.'

He moved further into the room so that he could see her properly. The result gave him a visceral jolt.

In the first place she was much younger than he had expected; twenty or a little more perhaps. In the second she was stunning. The soft light fell on glossy brown curls whose colour reminded him of newly hulled chestnuts. They framed a lovely face dominated by huge dark eyes and the most seductive mouth he had ever seen. She was just above the average height for a woman and her figure slender. The details were hidden beneath her cloak. For a second or two he indulged the fantasy of removing it. Any man would want to do the same, he thought. Genet was clearly growing more subtle in his recruitment. In keeping with French tradition he employed women as well as men for intelligence work, but the women in question didn't usually look like this one. Nor was her manner that of a courtesan. No doubt he utilised her beauty and apparent innocence in higher spheres. After all, government ministers and foreign ambassadors were no more immune to female charm than any other man. Several of them patronised Madame Renaud's establishment. The connection was all too evident. He took another pace towards her.

'You came here to meet Alain Poiret.'

Claudine's heart thumped. She used to think she was tall but this man towered over her. In the confined space he was altogether an intimidating presence. However, she couldn't afford to let him see that. Lifting her chin she met his gaze squarely. 'What do you know of Alain? Who are you?'

'My name is Antoine Duval.'

She guessed it was assumed: real names tended to get people killed.

'You must be Claudine,' he continued.

'Perhaps. Where is Alain?'

'Fouché's men arrested him last night.'

Claudine paled. The name of Napoleon's Chief of Police was well known and with good reason. The ramifications filled her with silent horror. 'Arrested?'

'Alain suspected that he was being watched,' her companion continued, 'but he managed to get a message to me before they took him.'

'Why you?'

'Because I work for the same organisation as you do, and with the same aim in mind; to gather information for the British government.'

'Alain never mentioned you.'

'He never mentioned you either, until he feared that your safety had been compromised. I am come in his stead to warn you.'

Unnerved by the news as much as by the man before her, Claudine had to make herself think. The story seemed genuine. It was very much in keeping with Alain's character that he would seek to warn her somehow. If he had chosen Duval to do so it was because he trusted him. It went against the grain to be beholden to anyone, but she had perforce to acknowledge herself obligated.

'I am grateful, monsieur. You took a risk.' Then the rest of what he had said filtered through the chaos of her thoughts. If Alain was being watched did Fouché's agents know who his other contacts were? Did they know about her? Were they just waiting for the right moment to spring the trap?

As if he had read her thoughts Duval went on, 'It is a matter of conjecture as to how much Fouché's men have already discovered. What is certain is that Alain will eventually be made to talk. It is too dangerous for you to remain here.'

'I can't just leave him to his fate.'

'There's nothing you can do to help him now, except to make his effort count. You must heed the warning and get away while you still can.'

That went against the grain too, but she knew he was right. 'I must return to my apartment. There are things I…'

'You can't go back there. It's the first place they'll look. We must leave at once—tonight.'

Claudine's chin lifted. 'We?'

'I gave Alain my word I'd get you to safety. There's a carriage waiting at the end of the street.'

Having no intention of putting herself in the power of this stranger, she shook her head. 'I can take care of myself.'

'A woman alone? I think not.'

'How do you think I got here in the first place?'

'It's easy enough to fall into a trap,' he replied, 'but a lot harder to get out.'

'I have my own contingency plans for leaving France. The matter need not concern you.'

'It does concern me, in every way.'

'I can manage. You have done your part, monsieur.'

'My part is just beginning.' His hand closed on her arm and drew her towards the door. Feeling her resist he frowned. 'We don't have time to argue.'

'I said I wasn't going.'

'Don't be a fool.'

The cutting tone and accompanying look raised her hackles at once. She stopped, swinging round to face him. 'How do I know that this isn't a trap?'

'If it were you'd be under arrest already.'

In spite of her protests, Duval threw open the door and drew her with him along the passage towards the staircase. Madame Renaud was waiting on the landing. She started to speak but the words were drowned out by heavy fists pounding on the door below. Then a man's voice called out.

'Police! Open up!'

Before anyone could say more they heard the unmistakeable order echoed from the rear of the premises. Claudine's stomach lurched. Duval swore softly. Then he looked at Madame Renaud.

'Is there another way out of here?'

Madame shook her head. The banging on the

door intensified. She leaned over the balustrade
and called softly to the flunky below.

'Wait another minute and then open it, Raoul.'
Then she turned back to her companions. 'Come
with me. Quickly.'

They needed no urging and moments later found
themselves back in the room they had so recently
vacated. Claudine looked round in bewilderment.
The only way out was the window but they were
on the first floor. Even if they weren't seen by
those outside, such a leap meant a broken leg at
the very least. It was crazy. She saw Madame look
at Duval and knew that some silent message had
been passed and understood.

'What?' she demanded.

'Take your clothes off and get into bed,' he replied.

Madame nodded. 'I'll delay them as long as I
can.'

With that she was gone.

Chapter Two

Claudine stared after her in stunned disbelief. Then she turned to speak to her companion but the words died on her lips for he had already thrown aside his cloak and was shrugging himself out of his coat.

She regarded him coldly. 'What are you doing?'

'What does it look like I'm doing?'

'You can't be serious.'

'Come on. We haven't much time.'

'If you imagine I'm going to…'

He paused, fixing her with a fierce glare. 'You have a better plan?'

'Well no, but…'

'Then do it or, by heaven, I will! This tardiness is like to get us killed.'

She knew he was right but that didn't make things any easier. She had never undressed in front of a man in her life. Reluctantly she unfastened her cloak and let it fall.

Seeing her comply, Duval continued undressing; coat and cravat joined his cloak and he sat down on the bed and began to tug off his boots. From below came the sound of raised voices. The police were in the hallway. Claudine fumbled with the fastenings of her gown. Her companion tossed his boots aside and dragged off his shirt. She had a swift impression of a hard-muscled torso and savage scars down the left arm and shoulder, and then looked hurriedly away resuming her struggle with the buttons.

Duval sighed. In two strides he was across the room. Strong hands turned her round and lifted her hair aside. In seconds the buttons were undone. Warm fingers brushed her skin as he slid the gown off her shoulders and, while she struggled out of the sleeves, unfastened the petticoat and stays beneath. It was accomplished with the smooth ease of one completely familiar with women's clothing. Moments later she was standing in chemise and stockings and his fingers were unfastening the pins that held her hair. Glossy curls tumbled in disarray about her shoulders.

Booted feet sounded on the stairs and she could hear Madame Renaud's angry protests. Then a man's voice barked orders.

'Search every room! The woman's here somewhere.'

Claudine's heart thumped painfully hard. It was her they meant. Alain must have talked. The poor man would have had no choice. She could only

imagine what methods had been employed to break
him. If they caught her she could expect the same.
For a moment cold terror replaced rational thought.
Her companion crossed to the bed and pulled back
the coverlets.

'Get in.'

Dumbly she obeyed, sliding across the chilly
sheets to the far side. As she pulled the covers over
herself Duval saw the soft gleam of metal on her
hand and, for the first time, noticed her wedding
band. He frowned.

'Take off the ring.'

She struggled for a moment or two and then
shook her head. 'It's too tight.'

'Then keep your hand out of sight.'

Swiftly he drew the bed curtains closed and then
came to join her. Outside, the booted feet came
closer, punctuated at intervals by feminine screams
and male oaths. Claudine shivered. He felt it.

'Don't be afraid,' he murmured. 'Just play your
part and say as little as possible.'

Inwardly he wondered how long her nerve
would hold. Alain had said she was a skilled operative but, just then, Duval was far from convinced.

The darkness inside the curtained bed made
it impossible for him to see her face, a circumstance for which Claudine was devoutly thankful. His words, though kindly meant, demonstrated
clearly what he thought her to be. It was all of a
piece with his casual assumption that she would

have no objection to their physical intimacy. Then all reflection was driven from her mind by the hands gathering up the fabric of her shift. Instinctively she reached to stop him.

'No.'

He gritted his teeth. 'If this is to be credible you must take it off.'

Another door crashed open, nearer this time, to be followed by more angry voices.

Claudine took a deep breath. 'All right, damn it.'

Hurriedly she struggled out of the chemise. He grabbed it and flung it aside. The immediacy of the cool linen sheet against her skin raised goose bumps along her arms and intensified the feeling of vulnerability. Never in her life had she been so glad of the darkness which hid her face. Then the mattress shifted under his weight and a lean hard body pressed the length of hers. Strong arms drew her closer, sharing his warmth. The musky scent of his skin sent a tremor through her that was nothing to do with their present peril. She could feel his breath against her neck and then the soft pressure of his lips. The skin seemed to burn where they touched.

'Kiss me.'

Claudine tensed. 'What!'

'Kiss me.' This time the tone was a quiet command.

'But I…'

His mouth slanted over hers cutting off protest,

gentle at first, then gradually becoming more insistent, ignoring resistance. Slowly, gently, his hands began their own exploration, their touch sending a wave of flaring warmth down the length of her. Gradually, of its own volition, her body relaxed a little and her mouth opened beneath his. His tongue teased hers. She knew it was wrong to be doing this and it should have been repellent; instead it shocked and excited.

As he felt her yield to the kiss Duval felt a familiar tightening sensation in his gut. Her body was exquisite, made for a man's touch and his own responded to it with a swiftness that astonished him. He didn't have to pretend. He'd wanted her from the moment he saw her. She filled his senses. The din from the next room faded to background noise. Suddenly, in the dark cocoon of the bed anything was possible. His lips travelled down her neck and throat to her breast, gently sucking and teasing until the nipple grew erect. He heard her gasp, felt her body quiver again. An answering heat flared in his groin. Then his mouth was over hers again, hot, ardent, seeking her response while his hands continued what they had begun.

The touch sent another flush of treacherous warmth the length of her body and triggered sensations she had never dreamed existed. An equally treacherous inner voice whispered thoughts of surrender, of submitting completely to his will, of pursuing this to its conclusion. And if she did she might become pregnant. It only needed one occasion. Horrified by her lustful response, she tried to protest but the sound was trapped in her throat. What emerged was a groan. Immediately the kiss grew deeper and more demanding. A hand caressed the length of her waist to her hip and moved thence to the secret place between her thighs, stroking gently. The touch sent liquid fire to her loins. Claudine gasped. The stroking continued. Her body quivered in response. She felt him unfasten his breeches and, moments later, his arousal hard against her leg…And then the door was flung open and booted feet tramped across the room. Ruthless hands dragged the curtains apart to reveal three uniformed officers. Duval turned and swore. That too had the merit of being genuine. Beside him, Claudine stifled a scream, dragging the sheet over her bosom, her eyes wide with shock.

Duval mentally prayed as his hand closed over her wrist in silent warning. If she lost her nerve now it was all over. Could she be relied on to play her part? Then Madame Renaud pushed past the intruders to address him.

'I'm so sorry, monsieur. It's all a misunderstanding.'

'It had damned well better be,' he replied. 'What the devil's going on?'

'We're looking for a woman,' replied the officer in charge.

'You've come to the right establishment then,' said Duval, 'only this one's spoken for.'

The officer ignored him and looked at Claudine. 'Who is this?'

With pounding heart she forced herself to return his stare, assuming what she hoped was a sufficiently brazen manner. Then she opened her mouth to speak, but Madame Renaud was before her and bristling with indignation.

'This is Fifi. She's one of my girls.'

'How long has she been in your employ?'

'About six months now.'

'Indeed.' The officer's gaze appraised Claudine silently, his gaze stripping the sheet away. 'Pretty girl.'

She wanted to slap the leering expression off his face. Instead she returned a provocative smile and fluttered her eyelashes.

'There are many pretty girls here,' replied Madame Renaud. 'And they can cater for all tastes.'

Sickened to the depths of her soul by the speculative looks directed her way, Claudine forced herself to sustain the role. Duval glared at the intruders.

'The only taste she has to cater for right now is mine.' He looked meaningfully at Madame Renaud. 'I paid you in good faith for the whole night with Fifi, and I mean to have my money's worth.'

The men standing behind their officer raised

their eyebrows and exchanged knowing grins. Madame nodded.

'Of course you do, monsieur,' she soothed. 'I can only apologise for the interruption. I hope she pleases you.'

'*Fifi* pleases me very much.' The inflection was impossible to miss.

'Monsieur Fouché says the same,' replied Madame.

The officer's head jerked round and his face paled a little. 'Monsieur Fouché? He is a patron here?'

'That's right. He values discretion, you see, and I run a discreet establishment. I don't suppose he'll be too happy when he learns about all this uproar. Nevertheless, learn of it he will because I shall certainly lodge a complaint.'

The man seemed much taken aback. 'I was merely doing my duty by acting on information received. However, it seems our information may have been wrong after all.'

Madame gave him a pitying look. 'I think someone's having a joke at your expense.'

That possibility was dawning on him too. Spots of angry colour appeared in his cheeks. 'We will withdraw.' He inclined his head towards the two in the bed. 'I beg your pardon, monsieur, mademoiselle.'

Duval eyed him coldly. 'Close the door when you leave.' Then, apparently considering the matter at an end, he turned his back on them and laid a hand over Claudine's breast. 'Now, *chérie*, where were we?'

For a moment the officer seemed rooted to the spot, not knowing quite how to respond. His men grinned broadly. Then Madame stepped in and chivvied them out into the corridor. Seeing the door finally close behind them Claudine let out the breath she had been holding and collapsed on to the pillows, trembling with relief. Duval smiled.

'Well done.'

'It is Madame who deserves our thanks,' she replied.

'She was wonderful. The police will have to look elsewhere for their spy.' He paused. 'Your performance too was…most creditable.'

'I can act a part when I have to.'

'A part you play to perfection if I may say so.'

Indignation flared. 'Yes, a part I play, and not at all what you think.'

Seeing the expression of amused scepticism that greeted these words, she squirmed inwardly. She was naked and in bed with a stranger in a brothel. Not what he thought? Dear heaven! He was only too justified in thinking it. Mortified now, she hurried on.

'This was a necessary ruse. If there had been any other way I would have taken it.'

'Of course.' The tone was gently mocking like his smile.

Claudine gathered together the last shreds of her dignity. 'I came here to meet Alain and to obtain the information he carried. The choice of venue was not mine. I would never have come here willingly any more than I would willingly have climbed into bed with you.'

She was unable to conceal the self-disgust she felt. However, Duval put a very different interpretation on her expression just then, and amusement ebbed. Despite his doubts she had indeed played her part well, but then the darkness hid all defects and she had been acting to save her life. The truth was that she found the thought of sexual congress with him to be abhorrent. The knowledge caused a sensation that was very like pain. He had thought himself past all this and it disturbed him to discover how far he was wrong. This woman had awoken something in him that he had believed dead. For a little while, in the forgiving darkness, he had thought she wanted him too. Now he felt angry with himself. His was no longer a face to attract the fair sex. That he had imagined such a woman might desire him was so pathetic it was laughable.

'You need have no fear that I would force myself on you, *chérie*,' he replied. 'I prefer my women willing.'

The tone was perfectly even but she sensed the anger beneath. It served only to increase her shame. Mingled with it was an emotion that was disturbingly like regret.

Duval turned away and swung his legs over the side of the bed. When he had fastened his breeches he glanced over his shoulder.

'Get dressed. We're leaving as soon as the coast is clear.'

Claudine located her chemise and drew it on hurriedly. 'I told you, I can take care of myself.'

She slid out of bed and reached for the pile of discarded clothing, supremely aware of the virile figure just feet away.

'I gave my word to Alain and I mean to keep it,' he replied.

'You have already kept your word.' She found her stays. 'I am grateful, truly. But this is where we part company.'

'We part company when I have delivered you safe on English soil. Now turn around.'

'Why?'

'So I can lace you up, why else?' he growled. 'Must you argue about everything?'

Claudine glared at him but, realising it would be impossible to manage alone, obeyed. 'I do not argue about everything.'

His hands moved deftly to the task. 'No?'

'No. I was just telling you…' She broke off with a startled gasp as the lacing was drawn tight.

'I know full well what you were telling me and you can save your breath.'

'I won't have any breath at this rate.'

The laces slackened a little. 'Better?' Seeing her

nod he fastened the stays and then stepped away to resume dressing. 'I don't intend to lose another English operative to Fouché's men.'

She donned her petticoat and reached for her gown. 'Why burden yourself with me since I cannot please you in any way?'

'You pleasing me or not is irrelevant.'

She sighed. 'Look, I know you mean well…'

'I mean to get you back to England.'

'You can't; not without my co-operation.'

'Your co-operation would be useful, but it isn't essential.'

Claudine stared at him. 'I'm not sure I care for the implications of that.'

'You're right; you wouldn't care for them at all.'

The words were casually spoken but something in his expression gave her pause. She had no idea what he was capable of and somehow didn't care to test the matter. He saw her uncertainty and nodded.

'You'll come with me, Claudine.'

Unsettled by that steady gaze she looked away and glanced round for her hairpins. They were strewn across the floor, scattered in the haste of undressing. She knelt and began to retrieve the nearest ones. Although fully dressed now he made no attempt to help. Claudine, quietly fuming, continued the search, only too aware of the booted feet in her line of vision and the powerful figure above whose gaze seemed to burn into her back.

The symbolism of their current positions didn't escape her. She was equally sure it hadn't escaped him either. Gritting her teeth she concentrated on her task. Eventually, when she had located enough pins, she got to her feet and moved away to the small mirror above the washstand.

For a moment or two she was startled by the face reflected there; by the rosy flush along her skin and the new sparkle in her eyes. Her lips were redder too and slightly swollen now. She could still feel Duval's mouth on hers, the touch of his hands on her naked flesh. Those five minutes in his arms had left her with an aching need, with feelings she could not afford and dared not pursue.

Confused now, and annoyed with herself as well, she turned her attention to the task in hand. However, without a brush or a comb the options were limited. Moreover, she could still feel the weight of Duval's gaze, intimate and unsettling. Hurriedly she drew her hair back and twisting it into a knot on the crown of her head, secured it there. The mirror revealed errant wisps curling around her neck and face. It was far from perfect but it would have to do.

Duval held out her cloak. He settled it over her shoulders and fastened it with unhurried deliberation. The gesture was both practical and quietly assertive. It was also unnerving, like his closeness now and the warmth of his fingers brushing against her skin.

He surveyed his handiwork and stepped back, meeting her gaze. 'Come.'

Chapter Three

Having ascertained that the coast was clear Duval led her downstairs and through the house to the back door. Madame Renaud was waiting here. Duval dropped a kiss on her cheek.

'Thank you. You were magnificent.'

'From what I could see, you weren't so bad yourself.' She raised an eyebrow.

He grinned. 'I take that as a compliment.'

'So you should.' She glanced at Claudine and her eyes gleamed. 'I knew I was right all along.'

'Right about what?' asked Duval.

'She can tell you later. You must get out of here while you can.'

Claudine paused on the threshold. 'Thank you for what you did today.'

'All part of the service.' Madame Renaud jerked her head towards the deserted street. 'Now go.'

The night air felt like an icy slap and Claudine shivered, clutching the edges of the cloak tighter. As soon as she and her companion had crossed the threshold, the door closed leaving them alone. Hearing it, she let out a long breath, never more thankful to leave a place in her life. Now all that remained was to get rid of Duval and put her own plans into execution. She turned to face him.

'I'm truly grateful for what you did in there, but this is where we part.'

For answer he resumed his grip on her arm. 'You'll do as you're told, my girl. We're not out of this yet, not by a long way.'

There was no way of knowing how far away the police were, and, without making the kind of scene that might attract unwelcome attention, Claudine had no choice now but to go along with Duval. They set off down the street, she almost running to keep pace with his longer strides. Neither one spoke. Once she tested his hold but it was like a vice. The physical contact was also a tangible reminder of what had passed. Every part of her being resonated to it and filled her with conflicting emotions. She pushed them away ruthlessly. What was past could not be altered. Just now she needed to focus all her attention on removing herself from the sphere of his unwelcome presence as soon as possible.

As they neared the end of the street she saw the waiting carriage. There was no way she was going any further.

'Please, you must listen to me…'

He might have been stone deaf. She was bundled unceremoniously into the waiting vehicle and pushed on to a seat. She heard him speak to the driver before climbing in and taking the place opposite hers. The carriage moved away. Claudine glared at her companion.

'How dare you do this?'

'You appear incapable of rational thought,' he replied, 'so I'm doing the thinking for both of us.'

'I don't need you or anyone else to think for me. I told you I had my own plans.'

'Well, now you're going to follow mine instead.'

The cool arrogance of this assertion was breathtaking. It was on the tip of her tongue to deliver a blistering reply but she bit it back. The words would roll off him like water from a duck's feathers. Instead she met his gaze.

'Where are we going?'

'St Malo,' he replied.

'St Malo! But that's days away.'

As if he hadn't heard the interjection he continued, 'From there I will arrange a passage to Jersey and thence to England.'

She knew that the Channel Islands were a favoured route into France for the British intelligence services. Even so, the thought of being shut up for the best part of a week with this man was beyond bearing.

'I'll be safe enough once we are out of Paris. I can…'

'You're coming with me. Get used to the idea.'

The tone was implacable, forbidding. Further argument would be fruitless since he was clearly impervious to reason, so Claudine lapsed into fuming silence, directing her attention to the window instead, watching the blur of streets and buildings as they sped past.

'Don't try giving me slip either,' he continued. 'I would find you very quickly and you wouldn't enjoy the consequences.'

She lifted her chin. 'No, but I'm sure you would. However, I have to tell you that you're doomed to disappointment there.'

'It's reassuring to know you have that much sense anyway.'

'I'm glad to have set your mind at rest.'

He surveyed her curiously. 'By the way, what did Madame Renaud mean when she said she was right?'

A wave of warmth flushed her neck and cheeks. 'I…it was nothing. A private joke.'

'Yet she said you would tell me.'

'Well, I'm not going to.'

Her gaze returned to the window and she missed the smile that flickered across his face.

A short time later the carriage began to slow. Glancing out of the window again Claudine's horrified gaze took in the flaring links and armed uniformed figures by the barrier at the city gate. Her stomach lurched. In the excitement of recent events she had temporarily forgotten about the routine security inspections governing travellers. Appalled, she looked at Duval.

'I have no documents. They are back in my apartment.'

'I have the necessary paperwork,' he replied. 'All you have to do is stay calm and keep your mouth shut. No doubt it will be a novelty for you.'

Claudine stared at him in impotent and dumbfounded silence. The carriage stopped and she saw him lower the window and hand the requisite documentation to the waiting official. The latter perused the sheet and glanced up. Claudine's heart thumped. Then he turned back to Duval.

'Your wife?'

'That's correct.'

'This is all in order, monsieur. You may pass.'

He handed the papers back and Duval returned them to the inner pocket of his coat. The officer touched his hat to Claudine and then called to his colleague. A moment later the barrier was raised and the carriage moved forward again. As it did so she let out the breath she had unconsciously been holding.

'I don't understand. How did you…'

Duval leaned back surveying her steadily. 'I called in a favour. Do you think I'd have attempted to conduct a rescue without some kind of forward planning?'

'No, I don't suppose you would.' She hesitated. 'Those papers describe me as your wife?'

'It was the most credible scenario I could think of, and the least likely to be challenged.'

'Yes, I can see that.' It was a detail that had other implications too, implications that caused a strange sensation in her stomach. She tried to see his expression but the dimly-lit interior made that difficult.

'I'm glad.' He paused. 'By the way, what were those contingency plans you mentioned earlier?'

Her face burned. As if her stupid oversight wasn't bad enough, it had just vindicated all his actions. How much he must be enjoying that.

'It hardly matters now, does it?'

'I'm just curious.'

'You're just gloating.'

She sensed rather saw him grin, and looked quickly away. The man was insufferable which made it doubly hard to be beholden to him. It would be pointless now to say that she'd never slipped up before today. One mistake was all it took and they both knew it. Her papers were in another reticule; she'd forgotten to transfer them before she left that evening and, after what had occurred, there would have been no possibility of going back for them. It was an elementary error but a potentially fatal one, and she could have kicked herself. No doubt it only served to reinforce his opinion that a woman alone couldn't cope.

Realising she wasn't going to be drawn further, he let it go. 'It will be a while before we stop so you should try and get some sleep, my dear. I mean to do the same.'

Claudine watched him settle back in his seat and then summoned her self-possession. 'Duval?'

'Well?'

'Thank you.'

Just for a second his expression registered surprise. 'You're welcome.' With that he drew his hat down over the upper part of his face and settled back again, bringing the conversation to a close.

Claudine shifted back into her own corner, closing her eyes, letting her body relax a little. The events of the day seemed unreal, as though she were held fast in a strange and disturbing dream from which she could not awake. Had it not been for her companion the dream might easily have become nightmare. *I can take care of myself.* She had to admit that the words sounded hollow. Her companion might be one of the most arrogant and overbearing men she had ever met, but he had done her a great service all the same.

At some point amid these thoughts she must have drifted off because the next thing she knew the carriage had stopped and the night was full of voices. She came to with a start.

Glancing out of the window she could see an inn yard and the shadowy figures of the ostlers leading the team away. Then cold air hit her face as the door opened and Duval returned.

'Where are we?'

'Just outside St Germain,' he replied.

'Are we stopping here tonight?'

'Only long enough to change the horses. I want to put a lot more distance between us and Paris before we rest.'

For once she had no wish to argue. Minutes later a fresh team was between the shafts and then they were on their way again. Since her companion seemed not disposed for conversation Claudine was left to her thoughts. Between that and drowsing occasionally the next few hours passed in a blur. It was just before midnight when they stopped again at another inn.

Duval bespoke accommodation and conducted Claudine to hers, pausing a moment on the threshold. 'Get some rest. Tomorrow will be a long day and we will be leaving early.' He paused. 'If you need me I'll be in the next room.'

With that he left her, closing the door behind him. Claudine let out a long breath. It had occurred to her that he might try to take advantage of the situation in the light of what had already happened, but it seemed she was wide of the mark. He had made no further allusion to it. Perhaps like her he thought it was a complication they do without.

Since she had no belongings with her she was forced to make do with washing her hands and face. Then, having removed her gown she sat down on the bed and emptied her reticule. Apart from the pistol it contained a handkerchief and a handful of coins. At some point in the near future she was going to have to purchase a few necessities. There was nothing to be done about her clothes since the rest were in Paris. She smiled wryly. A few dresses were a small price to pay for her freedom, perhaps even her life. Having replaced the contents of the bag she climbed into bed and extinguished the candle.

The sheets were chilly and she shivered, drawing the covers higher. It was a pointed contrast with the last time, and her treacherous thoughts conjured the memory of a man's warmth and a lean hard body pressed against hers. Unbidden she lifted a hand to her lips. She could still feel Duval's kisses there. The recollection caused a pulse of heat in the region of her pelvis, and with it forbidden thoughts. She couldn't go there, must not go there again. To do so would be disastrous and she mustn't forget it.

They left early next morning. Thus far there had been no sign of pursuit, a circumstance for which Claudine was devoutly thankful. Now that the immediate sense of urgency was gone and since her companion was still disinclined for unnecessary conversation, she began to look about her with more interest. The carriage they were travelling in was surprisingly comfortable and the driver, Matthieu, highly experienced. At first she had assumed the man had merely been hired for this journey, but now she wasn't so sure. Although he was courteous and deferential, his attitude towards Duval wasn't that of a stranger. The relationship was more like master and trusted servant. He also seemed to know the route well; where they could change horses and where the decent inns were to be found. And then there was Duval himself. He was no common adventurer. She never heard him raise his voice, but when he spoke servants leapt into action. His whole manner was that of a man used to command and to being obeyed. He had the upright bearing of a military man but his movements were almost graceful and characterised by a touch of arrogance. Yet in spite of his intimidating manner he spoke like a gentleman.

The light of day had revealed all the details of his appearance to her curious gaze. She could see now that his skin was lightly tanned and the hair that in candlelight looked to be between brown and blonde was the colour of ripe wheat. Moreover, the contrast between the injured and uninjured sides of his face was stark. It reinforced the notion that he must once have been classically good-looking, the kind of man that women noticed. His injuries had changed that significantly: he was not just attractive; the damaged face lent him a sombre and dangerous edge that was both enigmatic and exciting. He roused her curiosity as no other man had ever done.

Becoming aware of that intense scrutiny he turned from the window and his gaze locked with hers. His good eye was a clear and vivid blue, the blue of a summer sky. Just for an instant it seemed disturbingly familiar. The familiarity wasn't concerned with him since they'd only met for the first time yesterday; rather he reminded her of someone. An old memory stirred and struggled to surface, but the more she tried to retrieve it the more it eluded her. Then he spoke and the thought disappeared as quickly as it had come.

'You look worried. Are you?'

'No...at least not so much as I was. Do you think we are being pursued?'

'I think we'd have seen some evidence of it by now. All the same we can't afford to be complacent.'

He was certainly right about that. There were many other things she wanted to ask him too. His manner just then didn't seem quite so forbidding so she put a toe in the water.

'How did Fouché's men find out about Alain?'

'Someone betrayed him and, along with him, potentially an entire section of the British intelligence network in Paris.'

'A double agent?'

'It looks that way,' he said.

'Do you have any idea who it might be?'

'Not yet.'

'I never knew who Alain's other contacts were. Do you think he managed to warn them in time?'

'Let's hope so.'

'Yes.' She felt suddenly cold as the full implications became apparent. More than ever she was aware of the narrowness of her escape and, like it or not, of how much she owed Duval. 'It still begs the question though: why were they betrayed?'

'For knowing too much. Alain was on to something of great importance but he wouldn't say what it was until his sources had verified the facts. Unfortunately, they must have aroused suspicion somehow, because the police closed in before anything more could be passed on.'

'I see.'

'How on earth did you get involved in this débâcle?' he asked.

Claudine hesitated. She had never been able to talk to anyone about her clandestine activities. Indeed to have breathed a word of it would have brought ruin and disgrace. At first she had hugged the secret with quiet glee, but as time went on it became something of a liability. The chance to be able to speak freely to someone who understood was almost irresistible.

Duval heard her hesitation. 'You need not be afraid. Whatever is said here stays here.'

Something in his tone made her want to believe

it. She knew so little about him but, in spite of everything, her instinct was to trust him.

'My brother was with the army in Spain. He was killed at Talavera.'

'I'm sorry.'

She smiled sadly. 'Henry had given his life for his country while I was living in luxury and ease far from the dangers he had faced daily. His death made me question the life I was living, and suddenly it seemed shallow and worthless. I wanted to do something for the war effort on my own account but, short of joining the army myself, I could not imagine how.' She paused. 'Then I remembered that Peter, one of my cousins, worked at the Foreign Office. I wrote and asked him to call upon me.'

'I imagine he was surprised by the nature of the conversation.'

'He was at first, but he had also been very fond of Henry and perhaps that inclined him to listen sympathetically. Anyway, some days later he returned with a colleague, a man called Gabriel Viaud.'

Duval's brows drew together. 'Viaud?'

'Yes. Do you know him?'

'We've met.' He paused. 'But I'm interrupting. Please, go on.'

'I have a property on the south coast of England, an ideal location for getting informants into and out of the country unseen. Viaud asked if I would sanction the use of the coastal access for that purpose. Of course I agreed.'

Duval had been listening intently, his curiosity thoroughly roused. Was she English then? Her spoken French was impeccable. Her use of the first person hadn't escaped him either and yet she wore a wedding band. The reminder was oddly unwelcome although he had no right to find it so.

'Did your husband not have something to say about the matter?'

'I live alone, apart from the servants of course.'

'You are a widow?' Unaccountably he found himself hanging on the answer.

'Not exactly.' She hesitated. 'It's just that I haven't seen my husband for…some time. He has been serving abroad with the army.'

'I see.' It was not unusual. He should have expected it. The knowledge brought him back to earth; she was forbidden fare in every way.

Claudine said nothing. He did not see at all, but she wasn't about to go into a lengthy explanation of her personal circumstances.

He sensed her reticence and knew he had no right to probe. 'Forgive me. I digress. You were saying that you allowed your property to be used…'

'Yes. Then, a few months later, while I was in London, I was approached again by the same gentleman to find out whether I was willing to become more closely involved. The work involved minimal risk—it was merely to act as a courier taking coded messages between London and the coast.'

'And you agreed.'

'It was easy and it was something worthwhile, far removed from the giddy social round.'

'And then?'

'Then, about six months ago, I was introduced to Paul Genet. His department was looking to recruit suitable candidates for overseas intelligence. He knew of the work I had done for his associates; I could speak French and was then entirely unknown to the authorities in Paris. I was ideal for what he had in mind.'

'I can well believe it. He must have rubbed his hands in glee.'

'What's that supposed to mean?'

'He recognised a tool he could use for his purpose.'

Her eyes sparkled angrily. 'It wasn't like that.'

'No?'

The sarcasm was overt, as Duval had intended. Could she really be so naïve as to think Genet hadn't used her? Part of the émigré population who had fled their homeland during the revolution, he had lost no time in establishing a new spy network, this time providing valuable information for the British. However, he was also working with those who sought to overthrow Napoleon and restore the French monarchy. Genet and his confederates were prepared to use any means to achieve that end.

'No,' she retorted. 'It was my choice. I could have refused.'

'The adventure could have got you killed.'

'I was aware of that.'

'And it didn't deter you?'

'No, why should it? The risks were explained and I chose to accept them. Genet is not to blame.'

'Women should not be placed in dangerous situations.'

Claudine lifted one finely arched brow. 'And yet men do that to them all the time.'

'How so?'

'Men expect their wives to bear children, do they not? Yet there is no more dangerous activity for a woman.'

He frowned. 'It's not the same thing at all.'

'No, on balance, this is much safer,' she replied. 'In any case, it's my life and I'd rather spend it doing something to benefit my country than living some kind of butterfly existence in London.'

'It's a laudable aim, but it's over now,' he replied. 'This part of the network is finished.'

'This part perhaps, but I'll find another posting eventually.'

He stared at her in disbelief. 'Was this not a close enough brush with disaster?'

'It was unfortunate, but it's the nature of the business.'

'A business you would do well to stay out of in future.'

'Will you stay out of it in future?'

The tone was quietly challenging, something that rarely happened in the sphere of Intelligence work, and it provoked in him an upsurge of annoyance. 'This is my occupation, not an amusement that I took up to help me overcome boredom.'

Claudine's hands clenched in her lap. 'I do not deny boredom, but I do deny that this is mere amusement.'

'I'm relieved to hear it.'

'Genet employs me because I am good at what I do.'

'You still required rescuing.'

'And of course no-one else ever does.' The sarcastic tone was an exact imitation of his. 'In the entire history of espionage I'm the first.'

'I don't know about the first, but I'd wager that you're the most argumentative.'

'Oh, I'm sorry. I forgot. A woman mustn't do that, must she?'

The lowered eyes and dulcet tone didn't fool him for a minute. Her manner was impudent and provocative in equal measure, the kind of quiet insubordination that would have been easy to deal with in a man. In this case the options were severely limited.

'I cannot imagine what is troubling you,' he replied.

'It doesn't.' She eyed him speculatively. 'May I ask how you came to be involved in all of this?'

He was tempted to refuse; the past was an area he preferred to leave alone. However, she had been open with him to a surprising degree.

'Originally I was with Wellington in Spain,' he said, 'but then I was injured and rendered unfit for active service.'

For a brief instant he was back in the field hospital after Vittoria, lying on the makeshift operating table in the surgeon's tent where the air was heavy with the stench of blood and sweat and fear. Through the red haze of pain he could hear the screams of the poor wretches under the knife and the saw. He'd lost an eye that day along with half his face and a large quantity of blood from the sabre slashes to his shoulder and arm. They'd stanched the bleeding and sewn him up as best they could. Initially, he had lost much of the function in his left arm, although time and careful exercise had mended it eventually. Nevertheless it was the end of his army career in the Peninsula.

'Do you miss it?' she asked. 'Active service, I mean?'

'At the time it was a blow, but there is no point in lamenting what cannot be changed.'

He had understated the case. Separated from his erstwhile comrades and the life he had loved it had been like a form of exile. Having to deal with men like Genet did nothing to enhance the experience. Even so, what was the alternative; to go back to England? To go home? He hardly thought he'd be welcome there, given the circumstances. In any case it was too late to mend fences now.

Although she could not follow his thoughts, Claudine sensed the tension in him and sought to change the subject.

'Have you relatives in England?'

'Yes, though I have not seen them for some years.'

'That must be hard.'

'There was little affection in our family, especially not between me and my father. Besides, he is dead now and I am quite sure that my absence has occasioned little heartache for the rest of my relations.'

The words were spoken in a matter-of-fact tone but, again, she had the sensation of having moved into dangerous territory.

'Families ought to be united, although I know it is not always the case.'

'Have you any other brothers, or sisters perhaps?' he asked.

'None who survived into adulthood.'

'Then you must have been all the more precious to your parents.'

'My mother died when I was eight. My father hired a governess and considered his paternal duty done. It wasn't until I grew older that he took any interest in me, and then only as a commodity in the marriage market.'

'He arranged a match for you?'

'Yes. I had no say in the matter.'

The words sounded quite dispassionate but he sensed anger beneath them. His curiosity increased. There were so many things he wanted to ask, all of them intrusive. It was none of his business. Arranged matches were commonplace, and, if love followed, the couple might consider themselves fortunate. If not they made shift as best they could, as he knew all too well.

'And your husband?'

'He was likewise compelled to the match by his family.'

The story was so similar to his own that it struck a chord. Yet, in spite of her outspokenness and misguided thirst for adventure, there could be few men who would complain about gaining such a wife; unless of course their affections were engaged elsewhere. However, Duval wasn't about to delve there. To do so would be to awaken sleeping dogs. At the same time he could empathise with her situation; it seemed they had a surprising amount in common.

'Even so, he could not willingly have left you.'

The tone brought warm colour to her face. 'He went without a backward glance. I think he could scarcely wait to go. Oh, we exchange dutiful letters from time to time, but he has never given any indication of the desire or intention to return.'

'I'm sorry.'

'Don't be. He has his life and I have mine.'

Again Duval felt the words chime, but then it was familiar territory. 'Did you never feel lonely?'

'Sometimes,' she admitted, 'in the early days, but not now. Besides, I have grown accustomed to having my own independence and would not willingly relinquish it.'

'I can see why you might not wish to, but the war in Spain is over.'

The implication brought with it a twinge of unease. She had meant it when she said that she valued her independence. The advent of a husband after all this time was distinctly unwelcome. Had there ever been the least affection or esteem in the case, anything on which they might have founded a hope for the future, she might have been willing to try and build bridges. However, there was no shared experience to build on, no affection, nothing to bind them but a piece of paper. She found it hard now even to recall what Anthony looked like. Besides, time had a way of changing people. What he had looked like then might not be what he looked like now. He was a stranger to her in every way.

Although he could not follow her thoughts Duval could see the inner disquiet that they created. Had she disliked the thought so much? If so, her husband had much to answer for. Not that it was any of his business. Nor did he have any right to criticise.

'We have lived separate lives up to now,' she

replied. 'I see no reason why we cannot continue to do so.'

'The situation is not unknown.'

'No.'

He saw the fleeting expression of bleakness in her face and with it her vulnerability.

Both touched him more deeply than he had expected. The future she described was bleak indeed; an ocean of emptiness in which love and fulfilment had no place. The years would claim her youth and her good looks but they would not offer the consolations of a loving relationship and children. It was, he thought, a criminal waste.

'You might take a lover,' he said.

Claudine reddened. Ordinarily the very suggestion would have been an insult to a lady, but a second's reflection showed he hadn't intended it that way. The words had been spoken with casual ease and they served to underline what he thought her to be. Under the circumstances she could hardly blame him though. To express indignation now would sound like total hypocrisy.

'And leap from the frying pan into the fire?' She shook her head. 'The thought does not appeal.'

Her reply surprised him, not least because it had sounded genuine. He searched her face but could see no trace of duplicity there, only a very attractive blush. That surprised him too. All the same, it was hard to believe that she had never taken advantage of the relative freedom that her situation afforded. After all, had he not briefly experienced the heady sensuality beneath her outwardly cool demeanour?

'What will you do then?' he asked.

'I will go back to Sussex.'

'To your house by the sea?'

'Yes.'

'In what part of Sussex does it lie?'

'About ten miles from Hove.'

He stared at her intently for a moment, an expression that did not go unnoticed.

'Are you familiar with the area at all?'

'Yes,' he replied. 'I know it, but I have not been there for many years.'

'Of course, how should you?' She paused. 'You have family there perhaps?'

'No, my relatives reside in London for the most part.' It was true as far as it went, he thought, and he was reluctant to embark on a more detailed explanation. Family was a complex and difficult topic. As for the rest it was merely coincidence. Thousands of people lived in Sussex.

'I also have a house in London,' she went on, 'although I spend only part of the year there.'

Again he experienced the sensation of buried memories stirring. 'You stay for the Season?'

'Yes.'

Duval mentally rebuked himself again. All of fashionable society went to London for that purpose and many of them owned a house there. Her being among their number should come as no surprise. Such a woman would blend effortlessly into the social scene. His work had accustomed him to making connections between seemingly unrelated pieces of information, but now he was seeing coincidence where there wasn't any. He had to admit that she aroused his curiosity; indeed she had aroused a lot more than that. He had never met anyone quite like her. Being wed to his career, his experience of women was limited, but those he had met were decorative creatures with quiet and biddable natures. Claudine was undoubtedly decorative, but she was also argumentative and difficult, in short the most troublesome female of his acquaintance. It was just as well that his connection with the little baggage was to be of short duration.

'I should have thought that the Season would have offered plenty in the way of entertainment,' he said.

'Up to a point, but after a while it becomes dull and repetitive.'

'I can see how it might. All the same, it seems a fitter setting for a young woman of means and beauty.'

'Fit in whose eyes?'

The words were quietly spoken but, once again, he heard the challenge beneath. It prompted him to play devil's advocate.

'Your husband's perhaps?'

'His opinion is of no interest. He forfeited all

right to express any views on the subject long
since.'

'The law would say otherwise.'

'The law can say what it likes,' she replied. 'I
will never let any man treat me as a chattel again.'

Duval was intrigued. The passion he had just
glimpsed was not only genuine, it ran deep.

'He hurt you badly, didn't he?'

'It hurt at first, but, as time went on, less and
less. Now I scarcely think of him at all.' Claudine summoned a smile and changed the subject.
'Will you stay in London awhile when we reach
England?'

'For a while I imagine.'

'Will you visit your family?'

'I would not be welcome.'

She glanced up at him. 'Time can change things.'

'It can also widen the gulf.' He sighed. 'I will
not pretend that my conduct has been blameless; far
from it. Perhaps if I had gone back before it might
have been possible to heal the breach. Now...I
doubt it.'

'May I ask how long you have been absent?'

'Eight years.'

'Oh.' She paused. 'That is a long time.' If anyone should know about that it was she.

'Too long.'

'Still, it's said that blood is thicker than water.'

'You think so?'

She smiled wryly. 'Well, the prodigal son was welcomed back, wasn't he?'

'The prodigal son perhaps; not the prodigal husband.'

Claudine froze, rendered temporarily speechless as her mind struggled to assimilate what he had just said. What followed was a flood of conflicting emotions.

'I see.' She was surprised to discover how steady her voice sounded.

He had not missed her initial response. 'The situation is not as it may first appear. My wife and I have long been estranged.'

'I'm sorry to hear it.'

'Our marriage was arranged by our respective families and neither of us had any say in the matter. It was a disaster from the outset. As a result we live quite separate lives.'

She drew in a deep breath, trying to gather her scattered wits. She had made assumptions about this man that had no foundation in anything, except perhaps wishful thinking. It shouldn't have hurt but it did.

'And so you are free to amuse yourself elsewhere,' she replied. 'That must be convenient.'

His brows drew together. 'My career has taken the place of marriage and has been a most demanding mistress. Even if I'd felt so inclined, I have had little time to amuse myself elsewhere, and certainly would not do so with you.'

'Just how gullible do you think I am, Duval?'

'What happened in Paris was unavoidable, in the circumstances.'

'What happened was indefensible, in the circumstances.'

His gaze locked with hers. 'I'm not going to pretend I didn't want you, Claudine. What red-blooded man would not?' He made a vague gesture with his hand. 'Nevertheless, I never intended things to go so far. It's just that I got somewhat carried away by your charms. If you were offended then I apologise.'

There were so many things she could have said in reply, but none of them would have sounded in the least convincing. It horrified her now to think how close she had come to disaster with this man; a man who clearly regarded her as a whore. Gathering every last shred of self-control she faced him.

'The situation that occurred in Paris was unfortunate. I wish it had never happened, but the past cannot be changed. All I want is to forget it.'

He winced inwardly. 'In that case I will do nothing that might cause you to remember.'

She nodded. 'Thank you.'

He made no reply but turned away towards the window instead. It was an unstudied gesture but it unwittingly presented the unmarred side of his face. Claudine caught her breath. His profile was as strong and clear as a piece of marble statuary. The thought of Apollo returned unbidden. As she stared the buried memory stirred again. This had nothing to do with Paris. It was much older; a memory of another face in another place and time. Her heart beat a little faster in response. Who? Where? When? She frowned, trying to grasp the information, but, as before, it slid away from her leaving in its wake a sense of vague disquiet.

Chapter Four

The conversation had given Duval a great deal to think about over the next few days, not least the matter of his private life. It was a confounded mess but, much as he dreaded the thought, fate was dragging him back to England and he was going to have to address it. Could he return after so long an absence and expect to assume the mantle of husband? The law said he could. Legally his wife belonged to him still. He could compel her to live with him if he chose; could compel her to share his bed, bear his children and obey his every command. Legally his power was absolute.

In reality, he had no idea what he was going to do about the situation, only that he did have a responsibility. At the very least he must ascertain that his wife was still well and ensure that his financial obligations were being met. More than that, they needed to have a serious discussion. He had no more wish to live with her than she with him. It was entirely possible that she had found consolation elsewhere; that she might ask for an annulment. Then they would both be free to move on with their lives. And if he were free, what then? Involuntarily he glanced at his companion and sighed inwardly. Before he could put his life in order he had first to fulfil his present obligation to Claudine. After that they would go their separate ways and he would be able to concentrate unhindered on the problem of his future. He might have resumed his career in the army had not Napoleon been sent to Elba. As it was, thousands of British soldiers had been demobilised so that door was closed. Although it was far from ideal, espionage looked to be the only other option at present. There were loose ends to tie up as well, and he couldn't do that now until he'd dealt with personal matters.

It was therefore with considerable relief that he caught his first glimpse of the sea. The distant expanse of grey-green water represented safety. Once on English soil, Claudine would be beyond the reach of Fouché and his agents. That much was sincerely pleasing. The thought of her, or indeed any woman, in such hands was repellent. However, the sea also brought parting much closer. Duval guessed she would not be sorry. Her manner of late, though correct and courteous, was also distant. He understood why. For both of them the imminent separation would be welcome. Once he had resolved the issues surrounding his personal life, he would ask for another posting. Work would provide the means to keep his mind occupied. He suspected that Claudine would be hard to forget, but he meant to try all the same. For all sorts of reasons he too would be glad to reach England.

The passage to St Helier was arranged without undue difficulty. The owner of the boat was quite willing to undertake the journey for the fee that was offered. Claudine eyed him dubiously. The man, who gave his name as Pierre, was a rough-looking individual whose swarthy face and dark beard wouldn't have seemed out of place on a pirate sloop. She said as much to Duval when they were out of earshot.

'Pierre is trustworthy,' he said. 'He and I have worked together before.'

'Now why doesn't that surprise me?' she replied.

'What's that supposed to mean?'

'You both have a piratical air about you.'

Duval's good eye glinted. 'Be thankful I'm not a pirate, my sweet.'

'You would make me walk the plank, I have no doubt.'

'Tempting, I admit, but pirates don't throw money away like that; not when you would fetch such a handsome profit in any slave market in the Mediterranean. You would be an ornament in any man's harem.'

She glared at him. 'That is a vile thing to say.'

'It's the truth.' He paused. 'Of course, I might decide to keep you instead.'

'What, and lose a handsome profit?'

'There would be other compensations.'

The implications of that outrageous remark rendered her temporarily speechless. No doubt it had been made with the intention of provoking her into an unguarded reply that he could exploit to his advantage. However, she had no intention of obliging him. The conversation was already in dangerous waters and he was probably enjoying the fact. She darted another look his way, but his expression remained inscrutable.

The passage to St Helier was chilly but uneventful. Claudine was so eager to reach their destination that the discomforts of a small fishing boat were rendered negligible in comparison. She spoke little to her companion on the journey, partly because it wasn't practical to move around in the limited space, and partly because she was too preoccupied to wish for speech. Duval too seemed preoccupied, when he wasn't engaged in private conversation with Matthieu or Pierre. He barely even glanced her way. Their earlier conversation might never have happened. No doubt such teasing came easily to him, but it had resurrected memories that she would have preferred not to revisit. Moreover, it seemed that he had not forgotten either. His words were a further demonstration of how he regarded her. If she were to give him the least bit of encouragement…

For a moment her treacherous thoughts returned to the intimacy they had shared and the touch of his hands on her body, and in spite of the chill she felt hot inside. You could take a lover. Was it himself he had meant? Probably not, in the light of what had occurred between them. *I prefer my women willing.* No doubt there were many such, but she wasn't one of them. She had got carried away for a while, that was all. When she got home she could put all this behind her. She glanced in Duval's direction but his attention was apparently focused on the horizon. No question but he was looking forward to the end of their journey as much as she was.

On arrival at their destination they bade farewell to Pierre and then repaired to a quayside inn. Hot food and a cheerful fire acted as restoratives against the chill and counteracted the effects of the voyage. It was replaced by a feeling of well-being in which relief played no small part. She was safe; the chances of anything untoward happening now were minimal. It occurred to her again how much she owed to her companion. He might be a rogue, but, having stood between her and disaster, he had risked much on her account. That realisation did much to dampen the anger she had felt earlier. It had come as a shock to discover that he was married but it shouldn't have. He had always been forbidden fruit. When they reached England and said their goodbyes she would never have to see him again.

Sensing himself observed Duval looked up and then found his gaze lingering. The view across the table was very agreeable indeed. Warmth had brought a delightful flush of colour to her cheeks and lips and enhanced the beauty of those huge dark eyes. Tendrils of hair had escaped from the confining ribbon. They curled about her face and neck in a manner that was both artless and damnably alluring.

Under that intense scrutiny Claudine was more than ever aware of her dishevelled appearance. Apart from wearing the same clothes for days she had been able to make only the most basic toilette at each of the inns where they had stopped. She returned a wry smile.

'I know. I look like a gypsy.'

'Not the word I was thinking of,' he replied with perfect truth.

'I won't ask what that is.' She glanced with distaste at her gown. 'The first thing I shall do when I get back to Oakley Court is to take a leisurely bath.'

Duval was suddenly very still. 'Oakley Court?'

'My house...in Sussex.' She looked up and saw his expression. 'Do you know it?'

'I know of a house of that name.'

Claudine nodded. 'Of course, I remember you saying that you were familiar with the area.'

'The house I speak of belonged to the Earls of Ulverdale.'

'That's right. It still does.'

He strove to keep his voice level. 'Then…I think that Claudine may be an assumed name.'

When she saw his expression some of her cheerfulness faded. 'I would have said something earlier only…well, you never asked so I assumed you didn't want to know.'

Duval mentally cursed himself. 'I'm asking now.'

'My real name is Claudia…Claudia Brudenell, Countess of Ulverdale.'

His heart seemed to miss several beats and suddenly all the apparently unconnected pieces fell into place with appalling clarity. As the memory of their previous conversations returned, all the small coincidences rose up to taunt him: the houses in Sussex and London, the estate in the north and, of course, the estranged soldier husband. Only a prize idiot could have failed to make the connections.

Mistaking his silence entirely Claudia experienced a twinge of guilt. 'Forgive me, I should have told you…'

'It's not your fault,' he replied.

'Surely it doesn't make any difference now.'

The blue gaze locked with hers. 'I rather think it does.' He rose from the table. 'Now, if you will excuse me, I must go and see about our passage to England.'

Claudia rose too. 'Of course.'

He headed for the door, his face unwontedly grim.

'Duval, please don't be angry with me.'

He paused on the threshold and turned, surveying her in silence for a moment. Then the blue gaze lost a little of its hard glint. 'I'm not angry with you.'

With that he was gone leaving her staring at the closed door. Claudia frowned. In spite of that parting reassurance she knew that he was angry, and it sat ill with her to have incurred his displeasure in that way. It had never occurred to her that he might wish to know her real name; in their line of work it was something people didn't ask. His reaction to the truth had been totally unexpected. Perhaps he had been genuinely shocked to discover a lady of rank so far embroiled in such a shady business.

The more she thought about it the likelier that seemed. Everything he knew about her now must only serve to confirm his first opinion of her. It was an oddly lowering thought.

It took less than an hour for Duval to arrange the next passage to England, but the boat wouldn't leave for a while yet and he was in no mood to go back to the inn just then. Needing time to put his thoughts in order he went for a walk instead. For a long time he stood by the sea wall staring out at the white-capped water, but in truth he saw nothing. As he had told Claudia, the revelation of her identity made a great deal of difference. It was just that he had no idea what he was going to do about it. Each possible course of action seemed more unsatisfactory than the last. Perhaps he should have spoken up when she told him who she was. A part of him had wanted to, but another part of his mind recalled what she had said before: *The past cannot be changed. All I want is to forget it.* And he had given his assurance that he would not do anything to remind her of it. He sighed. Could he now go back on that? In the light of the morning's revelation how could he not go back on it? Whatever he did next was going to cause hurt.

The remainder of their journey was memorably uncomfortable: the crossing was rougher this time and most of the other passengers on the little packet boat succumbed to sea-sickness. Conversation was reduced to what was absolutely necessary. In spite of the poor weather conditions, Duval remained above deck with Matthieu for much of the time, returning only occasionally, so Claudia wrapped herself in her cloak and tried to sleep. However, her troubled mind refused to allow it. Ever since he had returned to the inn Duval's manner had been different. She couldn't identify exactly what had changed but knew instinctively that there had been a fundamental shift which could never be reversed.

She wasn't in the least bit sorry when they

reached dry land again. Moreover, it was English soil this time. The knowledge gladdened her immeasurably.

Duval accurately surmised the source of her smile. 'I think you will be glad to see your home again.'

'Yes, although there were times when I thought I might not.' She looked up at him. 'But for you that would have been a self-fulfilling prophecy. I owe you much.'

He guessed that it hadn't been easy for her to say, and yet the tone was sincere. It took him by surprise.

'I am glad to have been of service, truly.' He paused. 'All that remains now is for me to organise a post chaise for your onward journey.'

He was as good as his word. Within the hour the vehicle was ready at the inn door. It reinforced her earlier surmise that he wanted to be rid of her as soon as possible. In the light of events it was hardly surprising. She felt much the same.

Pausing by the waiting chaise, she turned to face him. 'Will you go on to London now?'

'Yes, for a while. I have urgent business there.'

'I can imagine.'

He seriously doubted that, but forbore to say so. 'It will take a few days to sort out.'

'Well, don't let me delay you.' She held out her hand. 'Goodbye, Duval.'

Warm strong fingers closed round hers and re-

tained their hold. 'When my business there is concluded I shall do myself the honour of calling on
you at Oakley Court.' Seeing her startled expression, he added, 'There will be important matters
to discuss.'

'Don't put yourself to any further trouble on my
account. I'm sure Genet will write to me himself.'

'The matters I spoke of do not merely concern
Genet.'

'What then?'

While she was grateful to him for getting her
out of France, she had no wish to meet him again.
Time and distance would help to put him out of her
mind and let her forget about what had happened.

'I am not at liberty to say at present.'

It reinforced the notion that he was seeking an
excuse to continue their relationship. If so, he could
have only one possible reason for doing so. That
she should have been instrumental in putting such
an idea in his head was mortifying. It was also extremely awkward. Moreover, he still had hold of
her hand and she couldn't break free without causing a scene.

'I think you had better,' she replied.

'I ask your patience for four days more. Then
we will talk.'

'No, we will not. Our association is at an end,
Duval. You must know that.'

'I'm afraid it isn't over yet, my sweet.'

The soft tone was deeply disquieting. Given

what had occurred, he had the power to ruin her if he chose; he could demand money or other favours, or both, in exchange for his silence. She was reluctant to think him so underhand, but what other reason could there be for his wishing to pursue a connection so clearly unwelcome to her?

'There is nothing for you here, Duval. I really think it would be better if you did not call.'

'And I really think I must.'

It was quite evident that he wasn't going to be deterred. Claudia shrugged.

'Very well, though I fear you will have a wasted journey.'

'We'll see about that when the time comes, won't we?' He led her to the chaise and handed her in. 'Until then, my lady.'

Chapter Five

Claudia saw nothing of the passing countryside on the last leg of her journey. Instead she was entirely preoccupied with the spectre of the man she had just left. The cool and civil parting she had once envisaged could scarcely have been further from reality. Now, instead of putting the whole business behind her, it hung overhead like the sword of Damocles. Nor could she see any way out of the situation.

The sight of Oakley Court had never been so welcome. It seemed like a sanctuary after the adventures of the past week. Her first act was to order a hot bath and, having done so, to scrub from head to toe before luxuriating in the suds for another hour. It was a delight to don a fresh gown and, with her maid's help, to arrange her hair properly. When at length she looked in the mirror the dishevelled hoyden was gone and in her place was an elegant woman of fashion. Only the memories remained. Memories that she was going to have to deal with, somehow.

The maid's eyes met hers in the mirror. 'It's good to have you home, my lady.'

Claudia summoned a smile. 'It's good to be home, Lucy.'

The girl glanced in disgust at the pile of dirty clothing on the floor. 'It's plain that some maids don't know how to care for a lady. Next time, take me with you, ma'am.'

'I am not planning on going anywhere for a while, but when I do I'll certainly take you with me. It just wasn't possible last time.'

Lucy beamed. 'You won't regret it, my lady. I swear it.'

Gathering up the discarded clothing the maid retired. Claudia watched her leave. While it would have been wonderfully convenient to have taken her along, she could never have justified putting Lucy's life at risk; nor could she tell the maid why her presence wasn't required. The girl's feelings had been hurt, but better that than the possible alternative.

Try as she might, Claudia could not rid her mind of Alain Poiret and the others, or of what had happened after their arrest. Although they were beyond help, it went against the grain to leave the matter there; to let a traitor escape justice. What other evil deeds might he perpetrate as a result? She wondered if Genet had any information, any clue at all that might point to the betrayer's identity. It occurred to her that a talk with Genet might be both useful and productive.

In the meantime, there were more immediate tasks awaiting her attention. Having spoken to the cook and the housekeeper, she took herself off to the salon to deal with a pile of correspondence. With its south-facing aspect and the view over the garden it was a pleasant place to work, particularly now that the spring flowers were in evidence. Snowdrops were giving place to daffodil foliage. Soon the tight buds would burst into soul-warming gold and banish winter dullness with glad colour. Save for hazel catkins and pussy willow, the trees were still bare but each branch and twig was covered with new buds. Later perhaps she would go for a walk. The day, though cold, would stay fine. The clouds were high, like fleecy islands in a sea of blue. The blue of a man's eyes…

The sky faded and without warning she was looking into Duval's face. With it came the memory of a bed chamber in Paris; a lean hard body pressed close to her nakedness; the pressure of his mouth on hers, searing, persuasive, his arousal, hard and shocking, awakening a throbbing pulse of warmth between her thighs. She drew in a sharp breath, forcing the image away. It was shameful to think of it let alone to have enjoyed it. She was no different from any of the other women in Madame Renaud's establishment. *I knew I was right.*

The mocking voice returned with force. Duval suspected the same. How could he not? Claudia felt her cheeks and neck grow hot. Her brief liaison with him was immoral, wrong in every way, and yet she knew now that he had awakened something in her that would never sleep until he was out of her life for good.

The thought of his forthcoming visit filled her with unease. She had no idea how she was going to handle it, only that it must be faced and decisively too. He was not entirely without a sense of honour. Perhaps she could appeal to it; make him understand that she meant what she said. He could have no hopes of her. She could not suppose he would be easily persuaded, but she must succeed in this. He represented danger in too many ways.

With a determined effort she returned her attention to the pile of correspondence, forcing herself to concentrate. It took her some time to read through all the letters and then to prioritise the replies in order of importance. A missive from Lady Harrington lightened her mood a little. It contained news of their mutual acquaintance, including a witty and entertaining account of a hunt ball, and expressed the hope that she and Claudia would meet in London: '…for the winter has been tedious, and I long for your lively company again. It seems an age since I had any word from you. Do let me know soon how you go on.

Your affectionate friend,

Anne.'

Claudia smiled to herself and set about writing a reply. She could not tell her friend where she had spent the last few weeks, but did provide as much local news as she felt would be of interest. In truth she would be glad to have some female company again, and Anne's was particularly agreeable.

By the time she had written the letter, her sense of shame had faded a little. She wrote a few more, shorter, replies and seeing the pile diminish a little did something to ease her conscience. She spent the majority of the morning on the task and then, needing some fresh air, rose and retrieved her shawl from the back of the chair.

As she turned she glanced towards the fireplace and the portrait hanging above it. A tall, slender figure in scarlet regimentals returned her gaze. His expression was cool, aloof, giving no clue as to the thoughts behind those vivid blue eyes. Deep gold hair complimented the face with its chiselled lines and almost sculptural good looks. Claudia surveyed it steadily. How old had Anthony been when it was painted? Twenty, perhaps? It was probably an accurate likeness, but somehow it gave no real sense of the young man she had known so briefly. No doubt he looked different now anyway. Eight years of military campaigning must have left their mark. The picture was all that remained. But for that, she might have forgotten what he looked like. She sighed and turned away.

A discreet knock at the door announced the arrival of the butler. 'The newspapers have arrived from London, my lady.'

'Thank you, Walker. Leave them over there on the table.'

'Begging your pardon, my lady, but I thought you'd like to see them at once.'

'Why? What has happened?'

'Napoleon has escaped from Elba.'

'What!'

'It's true, my lady. Apparently he landed at Cannes on the first of March, and is now trying to rally support.'

'Good gracious.'

Claudia seized *The Times*, scanning the front page. It was apparent that Walker had spoken the truth. She frowned. The paper was already several days old and the news older than that, so Napoleon had been at large at least a week. If he managed to rally enough men and raise an army it would mean war again. They'd had less than a year of peace, and now this. In addition there was a French spy on the loose who already knew too much about the British network. It had all manner of far-reaching ramifications that she didn't like in the least.

She was afforded little time to dwell on the matter because, having been away for some weeks, there were matters of estate business requiring her attention. A meeting with the land agent turned her mind towards spring planting, lambing, and

the purchase of a new seed drill. After that she sat
down to study the account books. She was in the
study with a pile of ledgers when Walker entered
to say that a letter had arrived.

Somewhat reluctantly she took it from the sal-
ver, assuming it was from Duval to confirm his arrival the following day. However, one glance at the
direction on the front revealed that it could not be
from him. Her mouth dried. Although she had seen
it on relatively few occasions, the elegant masculine hand was unmistakeable. With thumping heart
she stared at it a few seconds longer. Then, taking
a deep breath, she broke the wafer. The letter was
a single sheet and contained only a short message:

'My Dear Claudia,

I trust that you will forgive the brevity of this
letter but, since I am now returned to England, it
seems superfluous to write at length here. Rather
I shall look forward to speaking to you in person
when I arrive at Oakley Court tomorrow. You may
expect me by three in the afternoon.

Your obedient servant,

Brudenell.'

Claudia's stomach lurched. Anthony returning; coming here! Never! It had to be a mistake.
Hurriedly she scanned the words again, but their
import was unchanged. The realisation brought a
surge of emotion so powerful that it almost undid

her. Shaking, she sank onto the couch as her mind struggled to assimilate the news.

It took a minute or two and, as the initial shock wore off, it was replaced by cold fury. It was bad enough to discover that he was coming at all, but to announce his arrival thus, as though it were the most natural thing in the world; as though he had merely been away a week or two and not eight years, almost beggared belief. *You may expect me by three*...How dared he? The arrogance of it, the sheer brass-necked gall of the man was breathtaking.

'Damn you, Anthony Brudenell.'

She crumpled the letter into a ball and hurled it on the fire. Then she began to pace the floor, her mind in a whirl. Did he seriously imagine she would welcome him back? That the last eight years could somehow be expunged and she would fall into his arms? It was this thought which brought reality home and she realised with a sudden chill that no matter how many years had passed, he was still her husband in the eyes of the law. The implications caused a knot of dread in the pit of her stomach. Then her late father-in-law's voice spoke in her head:

'When your husband returns, you will have no time to think of frivolity. You will fulfil your wifely duty and bear his children. I have no doubt he will wish to make up for lost time.'

Claudia swallowed hard. Although she had

seen no outward sign of it in their brief association, would Anthony take after his father? Had the
intervening years brought out the same brutal traits
in the son? Her late father-in-law had no compunc-
tions about the use of force to compel obedience:

'Men are stronger than women and are therefore entitled to dominate them in whatever manner they see fit.'

Her fists clenched at her sides and she forced the
image away, trying to put her thoughts in some sort
of order. As more rational thinking returned so did
the recollection of Duval's intended visit. Claudia
checked in mid-stride. Of all possible timings, it
had to be the most disastrous. She had to put him
off. It was at that moment she realised that she had
no idea how to contact him. Foolishly, she hadn't
thought to inquire where he would be staying while
he was in London. He might be anywhere. She had
no idea when he meant to arrive either. The very
thought of him walking in just before, or just after,
Anthony didn't bear thinking about. Things were
difficult enough already.

Unable to bear the confines of the house any
longer, Claudia picked up her shawl and let herself out into the garden. The breeze was cool but
she barely noticed as her mind grappled with the
implications of the morrow. It soon became clear
that both of the forthcoming interviews must be
faced. Duval's visit would have to be brief, and
whatever he had to communicate said in the few-

est possible words. What she had to say certainly wouldn't take long. Then she could send him on his way and turn her attention to the larger problem of Anthony.

It was counterproductive to let imagination run away with her. All the evidence suggested he had no interest in her at all. She supposed that he would expect to stay for a day or two; given their history it was not likely to be longer. Now that she was a little calmer, the thought occurred that it might be no bad thing if he did stay a while, since it would allow them to talk about the future. It was pointless to put it off any longer; the problem must be addressed for both their sakes. She was quite sure that he had no wish to continue with this farce any more than she did. Divorce was out of the question of course: it was both difficult and expensive to arrange. Moreover, it would create a scandal that would hurt others as well as themselves. An annulment, however, might be managed more discreetly. Then they would both have their freedom. It was the ideal solution; the only solution as far as she could see. Anthony could have no reason to refuse. That knowledge made her feel marginally more optimistic.

Drawing her shawl closer, she walked slowly back to the house and turned her mind to domestic practicalities. She would need to speak to the housekeeper about arrangements for the morrow. A room would have to be prepared, a bed made up, fires lit, and there were meals to think about. She sighed. The notion of dining in her husband's company did not fill her with delight, but, if it helped to achieve the outcome she wanted, then it was worth the pain.

When the following morning passed without any sign of Duval, her heart sank. It would be just her luck that both expected visitors arrived together. The situation was rapidly descending into bad farce. She glanced at the clock and then at her dress. Protocol required that she change into something more suitable. It came as a relief to have something to do.

She paused before the mirror, her critical gaze taking in every detail of her reflection. The jonquil-yellow gown was not new but it was one of her favourites, and it suited her warm colouring. Moreover, she felt comfortable in it, an important consideration at a time when all else promised to be extremely uncomfortable. A matching ribbon was threaded through her dark curls. One small gold pendant and bracelet were her only jewellery. It was a simple and elegant outfit; perhaps too simple. She bit her lip. Should she have worn something more ostentatious? Her gaze went to the pile of discarded gowns on the bed and thence to the clock. A quarter to three already! No matter what her personal inclinations she would have to go down now. The jonquil gown must suffice.

She entered the salon a short time later, conscious of a growing knot of tension in her stomach. Involuntarily she glanced at the clock again; ten minutes to the hour. Still no sign of Duval, and Anthony was due at any moment. Just then, she could have wished both of them at Jericho.

From outside she heard the sound of carriage wheels and horses' hoofs. Those were followed moments later by men's voices in the hallway. One of them was Walker's; the other must be Anthony's. She closed her eyes for a moment and composed herself. Behind her the door opened and closed. Claudia turned, expecting to see the butler, and then her breath caught in her throat.

'Duval.'

The tall figure opposite was undeniably Duval, but now every vestige of the adventurer was gone. A coat of navy blue superfine was complimented by immaculate white linen and a cream satin waistcoat from which hung a single gold fob. Pale yellow breeches and highly polished Hessian boots completed an outfit that was at once simple and strikingly elegant. It accentuated every line of that lithe masculine figure. The dark leather patch that concealed his ruined eye lent him a wicked, rakish air whose effect was to enhance the aura of power that he wore as effortlessly as the clothes.

'Good afternoon, my lady.'

He bowed and then surveyed her steadily, the vivid gaze taking in every detail of her appearance.

Whether it found favour or not was impossible to tell, but the attention was utterly unnerving and Claudia felt perspiration start on the palms of her hands. She told herself firmly that she couldn't afford an attack of nerves now. What had happened between them was never going to be repeated. Why had he insisted on coming here? She supposed it was just possible that what he had to say was too sensitive to be committed to paper, but the uneasy feeling persisted that he had other motives for this visit.

Appalled by her reaction, and anxious to conduct this interview as soon as possible, Claudia came straight to the point.

'I hope that your visit to London proved satisfactory.'

'Yes, it did, I thank you.'

'You saw Genet, I collect.'

'Yes.'

'May I ask what he said?'

'It appears that two other operatives—Lebrun and Saunière—were warned in time to escape the trap in Paris.'

'I'm glad to hear it. Even so, Genet will have to start again; set up a new network almost from scratch. It won't be easy.'

'No, it won't, but he'll manage. Men of his stamp always do.' He paused. 'However, Genet isn't the reason I came here today.'

'Oh.' She tensed. Now they would come to it. 'What then?'

'Don't you know, Claudia?'

The tone was quiet, gentle even, but something about it caused a faint fluttering sensation in the pit of her stomach. The familiar use of her name caught her off guard too, although he had used it many times before. However, that was then. Circumstances were different now and the intimacy they had shared was over. He must be left in no doubt of that.

'No,' she replied. 'Perhaps you will be good enough to explain.'

For a brief moment his expression was quizzical. 'Do I need to explain?'

'Yes, you do. What is it you want to say?'

'Not to say, but to show you.' Under her puzzled gaze he strolled across the room and stopped before the hearth. Then he turned to face her. 'Look, Claudia. Look carefully.'

She stared at him, her eyes registering uncertainty. Then her consciousness moved past him to the portrait behind. For a moment the man and the portrait were juxtaposed. Then, slowly, inexorably, the two figures seemed to merge, their faces to blend and blur. Her heart leapt towards her throat.

'No,' she murmured, 'it isn't possible.'

She looked again at the man in front of her and, gradually, all the unconnected details of their earlier conversations fell into place. Her cheeks paled.

'Anthony?'

'Yes.'

Unwilling to trust her legs any longer she sank down on the couch, trying to assimilate the knowledge. Her companion frowned. She heard the decanter clink and then the sound of liquid being poured. Moments later he was beside her and placing a glass in her hand.

'Drink this.'

It was brandy, and a generous measure withal. Imbibing spirits was something she had done only rarely; the drink burned her throat and made her eyes water. She felt the fiery liquor carve a path all the way to her stomach but, gradually, it began to quiet the tremors there. With that came an increased awareness of the masculine figure beside her, of the arm around her shoulders transmitting a different kind of warmth, of the faint scent of cedar on his coat and beneath it the disturbing and familiar scent of the man. Together with the brandy it was a dangerously heady combination.

He watched her intently and, as some of the colour returned to her cheeks, felt inwardly relieved. For a moment or two he'd really thought she might faint. It was so unlike her as to be cause for concern.

'Forgive me,' he said, 'but it seemed better to let you see the truth rather than merely to tell you.'

Her fingers tightened round the glass. The truth. It had been under her nose for nearly a fortnight and she hadn't seen it. As the initial shock began to fade it gave way to other emotions, not least the sense of her stupidity. How could she have failed to make the connections between their respective backgrounds? Even Antoine and Anthony were two versions of the same name; Duval a loose pun on Ulverdale.

'There is much we need to discuss, Claudia.'

His voice dragged her back to the present. 'Yes.'

'But perhaps now is not the time. Later, maybe, when you've had a chance to recover.'

She heard him in disbelief. He spoke as though an hour's rest in a darkened room would some-how resolve this. While it was tempting to cut and run, to flee to the sanctuary of her chamber, that would solve nothing. It had to be faced, and pref-erably before courage ran out. With an effort she gathered her wits.

'I am not so poor a creature as you seem to think.'

'I have never thought so,' he replied. 'All the same, I know this has been a shock for you.'

She closed her eyes for a moment, thinking that shock didn't begin to describe what she felt just then. He had had far longer to make the mental adjustment. That realisation engendered others. Disengaging herself from his arm, she altered her position so that she could see his face.

'When did you first know the truth?' she de-manded.

'At the inn in St Helier, when you spoke of Oakley Court.'

'Yet you said nothing.'

'The truth came as a shock to me too. I needed to get my thoughts in order.'

'Among them, the possibility of saying nothing at all, perhaps?'

'That was never a real possibility.'

'Why not? It would have made little difference surely?'

'It made all the difference.'

'You could have gone back to your life and I to mine.'

'After what happened in Paris there could be no going back, Claudia.'

'Not there perhaps, but I'm sure Genet will find something else for you to do.'

'I am not talking about Genet, and you know it.'

Her chin lifted. 'No, I'm not sure I do.'

'I am talking about us.'

'There *is* no us. There never was.'

He sighed. 'I cannot defend my former behaviour. Nor do I expect you to forgive it. All we can do now is to move on.'

'I have already moved on. I have made a life for myself just as you have.'

'Circumstances have changed.'

'Nothing has changed, except that we now have a chance to discuss the future.'

'That is my intention,' he said.

'There can be no possible reason for things to continue as they are. Neither of us chose this marriage, but we can choose what we do about it now.'

'So I think.'

It was impossible to read his expression but the words gave her faint hope. 'I know that divorce is out of the question, but there could be an annulment.'

It wasn't unexpected, he had thought himself prepared, and yet hearing the words spoken was like being thrown into deep and icy water. He hadn't realised until that moment how far he had allowed himself to hope.

When he did not immediately reject the proposal she drew courage and hurried on. 'Our marriage is on paper only. Therefore, it has no force in law. It could be set aside and we would both be free.'

'Free to do what exactly?'

'Free to live as we choose. Free to love.'

His tone was studiedly neutral. 'Is there someone else, Claudia?'

The pink colour deepened in her cheeks. 'How could there be while I am married to you?'

'Perhaps I should have phrased that differently. Is there someone else whom you wish to marry?'

'Good Lord, no. How could you possibly think so? I have learned to value my independence too much for that.'

That stung too, and rather more than he'd expected. 'Was that why you left Ulverdale?'

'That's right.'

'Didn't our respective families have something to say about that?'

'Plenty, but once I had reached my majority the matter was out of their hands. Besides, my father was dead by then and yours too. Of course, your mother tried to persuade me to stay, but she could not prevail.'

'Was it so very bad then?'

Claudia's eyes sparkled with contained emotion. 'How can you ask me that?'

'Point taken. Yet there must have been compensations: parties, balls, soirées, the usual entertainments.'

'I was a married woman. Therefore such things were not deemed fitting for me. It was made clear that my role was to possess my soul in patience until your return, at which time I could look forward to providing future heirs for Ulverdale.'

Her tone was unwontedly bitter. He listened in appalled silence, realising for the first time how far off the mark his former suppositions had been. His imagination had created a picture of a young lady of fashion enjoying all that the Season could offer. The reality was horrifyingly different.

'I'm truly sorry, Claudia. I swear I had no idea…'

'How should you?' she replied. 'You never came to Ulverdale again.'

He took her hands in a firm clasp. 'You were not the reason I left. Please believe that.'

She wanted to pull away but his hold denied the possibility. 'How can I believe it?'

'My anger was directed at my father, not at you. It was through his thoughtless profligacy that my family was facing financial ruin.' He paused. 'His gaming debts were enormous, the estate was mortgaged to the hilt and the banks would extend no more funds. At that point he could no longer ignore what was happening. With his creditors closing in he became increasingly desperate. He would have done anything, I believe, to avert the impending disaster.'

'Yes, and thus he found his son a wealthy bride.'

Anthony nodded. 'I will not pretend that I viewed the matter with anything other than dismay. I had just turned twenty and marriage was the furthest thing from my mind. I had my heart set on a career in the army.'

'Evidently.'

'The fact that my intended bride was but fourteen made everything the more reprehensible…'

Without warning he saw his father's face again, grimly smiling. 'The knot must be tied fast. You must bed her.'

Sickened, he heard again his own angry refusal and felt revulsion rising in his heart; revulsion for his father, not for his innocent and frightened child bride. To have obeyed that brutal behest would have been no better than rape. The slender colt-ish figure had scarcely begun to show the first signs of womanliness. To have got her with child might have killed her. Her body was not ready for the rigours of childbed. Not that that would have troubled the old reprobate. Money cancelled out all moral qualms there. However, the countess had supported her son in this, standing up to her husband with unusual vigour. A fierce private quarrel had ensued but, under their combined strength, the Earl had backed down looking unwontedly shamefaced and muttering something about there being time yet. At least right had prevailed that far.

Unable to follow his thoughts, Claudia could only guess at their intensity. 'And so you protested.'

'I made my feelings known, but that cut no ice. My father was adamant. He painted me such a picture of ruin and disgrace as would have done credit to Hogarth. In the end, my agreement to the match was what procured my army commission.'

Claudia nodded. She knew much of the tale already. Hearing Anthony's side of things only reinforced what she had long suspected. Although she had misunderstood the direction of his anger, the conversation only served to reinforce the knowledge of his indifference towards her. It shouldn't have hurt any more, and she was appalled to discover that it did.

Withdrawing her hands from his she forced a brittle smile. 'Well, at least one of us was happy, then. It could have been so much worse, couldn't it?'

'It was bad enough for you, I think.'

'I don't want to talk about it, not now.'

He nodded. 'I know it's difficult; that you need time to think…'

'I've had eight years to think, Anthony. Frankly, it's enough.' She rose from the couch. 'Now I must ask you to excuse me. I have matters to attend to, and you must be tired after your journey. A room has been prepared for you. Walker will show you where.'

The Earl came to his feet as well. It was dismissal, for now. However, he had too much sense to protest. There would be time for discussion later.

'Dinner is at six,' she continued. 'I'm afraid we don't keep fashionable hours here.'

'Until then, Claudia.'

She nodded and then walked away, conscious of the gaze burning into her back. He watched her open the door, throw it wide and keep on walking. She didn't look back.

Having located his room and given Matthew instructions about unpacking the luggage, the Earl took a turn about the garden. Even after so many years' absence it was achingly familiar, a green sanctuary after the tension in the house. Yet he had expected nothing else. Having spent time in Claudia's company he had soon learned about her fiery nature. She had made it quite clear at their last meeting that she didn't want to see him again, that she suspected his motives. Far from causing dismay it had rather pleased him that she should wish to sever all ties with the adventurer called Antoine Duval.

The time spent in London had allowed space to think about what he was going to do. A part of his brain told him to walk away and, if they had not spent those days together in France, he might have been able to do it. But they had spent the time together and things weren't so simple now. He grimaced then, recognising an evasion. Even if France hadn't happened, he knew very well that things wouldn't have been simple at all, not after he'd set eyes on Claudia.

Chapter Six

He had half expected that she would refuse to appear for dinner that evening and keep to her room instead, so he was frankly surprised when she entered the drawing room just before six. He rose automatically and then caught his breath, letting his gaze travel the length of her. She was wearing an elegant evening gown of blue sarsenet, cut low in a tempting décolletage, offset by a spangled shawl carelessly draped about her bare shoulders. A sapphire necklace graced the slender column of her throat and matching stones adorned her ears.

His throat tightened. Somehow he found his voice.

'You look beautiful.'

She inclined her head in acknowledgement of the compliment. 'You are kind, my lord.'

'So formal, Claudia?'

'I am not like to be anything else.'

He sighed inwardly. Clearly she had no intention of making things easy. The impression lasted throughout dinner. Though her manners were impeccable and her behaviour correct in every way, she had retreated from him. It was, he knew, a defensive stance and one he understood. All the same he found himself missing her laughter and the lively banter of their former conversations. That had been a very different Claudia, far removed from the ice-cool beauty facing him now. Was this the face she showed to society or was there yet another, vivacious, teasing, possibly a little flirtatious? Whatever the truth it was intriguing; whatever face she chose to show was guaranteed to attract men in droves.

For no apparent reason the scene at Madame Renaud's returned; half a dozen men whose leering glances were directed towards the bed and the naked woman beside him. His fingers tightened on the stem of his glass and he tossed off the remains of the wine. He and Claudia had a great many things to discuss.

Not wishing to make the servants party to their conversation, he waited until the meal was over and the two of them could retire to the privacy of the drawing room before broaching any intimate topics. He had no intention of making their relationship the subject of backstairs gossip.

In fact Claudia was glad of his discretion. The next hour was not likely to be comfortable, but it had to be faced and it was better to do it in private. All the same, being alone with this man was harder now than it had ever been. Although she could not read his thoughts or guess at his feelings, she sensed purpose beneath the outwardly cool manner. Assuming what she hoped was an expression of calm she sat down on the couch and waited. Whatever happened she must govern her anger this time; must remain in control. To do anything else would hand him further advantage and he had too many of those already.

She helped herself to tea from the tray that the servants had left. Out of the corner of her eye she saw the Earl pour himself a glass of brandy from the decanter, and then return to take the chair opposite. For a little while neither of them spoke. Claudia made no move to fill the silence but let it stretch out instead, putting the onus on him. In fact, he seemed very much at ease, a circumstance that did nothing to improve her mood. He took a sip from his glass and then set it down on the small table at his elbow.

'So what now, Claudia?'

For some reason, the gentle tone was harder to deal with than arrogance. Collecting her wits, she made herself meet his eye. 'I have already told you what I think. In the circumstances the best solution would be to have our marriage annulled.'

'Would it?'

'You know it would. Neither of us wanted this

in the first place. We did it because there was no choice, but things are different now.'

'Yes, they are.'

'It was a business arrangement: money for a title. You can keep both if you will.'

'You cannot live without means, Claudia.'

'I have means. I was my father's sole heir; he willed everything to me.'

'I see.' The piercing gaze never left her face. 'You are aware that, in law, a woman's property belongs to her husband.'

Claudia kept her voice level. 'In law, yes, but you have more than enough now. We could both go our separate ways and live comfortably too.'

'Live comfortably? I doubt that.'

'I had not written you down as avaricious, Anthony. I thought that description applied only to our respective fathers.'

He winced inwardly. 'You misinterpret me. I was referring to the likely social consequences. I don't want your inheritance, Claudia. It's yours with my blessing.'

It hadn't been what she was expecting at all, and the words took the wind out of her sails. 'Thank you.' She took a deep breath. 'But it's still not enough. I want my independence too.'

'You already have that, do you not?'

'Up to a point.'

'A point that far exceeds what is afforded most other women.'

'What satisfies them does not satisfy me.'

'You have more courage than most,' he said, 'but it has brought you close to disaster.'

'I knew the risks and was prepared to accept them.'

'But I am not.' He paused. 'I am responsible for your safety now, Claudia, and I will not permit you to put yourself into any more perilous situations.'

The inflection in his voice was all too familiar and her hackles rose immediately. 'You will not permit?' With an effort she held on to her temper. 'Since when were you concerned for my safety?'

'Since Alain Poiret was arrested.'

'I told you, I am grateful for what you did. However, now that Napoleon is free there will be greater need for experienced operatives.' Seeing his expression, she added, 'All right. Next time I'll ask for a less dangerous posting.'

'There will be no more postings.'

'That is not for you to say.'

'It is very much for me to say.' The blue gaze locked with hers. 'Your involvement in espionage is at an end.'

'What do you mean?'

'I had a long talk with Monsieur Genet in which I made my views very clear. His department is not to approach you again for any reason.'

Claudia came to her feet at once. 'How dare you go behind my back like that?'

'Dare didn't come into it, only the intention to put you beyond the reach of danger.'

'I make the decisions about what I do or don't do, not you.'

'As I said before, circumstances have changed.'

She glared at him. 'Who do you think you are?'

'I am your husband, inconvenient as that fact may be.'

'Inconvenient doesn't begin to describe it. Say rather, intrusive, interfering, dictatorial, devious, arrogant…'

Far from rising to the bait he remained infuriatingly calm. 'My faults are many indeed, but in this instance my motives at least are good.'

'Your motives are doubtless as selfish as they have ever been.'

'Is it selfish to want to keep my wife out of danger? Out of brothels?'

Hot colour dyed her neck and face. 'I went there only because it was necessary. Genet knew my feelings on the subject.'

'And yet you went back, not only putting yourself in danger but your reputation too.'

'Mine or yours, Anthony?' She laughed softly. 'That's the real reason for this belatedly possessive outburst, isn't it?'

His expression hardened. 'Is that what you think it is?'

'Isn't it?'

'Does your reputation matter so little to you then?'

'Of course it matters.'

'I'm glad to hear it,' he said, 'because I can assure you it matters to me.'

She knew it was dangerous ground, knew it was unwise to push this any further, but Claudia's inner demon was now thoroughly roused. 'I suppose there's a first time for everything.'

That brought him out of the chair. Strong hands closed round her arms and drew her much closer. His expression sent a shiver the length of her spine. However, it was only partly fear. Underneath it was something much harder to define. Heart pounding, she continued to hold his gaze.

'Yes, there is,' he replied.

His face was very near to hers now. If he bent his head their lips would touch...The recollection sent a pulse of treacherous warmth to the core of her body. She fought it. She couldn't afford to hand him such an advantage. In the name of self-preservation she turned her face away.

Misinterpreting the movement he drew back a little. He wanted to shake her soundly for impudence; he wanted to kiss her until she begged for mercy. However, the idea was clearly repugnant to her, in daylight at least. A kiss with a stranger in the dark, however...

Claudia could feel the anger flowing through

him, hot and dangerous. It wouldn't take much to ignite it and then…She licked dry lips.

'What happened in Paris was…unfortunate.'

'Unfortunate? You were in bed with another man!'

It brought her gaze straight back to his. 'What are you talking about? I was in bed with you.'

'You didn't know my identity at the time. I was a total stranger as far as you were concerned.'

Claudia glared at him. 'It wasn't my idea, remember?'

'You shouldn't have been there in the first place.'

'Take it up with Genet.'

'I already have.'

'Did you buy his silence?'

'I didn't need to buy his silence. He knows it's more than his life is worth to breathe a word.'

'Oh, good. Think of the scandal otherwise.'

The Earl gritted his teeth, torn between several courses of action, all of them unwise and all of them deliciously tempting. With a serious effort he controlled himself. Claudia was confoundedly successful at provoking his wrath.

'I have neglected my responsibilities for far too long, but I mean to make amends.'

'And what exactly does that mean?' she demanded.

'It means that things are going to be different from now on.'

Hope leapt. 'Then you will permit the annulment to go ahead?'

'No.'

As quickly as they risen her spirits sank again, only to be replaced with an uncomfortable suspicion. 'Then what exactly do you intend?'

'To be a husband,' he replied.

'You can't be serious.'

'I was never more serious in my life.'

Her heartbeat accelerated dangerously as the recollection of the Parisian bedroom scene returned in vivid detail. 'It isn't going to happen.'

'I can assure you it is.'

'Do you really imagine that I'll allow you to walk back into my life as though nothing had happened?'

'Unfortunately, you have no choice about that, my dear. I am back and I intend to remain.'

Chapter Seven

Claudia lay awake, her mind in turmoil as it replayed all the details of that heated interview with Anthony. Turmoil was accompanied by impotent anger. He had no intention of letting her go, and it was quite clear that he intended to curb her independence as well. The knowledge that, in law, he was fully entitled to do it only added oil to flames. As to the rest of what he intended...The thought made her feel hot all over. It also revived shameful curiosity. She had often wondered how it might have been with them if he had remained at Ulverdale. The original contract stipulated that the marriage would not be consummated until she was sixteen, so they would have had time to get to know each other, become friends, maybe even fall in love. Her imagination had supplied a limited picture of what would happen after that. Certainly she had never envisaged anything like the sensations she had experienced that night in Paris; sensations that were impossible to forget. The fact that the incident meant nothing to him made everything so much worse.

Like Claudia, the Earl slept little that night but, as was his wont, rose early the next morning. A glance from the window revealed the start of a fine day; it provided a good opportunity to take a closer look around. No doubt in his lengthy absence there had been changes at Oakley Court. He turned from the window and glanced across the room to where Matthew was pouring hot water into a basin. The valet completed his task and turned round.

'Shall I shave you now, my lord?'

He assented. It was the part of the day he enjoyed least. The scarring on his face made shaving a lengthy and delicate operation. However, Matthew had a blessedly light touch which did much to alleviate discomfort. As the valet went about his task it left the Earl at leisure to reflect. His return was always going to be fraught with difficulty, but after the previous evening those had increased tenfold. The announcement of his intention to stay had resulted in his wife's stormy exit from the room. It had been tempting to go after her, but a moment's reflection showed him the folly of doing so. Claudia had been in no mood to listen to anything he might have to say. Knowing something of her fiery nature already, her reaction hadn't come as a complete surprise. It was also understandable. After having enjoyed her independence it had doubtless been a disagreeable shock to discover that she was subject to a husband's control. Given the choice he would have used a much lighter touch, but her involvement with Genet and his ilk was too pressing to ignore.

As to the rest, he was quite serious about that too—in spite of Claudia's outraged disbelief. His beautiful wife was going to have to accustom herself to his presence in her life.

By the time he got downstairs she had already breakfasted and gone. However, by dint of leaving the study door open, he was able to see who passed through the hall and thus, eventually, to intercept her.

'I must beg a few minutes of your time, Claudia.'

She stopped in her tracks, her attention fully arrested by the tall figure in the doorway. However, conversation with him was the last thing she wanted just then. 'Can it wait a little? I have rather a lot to do this morning.'

'I regret that it cannot.'

She bit her lip. It was tempting to walk away but a moment's reflection revealed that it might be unwise. He might have let her get away with it last night; he wouldn't do so a second time. The probable consequences for herself were disturbing. Accordingly she turned and bent her footsteps toward the study. He stood back to let her pass and then closed the door.

Aware of him to her fingertips, Claudia stood by the desk, surveying him with what she hoped looked like nonchalant ease. 'What is it, Anthony?'

He halted a few feet away. 'There are things I didn't get a chance to say last night.'

'Really? I rather thought we'd covered the essentials.'

'By no means.'

'What did we leave out?'

'It concerns my conversation with Genet.'

'Genet?' It wasn't what she had been expecting at all. 'What about him?'

'As yet he doesn't know how far the service has been compromised, but it is just possible that, although you escaped Paris in time, your identity is known anyway.'

Her brows drew together. 'How is that possible?'

'You have allowed use of the coastal access here in the past. This house is prominent in the neighbourhood. It would be child's play to discover the name of the owner.'

As she assimilated this the implications became more disturbing. 'Then the traitor may be English.'

'It's a possibility, and one that cannot be ignored.'

'I can see that, but not how it concerns me now. We're no longer in France.'

'No, but that only means you're further away

from possible danger, not out of reach.' He paused. 'While I don't want to cause undue alarm, you need to be aware of it, Claudia.'

She nodded. 'All right.'

'You also need to be careful.'

'Very well.' She regarded him quizzically. 'The same must also hold good for you.'

'It does, but I am better able to defend myself.'

'I can shoot straight.'

His lips quirked. 'I'm sure you can. Whether you will always have a pistol to hand is another matter.'

'Point taken. I'll be sure to carry it with me when I go out.'

'I'd be glad to know you did.' He paused. 'I'd hate to see you come to harm, my sweet.'

Something in his tone and the accompanying expression caused her pulse to quicken. Moreover, it lent a different dimension to their conversation last night. It seemed his apparent interference had a different motive from the one she had imagined. She had been so angry, that such a possibility had never occurred to her.

'Did Genet say any more about Paris?'

'Only that five people were arrested. Apart from ourselves, only Lebrun and Saunière managed to get away in time. To Antwerp apparently.'

'And those who were arrested?'

'Presumed dead.'

She shivered inwardly, knowing it might so easily have been her. He squeezed her shoulder gently.

'It does no good to dwell on it, Claudia.'

'I know, but I can't seem to help it.' The warmth of his hand was both reassuring and disturbing in equal measure, evoking memories of much closer intimacy. It would be all too easy to surrender to a momentary weakness and end up in his arms. The recognition that part of her wanted to was mortifying. She forced a smile and detached herself from his hold. 'The sooner I occupy myself again the better.'

His hand fell to his side. 'I'm sure you're right.'

'Please excuse me.' Claudia made for the door, needing to be gone now, every part of her aware of the gaze that followed her.

'Until later, then.'

She paused briefly on the threshold and nodded. With that she was gone. She did not hear the sigh that accompanied her departure.

The Earl watched her retreating figure until it was out of sight and then turned away. On one level it was a relief that they had been able to talk calmly this time; that he had told her the facts. On another, the little interview had underlined the distance between them. While she was prepared to engage with him to a degree, it was evident that she did not welcome physical intimacy, even when it had only been intended to comfort.

That thought engendered others; had his lovely wife found solace elsewhere during his absence? She had denied taking a lover, or even wanting to, but having glimpsed the passion beneath that cool exterior, he wondered. She must have had numerous admirers. She had a degree of freedom denied other women, and a thirst for adventure. It had taken her into many questionable places, including Madame Renaud's establishment. Had it also taken her into clandestine affairs, seeking the love she had been denied in her marriage? It wouldn't be the first time such a thing had happened. Once the first male heir had been born many married couples turned a blind eye to each other's infidelities. Had Claudia been unfaithful? He grimaced, knowing he had no right to criticise. People who lived in glass houses...

On the surface of things, dinner that evening seemed a little more relaxed. By dint of asking questions about the estate and its environs, the Earl encouraged Claudia to talk. She seemed willing enough to oblige him, glad to keep to neutral ground. After the meal they lingered over the remains of the wine.

'Do you never find yourself lonely here?' he asked then.

'No. I am used to my own company.'

The words carried no intended edge but they cut all the same. 'How do you entertain yourself?'

'I like to read and play the pianoforte. If the mood takes me I might sew, though it is not my favourite occupation. In the summer it is pleasant to walk or sit in the garden.'

'Do you invite friends to stay?'

'There is plenty of company to be had in London during the Season. This house is a welcome refuge after that. And, of course, I have various acquaintances in the neighbourhood who come to visit.'

'Do you not spend time at Ulverdale?'

'No.'

'I shall have to visit at some point,' he continued. 'I hoped you might accompany me.'

'I regret that I cannot.'

'Cannot?'

The apparent mildness of the enquiry did not deceive her for an instant. If she did not qualify the remark he might insist, and then they would quarrel.

'When, finally, I escaped from Ulverdale I vowed never to go back there.'

'I see.'

'Do you?' She set her glass on the table. 'I doubt that.'

Suddenly the tension was palpable again.

'Will you not tell me?' he asked.

'What can I tell you about your father that you do not already know?'

His brow creased. 'He did not hurt you, Claudia?'

'He did not physically raise a hand to me, though he left me in no doubt of my place in the scheme of things. Your mother was not always so fortunate.'

He stared at her, appalled. 'Good God! If I had

thought…I never once suspected that he would descend so far.' He paused. 'I had always been his whipping boy, you see.'

'You?'

'Yes. We were never close, but as I grew older and realised what his addiction to gaming was doing to our family, I came to despise him.' He smiled mirthlessly. 'I tried to talk to him about it, even remonstrated with him to make him see sense…'

'What happened?'

His jaw tightened. 'I got a beating for my pains.'

Having spent time in the proximity of her late father-in-law, she recognised the words for understatement. Being around the brute was like walking on eggshells. The least thing could trigger his temper, never mind a direct confrontation. That Anthony should have instigated one was certainly courageous, even admirable, albeit misguided.

'I'm sorry to hear it,' she said, 'though I'm not in the least surprised.'

'I used to think that I was the cause of most of his ill-humour, that if I was out of the way his temper might improve.'

'No, it merely found another target.'

'I swear I had no idea.' He paused. 'While I knew that my parents' marriage was unhappy, it was characterised by coldness, not violence.'

'I think by the end that your father was… unbalanced.'

'His behaviour was always unbalanced.'

'Yet, knowing that, you left me at Ulverdale, the very place you could not wait escape.'

'It was very wrong of me.' He sighed. 'Perhaps it's time to return and confront the demons.'

'You know nothing of my demons, Anthony. Do not presume to tell me how to deal with them.'

'You cannot run away from them.'

'You did.'

His jaw tightened. 'I am not proud of it.'

'I am. Leaving there I count as one of great achievements of my life.'

'It was not the fault of the place.'

'The Bastille can't help being a fortress, but that doesn't make it a desirable place to be.'

'Then since you feel so strongly, I withdraw my suggestion about your coming.'

They lapsed into tense silence for a while. Then she took a deep breath. 'I am thinking of returning to London next month.'

'By all means; we can go whenever you wish.'

We. Claudia lowered her gaze, avoiding his, conscious of increasing annoyance. She controlled it. After all, what had she expected? That he would permit her to return to London alone? That her old life would resume as normal? There was no chance of that now. Anthony's presence was all too real and he wasn't going to go away. The best that she could hope for was some sort of *modus vivendi* that would facilitate a peaceful co-existence. They had lived separate lives before, they could do so again.

'As you wish.' She rose from the table. 'And now if you will excuse me, I am feeling rather tired. I shall retire early.'

The Earl rose too, surveying her steadily. 'Goodnight then, Claudia.'

He watched her walk away and then resumed his seat with a sigh, mentally cursing his tactlessness. Each time he thought he was making progress he would suddenly find himself two steps back. It had been a mistake to mention Ulverdale, but then he could never have guessed at the depth of her antipathy for the place. It was quite evident that she thought of it as a prison. To have insisted on her accompanying him would only have alienated her further. The significance of her wish to return to London hadn't escaped him either. Apart from the numerous distractions on offer, it afforded the possibility of seeing less of him. He finished the rest of his wine. Why would she not wish to see less of him? She was trapped in marriage with a man she didn't love and whose motives for keeping her were questionable. Yet there had been a spark between them. He had not imagined it. The memory lingered and he clung to it, unable to help himself. If it could only be rekindled…He sighed. The way things were at present such a hope seemed forlorn.

Chapter Eight

The clock on the mantel showed that it lacked a few minutes till seven. Claudia slid out of bed and went to the closet, rummaging for her favourite riding clothes. Having located them she began to dress. It was quite quickly accomplished, leaving her only to tie back her hair with a ribbon. She paused briefly to glance in the cheval glass. A slim figure in boyish clothes stared back. In London she could never have enjoyed such freedom, but here, in the privacy of the park, it was possible to do as she pleased.

As a precaution she used the back stairs on her way out. There was little risk of running into Anthony; likely it would be hours yet before he made an appearance, and by the time he did she would look the epitome of respectability again. Meanwhile, she meant to enjoy herself.

Hurrying along the side path she turned the corner and headed for the stables, reaching her destination a few minutes later. As she did so, the head groom emerged from the stable building.

Seeing her approach he smiled, touching his cap in acknowledgement. 'Good morning, my lady. Shall I saddle Spirit for you?'

She returned the smile. 'Thank you, Jenkins.'

'Do you wish to be accompanied today?'

'No, I'll be staying in the park so I'll ride alone.'

'Very good, my lady.'

Five minutes later he led Spirit from the stable. The chestnut mare whinnied, her ears pricking when she saw Claudia. Jenkins grinned, watching as his mistress stroked the horse's velvety muzzle. Then he held the stirrup while she mounted, waiting till she was comfortably settled in the saddle before letting go of the bridle. Claudia thanked him and then, touching the mare with her heels, set off.

It had rained overnight, but the clouds had moved on leaving pale sunlight and translucent blue skies. She smiled to herself. In spite of everything, it felt good to be alive on such a morning. It also felt good to have some time to herself to enjoy at least the illusion of freedom.

She held the mare to a walk along the tree-lined track, but when they reached the open ground beyond, let her out to a canter. The faster pace felt good, like the feel of the wind in her hair and the cool air on her cheeks. The horse seemed to sense her enjoyment and to share it, her small neat hooves flying over the turf. Feeling her champ the bit, Claudia leaned forward.

'Go, Spirit. The pace will suit me well.'

With that she gave the horse its head and the canter accelerated into an exhilarating gallop.

When Matthew had finished shaving him, the Earl rose from the chair and finished drying his face on the towel. A cursory glance from the window stopped him in his tracks and, involuntarily, he followed the progress of the galloping horse. An elegant creature, it was finely made with a look of the Arabian breed, an impression borne out by its evident swiftness. He had no need to ask the identity of the rider. Nor was there any doubt of her skill. He might have guessed that Claudia would be a competent horsewoman. Knowing her as he did by this time, it should have come as no surprise that she should flout convention by riding astride or failing to take a groom with her. It was all of a piece with the rest of her behaviour. He did not imagine it was done on purpose to annoy him; the early hour suggested that her intention had been just the opposite; that she sought not to draw his attention at all. However, it did annoy him, particularly in the light of their recent conversation, and they were going to have to discuss the matter.

Claudia reined the horse in at the top of the slope and let her breathe for a minute before continuing at a gentler pace. As she rode she looked around, enjoying the peace and beauty of the new day. The rain had left water droplets on every twig and blade of grass so that they sparkled in the strengthening light. In the distance a patch of sea, gun-metal grey, was visible through a declivity in the wooded slope. As she looked, a movement caught her eye and she discerned a figure on the edge of the trees. It was a man but he was too far away to make out details, although he did seem to be looking her way. Perhaps he'd just noticed her too. Then he turned and, moments later, was lost to view in the wood. Claudia frowned. His behaviour seemed furtive somehow which argued the poacher. She would mention the matter to the land agent when next they met.

She returned from her ride feeling thoroughly invigorated by the exercise and fresh air. Giving Spirit a final pat she handed the reins to the waiting groom. Then she hurried back to the house.

When she emerged from her room half an hour later all trace of the hoyden was gone, and she was respectably dressed in a sprigged muslin frock with her hair neatly arranged. She went downstairs. The breakfast parlour was empty so she assumed that Anthony hadn't come down yet. After all, it was still early. Claudia relaxed a little. Helping herself to ham and eggs she turned her mind to the household tasks awaiting her attention. It was also time to take a look at the accounts. She liked to think that all the servants were trustworthy, but suspected that, in part, it was because they knew she kept an eye on expenditure.

Her mind was still engaged with the thought as she headed for the salon after breakfast. She was through the door before she realised that she was not alone and involuntarily stopped in her tracks.

Hearing her come in, the Earl looked up from the paper he had been reading and got to his feet.

'Good morning.'

Recovering her self-possession she returned the greeting. 'I beg your pardon. I didn't mean to intrude.'

'You're not intruding. As a matter of fact I've been waiting to speak with you.'

Something about his expression caused an uneasy fluttering sensation in her stomach. 'Is something wrong?'

'Did we not have a conversation recently about the need for sensible caution?'

'Well, yes, but…'

'Yet you rode out unaccompanied today.'

'I…it was only in the park.'

'Do you imagine that such distinctions will carry any weight with those who might wish you ill?'

Feeling uncomfortably on the back foot now, she reddened a little. 'No, I suppose not. I didn't think.'

'No, you didn't think. You laid yourself wide open to possible danger.'

'It wasn't intentional. It's just that I always ride alone if I'm going to stay in the park.'

'Not any more. In future you'll take a groom with you.'

She bit back the immediate reply that came to mind, knowing that it would only exacerbate the situation. Moreover, she knew that he was right; it had been foolish and she had been unthinking. Her annoyance turned inward.

Anthony took a step closer filling her line of vision. 'Am I making myself clear?'

'Perfectly clear. It won't happen again.'

'See that it doesn't.'

Unable to bear the weight of that fierce scrutiny she looked away. 'It was foolish. I'm sorry.'

Some of the tension went out of him. 'All right, we'll say no more about it.'

It was then she remembered the man she had seen earlier at the edge of the wood. However, to mention that now would only make things worse. It would keep for later. The silence stretched out a little longer.

'Was there anything else?' she asked.

'No, nothing else. Now if you'll excuse me, there are things I have to do.'

With that he left her. Claudia let out a long breath. No question but he was still very annoyed. The fact that his anger was justified did nothing for her peace of mind. No doubt he thought her a heedless little fool. She had always prided herself on professionalism where her work was concerned, and it was galling that, twice now, she'd given him cause to doubt it. Just why his opinion should matter was unclear, but she knew it did and she was resolved not to be careless again. It occurred to her then that he hadn't made any comment at all about her choice of riding clothes.

When he left Claudia the Earl headed for the stables himself, wanting to distance himself from the house for a while. Some fresh air would clear his head and that would be no bad thing either. It wasn't easy to maintain a cold and forbidding manner in his wife's presence, but he'd wanted to leave her in no doubt as to his mind. Her safety was paramount and it depended in part on her co-operation. Playing the repressive husband was no part of his plan, but nor could he allow her to think everything could go on as it had before. His talk with Genet had made that clear.

Claudia spent an hour on the household accounts, or, more precisely, staring unseeing at rows of figures. No matter how hard she tried, all that she could think of was her interview with Anthony. The recollection of his anger only enhanced her guilt. In the end she gave up on income and expenditure, and shut the book. It was a fine day and a walk would clear her head.

The steps from the terrace adjoined a path which ran alongside the lawn for a little way, leading thence through an archway in the yew hedge and coming at length to the edge of a broad grassy walk. At its end, some two hundred yards off, was a stand of mature trees. Claudia turned towards them, coming to the fringes of the grove a few minutes later. In the midst was a clearing where stood a small circular temple built in the classical Greek style. Open at the sides, its supporting pillars and upper stonework were darkened with rainwater and greened with moss. In the centre of the marbled floor beneath the dome was a plinth adorned with a semi-nude statue of the goddess Aphrodite. It stood only two feet high but the workmanship was exquisite. Claudia found herself drawn back to it repeatedly. She had no idea of its origin or how long it might have been there. It looked very old so perhaps it had been installed by whoever had built the house. She had no idea who that might have been. According to family legend the first Earl of Ulverdale had won the property from a rival at the gaming tables during the reign of Charles the Second, a tale she had little difficulty in believing. Whatever the truth of the matter she enjoyed coming here.

The temple was pleasant, conducive to quiet thought and the contemplation of art. Slowly she moved round the plinth, regarding the figure from every angle. It was as though the sculptor had captured a moment of intimacy, a woman disrobing to bathe perhaps, and translated movement into stone. Its simplicity was beautiful and arresting.

'I wonder who the sculptor was thinking of when he created that.'

The voice broke into her reverie and her heart leapt towards her throat. She turned quickly to see Anthony standing on the threshold. His horse was tethered to a bush some few yards off. The damp turf had prevented her hearing either of them approaching. She turned back to the statue again, mentally trying to compose herself, aware of booted feet crossing the marble floor behind her.

'Perhaps there was no particular person, only an idealised image in his mind,' she replied.

He came to stand beside her. 'Perhaps.'

'You doubt it?'

'She is so beautifully rendered and yet more lifelike than most classical statuary. This seems to me to be more like a tribute, as though a lovely woman were immortalised in stone.'

Claudia glanced up in surprise. She had never heard him speak in that way before, or in quite that contemplative tone. 'Do you know anything of her history?'

'Very little. Apparently my grandfather acquired the piece in Italy while on the Grand Tour. He claimed that it was a Bernini.' He smiled ruefully. 'I suspect it was wishful thinking; the old man was renowned for telling some tall tales.'

'And yet the Italian ladies are accounted very beautiful, are they not? Perhaps the sculptor had a secret lover who provided the inspiration for this.'

'It's a wonderfully romantic notion, isn't it?'

'There are precedents for such a muse,' she replied. 'Petrarch and Laura; Dante and Beatrice...'

'Bernini and Aphrodite?'

It was said deadpan, but then his gaze met hers and she caught the gleam in his eye and, unexpectedly, they both laughed. And then, gradually, laughter faded a little and was replaced by something much quieter and infinitely more intense. Her heartbeat quickened and she lowered her eyes in confusion, aware of him to the last particle of her being. Aware too that the place was some distance from the house and they were quite alone; aware of a danger that she could no longer name but recognising that its origins lay in her.

He drew closer. 'What are you afraid of, Claudia?'

'Nothing.'

'No?' His hands rested lightly on her shoulders, their touch warm through her clothing. 'Then why are you trembling?'

There were many answers to that, chiefly concerned with his nearness now and the sensations it gave rise to; sensations she ought not to be feeling.

Instead she sought safety in prevarication. 'I...it's a little cooler out here than I thought.'

A hand closed gently over hers and, feeling the temperature of her flesh, he frowned. 'You are cold, aren't you?'

'I thought a shawl would be warm enough. I'll go back now.'

He released his hold. 'In that case I'll walk back with you. Just let me fetch my horse.'

Drawing a deep breath, she watched him stride away, still feeling the warm imprint of his hands on her skin. She saw him retrieve the reins. Then, leading the animal towards her, he fell into step alongside. They walked in silence which offered a kind of refuge and which neither one made any effort to break.

Chapter Nine

In the course of the next week life settled into a quiet routine, on the surface of things anyway. Although there had been no more arguments, Claudia began to feel restless. In spite of keeping herself occupied each day, the familiar round of tasks offered no challenge. More than ever she missed the autonomy of her old life. More than that, she missed the adventure and the sense of doing something worthwhile. She had made a promise to Henry. Now, Napoleon was raising an army, all of Europe was in ferment and she was cooped up here, trapped in a loveless marriage with a man who would never let her go.

Realising how perilously near to self-pity she was allowing herself to become, her annoyance turned inwards. She needed to shake herself out of this and soon. A good walk would have helped to lighten her mood, but it had been raining all morning. Instead she went to the salon and ensconced herself in an armchair with a copy of *Camilla*.

However, it proved hard to concentrate and she found her attention straying from the novel to the alcove opposite where her brother's picture hung. The dark gaze held hers, steady, kind and understanding. Being only a year apart they were close as children, finding in each other the warmth and affection so lacking in their parent. It was always easy to talk to Henry. He was a good listener and he never judged her. She wished so much that she could talk to him now. What advice would he give? It might be impossible to answer that, but she could at least keep faith with him; could at least try to serve her country, as he had.

Being deeply engrossed in thought she failed to hear the door open and, as she was curled up in the chair, the Earl was halfway across the room before he noticed her presence. He checked abruptly, taking in the scene at a glance. At any other time he might have smiled at its artless charm, but just then what struck him most forcibly was the expression on her face. It was sad and wistful and achingly lonely. More than ever he would have liked to draw her close and kiss away the sadness he saw there, but he knew he could not. If he touched her he might not be able to stop at a single kiss and anyway she would not welcome the attention. Conscious of trespass, he would have retreated then, but some sixth sense warned her that she wasn't alone any more. She looked round quickly, her expression registering both surprise and wariness.

'Anthony.'

'Forgive me, my dear. I didn't mean to startle you.'

Keenly aware of him and of her informal position, she straightened and rose from the chair. 'Was there something you wanted?'

'I came in for those.' He nodded towards the papers reposing on the small table nearby.

'Ah. Yes, of course.' She summoned a brittle smile. 'Be my guest.'

He drew nearer and then glanced towards the picture she had been looking at before. It was head and shoulders portrait of a young man in army uniform. His warm colouring was very like Claudia's, and, although the lines of the jaw and brow were much stronger, he could detect similarities in the eyes and mouth.

'Your brother?'

'Yes. It was painted just before Henry went to Spain.'

'I can see a certain likeness between you.'

She nodded. 'I like to think there is one.'

'You and he were very close, I collect.'

'He was my best friend.' The words came out involuntarily. Moreover, they revealed rather more than she had intended and she was immediately aware of the attention bent her way. She averted her eyes to the painting again.

The Earl smiled faintly. 'My brothers and sisters died in infancy so I never got to know them, but I have often thought that it must be pleasant to have siblings close in age to oneself and to whom one felt an affinity.'

'I don't know what I would have done without Henry,' she replied. 'He was a rock in all the turmoil.'

'Your mother's untimely death must have been a dreadful shock.'

'It was, but the turmoil began long before. Like so many of their generation, my parents' marriage was arranged but it was not a happy union. Some of my earliest memories are of their rows. Those became increasingly bitter with time.' She sighed. 'Their tastes and interests were opposed, and my mother, though beautiful, possessed of a fiery temper. My father was authoritarian, a cold and undemonstrative man, though I think he did care for her in his way.'

'And what of you and your brother?'

'Henry was the heir. My mother doted on him. My father, though he could never be said to dote, was nevertheless very proud of him and took a keen interest in his education and his future career.' She smiled ruefully. 'Being a girl I was never of any consequence to either of my parents. After my mother died, my father hired a governess and considered his duty done. He never showed any interest in me, until I was old enough to be of use to him. Henry was the only person who ever made me feel that I mattered.'

'I see.' Suddenly he did see; indeed a great many things became clear.

Claudia glanced up at him. 'I think it is not uncommon. Sons always take precedence over daughters in terms of importance.'

'Even so, it does not excuse emotional neglect.'

'And yet, having met your father, I suspect that your own experience was not so very different.'

'It wasn't,' he replied, 'or not where he was concerned. My mother was affectionate when we met, though I saw little of her, and there wasn't a Henry around to confide in.'

'I was fortunate in that at least.'

'Yes, you were.'

'I used to be able to tell him anything, and he was never shocked or angry.'

'An ideal confidant then.'

'We would talk about all manner of things. He was always interested in politics, and especially the progress of the war. He said he wanted to serve his country, not sit in a dreary office surrounded by ledgers.'

'How did your father respond to that? Surely he wanted his son to go into the business after him.'

'Yes, but Henry refused. They had a fierce argument about it, but, in the end, my father backed down and agreed to buy him a commission in the army.'

'What about the business?'

'One of my cousins stepped into the role that Henry declined.' She shook her head. 'Sometimes I try to imagine how things would have been if he had stayed, but it's always much easier to see him leading a charge.'

'His love of adventure has rubbed off on you.'

'I suppose it has, although I still can't see myself leading a cavalry charge.'

Anthony smiled. 'Well, that's a relief anyway.'

'It was a great pity he never married. I should have liked to have some little nieces and nephews.'

He glanced down at her. 'Should you?'

'Yes. I like children.' As the implications of that remark dawned, she hurried on. 'I mean, I'm sure I should have liked them...if he'd ever had any. Which he didn't.'

The Earl's lips twitched. For a moment he fought temptation but it proved too strong. 'And should you not like to have children of your own, Claudia?'

Under that cool scrutiny her blush deepened. 'I...I really hadn't thought of it.'

'No?'

'Of course not. How should I? It was never relevant.'

'And now?'

She lifted her chin. 'It is no more relevant now than it was before.'

As soon as the words were out she knew them

for falsehood. The subject was going to become increasingly important because Ulverdale would require an heir. Moreover, Anthony would be within his rights whether he demanded one or many children. Her entire body turned hot at the thought. Out of nowhere came the thought that it might be pleasant to have a family of her own. Then the spectres of pregnancy and childbirth returned with force. She had no intention of becoming a brood mare to satisfy the Brudenell family's dynastic interests. However, there was more involved here than just her feelings. Given the situation, what were the odds that history would repeat itself? Even if she braved childbirth and survived, would Anthony love his children, care for his children, or would he reveal the same indifference to his offspring as his father had shown? As indeed her father had shown? How would Anthony regard her once he had the heir he needed? Would he abandon her as he had before? The possibility was chilling.

Although he was unable to follow her thoughts, her expression was more eloquent. Therefore, instead of the verbal challenge she had been expecting, he merely returned a wry smile.

'You're right of course, my dear.' He retrieved the papers from the table. 'And now if you'll excuse me, I'll go and read these and leave you to your book.'

She waited until the door closed behind him and then hurled her novel on to the chair, furious with herself for rising to the bait. He must have enjoyed that little scene immensely. The wretched man always seemed to know exactly how to provoke her, and she fell for it. She already knew he didn't love her; he didn't even want her apparently. Her unwillingness to share his bed was a matter of supreme indifference to him. It shouldn't have mattered to her either, but the knowledge rankled deeply. To be an unwanted wife was bad enough, but to be a virgin wife took a bad joke to a new dimension. Of course, Anthony had time on his side. They were husband and wife and he was no doubt calculating that, eventually, she would yield. Even worse was the inability to forget how it had felt to share his bed. Her treacherous thoughts kept returning there giving rise to sensations that were as shocking as they were unexpected. It was like a sickness that had no cure.

Anthony scanned *The Times*, his mind rapidly assimilating the details of the latest news from France. Given the rapidity with which Napoleon was gathering his forces together, confrontation was inevitable. The only question was where? No doubt Genet's spies were kept busy trying to learn the details of troop movements, and the most likely route for an invasion. If the work had been dangerous before it was much more so now. For a moment Alain Poiret's face came to mind. *You must warn Claudine...get her safe away.*

The Earl frowned. Thank heaven the warning had come in time to get her out, in spite of her initial efforts to thwart him. His former career had led him to the expectation of instant obedience from those in his command. Nothing had prepared him for Claudia. Of course, he'd fondly imagined then that their relationship would be of short duration. How wrong could a person be? Yet being wrong, would he change things?

It took but a moment to know the answer. She was in his blood; had been from their meeting on that astonishing evening in Paris. It was vain to deny it. He wanted her as he'd never wanted a woman in his life, but it meant nothing without her full and free consent. He sighed. Once he might have rated his chances more highly; might have been able to woo her and win her, but that was before a French cavalry sabre had destroyed his face.

An improvement in the weather next morning provided all the excuse Claudia needed to get out of the house. However, when she arrived at the stables it was to find that Anthony was already there and a groom leading out his horse. The bay was a beautiful animal standing over sixteen hands and, quite evidently, being possessed of a spirited temperament. She guessed that it wouldn't be an easy horse to ride. With its small head and powerful neck and flowing mane it had the look of the

Spanish breed. Had Anthony brought it back with him? Suddenly she was curious.

The Earl swung into the saddle and was about to depart when he looked up and saw her. His gaze lingered. The full-skirted green habit was elegant and in the first stare of fashion. It also showed off her figure to advantage. The jacket was cut in the latest military style, its severe lines relieved by gold frogging. A dashing feathered shako completed the outfit.

He smiled. 'Good morning, my dear.'

Feigning nonchalance, she returned the greeting. Then, to divert his attention, she nodded towards the horse. 'That's a beautiful animal. Andalucian?'

'That's right.'

'What do you call him?'

'Diablo.'

'And is he a devil?'

'He can be, when he feels like it.'

She could well believe it. The bay was no mount for a novice. As the groom led Spirit out the mare looked small in comparison.

The Earl glanced at the chestnut and then at Claudia. 'Come with me this morning.'

She hesitated, but it was impossible to refuse without seeming sulky or petulant. Better to let him think she attached no importance to the matter one way or another.

'As you wish.'

He waited while the groom helped her into the

saddle. Supremely conscious of the Earl's undivided attention, she casually arranged her skirts and gathered her reins.

'Ready?' he asked.

'Yes.'

As they set off he reined the bay alongside. For a little while they rode in silence. For all her feigned indifference Claudia was aware of the man to her fingertips. From time to time she darted a glance his way. He had an excellent seat, she noticed, but then it was hard not to when the close fitting riding clothes accentuated every line of that hard, virile frame. A frame whose strength she had already experienced. The hands that held the reins with such deceptive lightness now were also capable of punishment—and arousal. Far from being an imposition, his presence was both stimulating and exciting. Embarrassed by the direction of her thoughts and annoyed with herself for thinking them, she looked quickly away.

In fact the Earl hadn't noticed that covert inspection. His attention was temporarily elsewhere, taking in the prosperous and well-tended look of the whole demesne. It was everywhere apparent from the neatly-laid hedges and clear, free-running ditches to the cultivated fields in the distance where the new green wheat showed above the dark earth. He looked across at his companion.

'Is Charles Trevor still the land agent here?'

'He retired four years ago,' she said. 'His son, Hugh, now occupies the position.'

'I see. An appointee of my father's, I presume.'

'No, an appointee of mine.'

The Earl knew he shouldn't have been surprised, but all the same he was.

'Hugh Trevor learned the business from his parent,' Claudia went on, 'and bids fair to be every bit as good.'

'You say that with great confidence so you must be familiar with the quality of his work.'

'Of course. We have regular meetings, and I have ridden out with him and his father on numerous occasions.' She smiled reminiscently. 'Hugh has the same love of the land. He is so enthusiastic and energetic, and very knowledgeable about the latest farming methods.'

The warmth of her tone combined with the smile didn't escape her companion. However, he was also curious and didn't want to stop Claudia in this expansive mood.

'Is he indeed?'

She nodded. 'His introduction of the new plough and seed drill paid dividends on the wheat harvest last year.'

'Did it?'

'Yes. The yield increased by about five tons to the acre.'

The Earl became more intrigued by the moment. That any young woman should take an interest in such things was entirely beyond his experience. He decided to probe a little further.

'And what did you do with the extra profit?'

'Most of it was invested in more up-to-date machinery. There was a new harrow that Mr Trevor was particularly keen to acquire. The rest paid for replacement thatch on the farm labourers' cottages in Thorney Lane.'

As he listened the Earl was quietly impressed. It was quite apparent that she had involved herself fully in the running of the estate, and he applauded that. She was interested and knowledgeable and, he suspected, competent. That she should have undertaken such a role only served to revive his guilt.

Unable to decipher his thoughts, Claudia wondered if he were displeased. Now that he was back perhaps he felt it was not her place to make financial decisions on that scale.

'Do you mind?' she asked.

'Do I mind what, my dear?'

'That the money should have been spent in that way.'

'Certainly not. You have made all the right decisions. Not many young women would concern themselves over such things.'

'Well, someone had to.' As soon as the words were out she could have bitten off her tongue. 'I'm sorry, I didn't mean…that is, I…' she broke off, floundering.

'Don't be uneasy. You were right: someone had to and I wasn't here.'

Spots of colour appeared in her cheeks. 'The work was overdue. I would have done something about it before if I'd been able to. However, it was out of the question until I attained my majority. Your father had no interest in Oakley Court, or his tenants.'

'I can quite believe it. He had no interest in anything besides gaming and hunting.' He smiled wryly. 'When I was a child I used to hope he would take me out riding or shooting or fishing. He never did.'

'Why would any man let such opportunities slip? He might have established a much closer bond between you.'

'He never saw them as opportunities, only as potential hindrance. Besides, he didn't want a close bond.'

'But your mother cared.'

'Yes, but she was dominated by him. I was left first in the care of a nursemaid and then a tutor, and brought out for inspection once a day. If the tutor reported any deficiencies in my behaviour or studies my father would administer a beating.'

'Good heavens.'

'When I was nine I was sent away to school. My father said the discipline would do me good.'

Claudia paled. 'That's dreadful.'

'Not in the least. It was a blessed relief since

the regime at Eton was much easier and far more pleasant.'

The tone was light enough but she glimpsed the hurt that lay beneath. It revealed an unexpected vulnerability. The lonely, brutal childhood had in part shaped the man he had become. The conversation shed light on an area of his life about which she knew nothing, and it whetted her curiosity.

'What happened after Eton?'

'Cambridge; at my father's insistence. I wanted a career in the army, but that is usually the preserve of younger sons and the old man wouldn't hear of it.' He paused. 'Then, at the end of the second year I was summoned home and informed that I was to marry.'

'I can well imagine how that was received.'

'Yes, I expect you can. There was a fierce row, of course, and I refused point blank to comply, until the full extent of the financial situation was revealed. After that I knew there was no choice.' He shot a swift look her way. 'Hardly a flattering description of events, is it?'

'How could it be? The entire arrangement was about money.'

'Nevertheless, it offered the opportunity I had been seeking with regard to a career in the army.'

'You agreed to the marriage in exchange for a commission.'

'Exactly.' He met her gaze. 'I'm not proud of my actions, Claudia.'

She sighed. 'Well it's all water under the bridge now, isn't it?'

They rode on in silence for a while. Claudia had no difficulty in identifying with what she had heard, or with the emotions beneath. She had been terrified to learn of her father's plans for her future; terrified by the thought of leaving her home to live among strangers to whom she meant nothing more than a financial package. So much so that she had found the courage to confront her father.

'I don't want to be married yet. I'm not ready.'

'Ready or not, you most certainly shall be married,' he replied. 'This match is more than I could ever have hoped for. It allies us with one of the oldest and most respected families in the land.'

'I don't care about that.'

'You will learn to care, you silly girl. In the meantime you will be guided by me.'

'If I must marry let it be later; when I am seventeen or eighteen.'

'It cannot be later. The Earl's financial problems are pressing and must be resolved as soon as may be. Besides, the contracts are signed and sealed. The wedding will go ahead as planned.'

And so it had, regardless of tears and entreaties. The marriage ceremony had been brief and confusing, the groom distant and grim-faced. He'd rejoined his regiment almost immediately afterwards, abandoning her at Ulverdale. Claudia swallowed hard. Her feelings had counted for nothing.

But then nor had Anthony's. He too had been a pawn in a larger game. The only difference was that he had found an escape route, of a kind.

These thoughts occupied her until their return to the stables. She was abruptly jolted out of them when her companion dismounted and, having handed his horse to a groom, came to help her. Claudia feigned nonchalance but, as always when he was near, it was much harder to maintain an outward show of calm. Strong hands closed on her waist, lifting her without any apparent effort and then set her down gently. The hands lingered on her waist.

'I wonder, would you like to see the other horse I brought back with me?' he asked.

Keenly aware of this prolonged proximity and of its potential danger to herself, Claudia hesitated. Caution vied with curiosity and lost. 'Is he another Diablo?'

'It's not a he this time, and she's not in the least like Diablo.'

'I'd like to see her.'

He relinquished his hold then and they went together into the stable. In a stall at the far end was a pretty grey mare. Standing at 15.2 hands, she was a little bigger than Spirit, but she had the same dark, intelligent eyes. Claudia regarded her with quiet delight.

'She's beautiful.' Moving quietly to the horse's

head she let the animal breathe her scent. 'What do you call her?'

'Jarilla: she's named after a white flower that grows in the mountain regions of Spain.'

'It suits her.'

'I think so.'

'May I try her sometime?'

'Whenever you like. She's keen but she's well-mannered.'

'You have an eye for a good horse,' she said.

'Yes, but fortunately one eye is enough.'

Claudia looked up quickly and catching his expression, smiled too. 'So it would seem. After all, it was no impediment to Nelson.'

'Hmm. Perhaps I should point out that Nelson is dead.'

'All right, the Norse god, Odin, then. Did not he give an eye in exchange for wisdom?'

'So the story goes. I cannot claim to have done the same.'

She lifted a hand towards his face. He tensed, holding his breath, forcing himself to remain still as her fingertips came to rest lightly on the leather patch.

'You lost yours in the service of your country. To my mind that's a far nobler thing.'

For an instant a shadow crossed his face, a shadow composed of pain and horror. Then it was gone. He smiled wryly. 'There was nothing noble about it, believe me.'

'There is from where I'm standing,' she replied.

His smile faded a little and the gaze holding hers became intent. Her pulse quickened. He stepped a little closer, and his hands slid round her waist drawing her to him. That sudden, unexpected contact sent a charge through the length of her. His face drew nearer her own, its expression unmistakeable, and then his mouth brushed hers, gentle, tentative, seeking her response and then, when she did not pull away, becoming more assured. Her breath caught in her throat and deep inside a familiar spark leapt into being. She forgot to resist; forgot that this was folly; forgot everything except the man and the knowledge that she wanted this. As her mouth yielded to his the kiss grew deeper, his tongue seeking hers, tasting its sweetness, his hands caressing her back, warm and strong and sensual, sending a delicious tremor along her spine. He felt it and the hold tightened, pulling her closer. The response was an immediate flood of heat in her pelvis, fuelled by the faint spicy scent of sandalwood on his coat and beneath it the scent of the man, erotic and exciting. Her arms slid around his neck, her body moulding itself to his. At once the spark leapt into flame and the kiss became passionate and hungry and dangerous.

Every bodily instinct was to yield herself up to the fire and to be consumed, but, in the back of her mind, it also illuminated disturbing memories of Paris. Anthony might desire her but he didn't love her. To him she was a means to an end as she had always been. Once it had been about money, now it was about getting an heir, and, seeing his opportunity, he meant to see his will met. Ashamed of her collusion in that design, she tensed, turning her head aside so that his lips grazed her cheek.

'I'm sorry, I…I should never have…'

The effect was like a bucket of cold water and he drew back a little, regarding her averted face. His heart sank. It was impossible to mistake the expression there. Desire ebbed and he slackened his hold. For a second or two, neither one moved or spoke. Then he stepped back and she was free.

'Forgive me,' he said. 'I didn't mean to get carried away like that.'

Heart pounding, she turned her head to meet his gaze, unable to form a coherent reply. However, the look on her face was far more eloquent.

He surveyed her steadily but his expression was cool now, almost mocking. 'I should have remembered that your preference is for intimacy in the dark.'

With that he turned and walked away. Speechless and trembling with reaction, Claudia stared after him in disbelief. And then, slowly, disbelief gave way to appalled realisation. How could she have been such a fool? After everything that had gone before, after all that experience had taught her about marriage, how could she have allowed herself to be so easily seduced? Yet when he kissed her she hadn't been able to help herself; worse she hadn't wanted to help herself. Her entire body still resonated to the touch and scent and taste of him. A few minutes more and he'd have taken her right here in the straw like any common trollop and she would have yielded. Even the dread of pregnancy would not have swayed her at that moment. Was physical desire so strong a passion that it swept all other considerations aside, or was this really about her moral frailty? He must have recognised that and been disgusted by it. Cringing inwardly, Claudia wondered how she was ever going to face him again.

The Earl strode back to the house, his expression grim. It hadn't been his intention to touch her, but somehow he hadn't been able to help himself. He'd wanted her so badly it almost frightened him. He only had to be in the same room for passion to awaken. Having then indulged it, he should not have been surprised by her response. While she managed to conceal her distaste most of the time, she could never entirely do so when intimacy beckoned. When it became clear that his feelings were not returned he had concealed shame and embarrassment with a cool set down. The memory burned, fuelled by self-disgust. What woman could regard him now with anything other than repugnance? Rather than risk rejection, or worse, pity, he had always avoided putting himself in that situation, throwing himself into his career instead. Having broken that rule he should have been prepared for the consequences. Once, not so long ago, he had told Claudia that he intended to be a husband. He wondered now how he could have spoken with such confounded self-assurance.

Chapter Ten

Claudia was tempted to stay away from the dining room that evening. After all that had passed between them the thought of meeting Anthony filled her with dread, but, short of taking every meal in her chamber from now till kingdom come, there was no way of avoiding it. Glancing at her reflection in the mirror she smoothed a small wrinkle from the bodice of her gown. It was one of her newest, and already one of her favourites, a confection of white crepe with an overdress of lace. It was both modish and, with its deep décolleté, exquisitely feminine. She knew it became her well and, just then, needed every boost to self-confidence that she could get. Goodness knew it was little enough. She sighed and, turning from the mirror, slid her feet into white satin slippers. A touch of perfume completed the toilette. Then, gathering the shredded remains of courage, she went down to dinner.

* * *

Hearing a light footstep he looked round and then came slowly to his feet. He must have breathed, though it seemed to him that he could not. He hadn't expected her to appear at all this evening, perhaps not for several days. After what had happened earlier, most women would have taken refuge in hysterics and smelling salts. He might have known that she would do exactly the opposite. Not only did she have the nerve to face him, she managed to look completely unruffled. Butter wouldn't melt. As for that gown…One look was enough to fire a man's blood. Had that been deliberate too? A taunting reference to what had passed? He wouldn't be surprised; she had mettle enough. It ought to have increased his ire, but what he felt instead was more like admiration.

'Good evening, my dear.'

'Anthony.'

She inclined her head in acknowledgement of his presence. Recollecting his manners he made her a belated bow. As she moved past him he caught a faint whiff of her perfume; heady, exotic and fascinatingly elusive. In spite of himself his lips quirked. He had to hand it to her, when Claudia went to war she gave no quarter.

They dined in silence for the most part. In truth she had little appetite and her stomach seemed knotted, but she would rather have died than let him see it. The brute looked so completely at his ease. When at length he had finished eating, he leaned back in his chair, surveying her steadily, his hand toying with the stem of his wine glass.

'I am planning to leave for Ulverdale in the morning.'

Her heart sank. She had temporarily forgotten about the arrangement, but she wasn't naïve enough to think the timing a coincidence. It was clear that he couldn't wait to be away from her now. With an effort she recovered her self-possession.

'Will you be away long?'

'A week or two, I imagine. There will be much to re-acquaint myself with.'

'Yes, I expect there will.'

'If I need to remain longer, I'll write and tell you.'

'Very well.'

'Is there anything you need before I leave?'

'No, I thank you.'

'I'm planning an early start.'

'Then I had better not detain you.' She rose from her chair. 'I'm sure you must have many things to do.'

He rose with her. 'Yes.'

'Goodnight then, Anthony.'

'Goodnight, Claudia, and goodbye—for the time being. I shall probably be gone before you rise tomorrow.'

'I wish you a pleasant journey.'

With that she turned and walked away, unaware of the gaze that followed her every step of the way.

He left in the grey light just after dawn. Tendrils of mist floated round the trunks of the trees across the driveway and clung to the hollows, investing the landscape with a strange eerie quality. Claudia stood by the drawing room window and watched the Earl's tall familiar figure descend the steps to the carriage. He paused for a moment to say something to Matthew who was on the box with the driver, and then climbed in. The door slammed shut behind him. She heard the coachman speak to the horses and then the carriage pulled away. She watched until it disappeared round a bend in the drive. Feeling strangely forlorn, she drew the shawl closer about her shoulders and made her way back to her room.

The maid had not been in to light the fire yet and the air was chill. Claudia climbed back into bed and huddled under the covers to get warm, trying to think positively. The house was hers again now; independence too. She could do as she pleased; see whom she pleased; go where she pleased and all without reference to him. She would have a week at least, without being subject to Anthony Brudenell's authority. It ought to have filled her with unalloyed delight. She closed her eyes, trying to blot him out, but that only served to reproduce his image in sharper focus. She turned over and thumped the pillow. There were plenty of things to think about that didn't involve him.

A brief diversion arrived later in the form of a letter from Anne Harrington informing her that it was her friend's intention to go to the Continent for the Season this year: '...for I am persuaded that, since Wellington is to be recalled from Vienna and is to set up his headquarters in Brussels, most of the *ton* will be there, and London very flat as a result. Do say that you will come too, dearest Claudia. It promises to be such fun and a complete change of scene...'

Claudia looked thoughtfully at the missive. If Wellington had been recalled it was because he meant to gather an army. He would need as many men as he could get, especially veterans who had served with him in the Peninsular Campaign. That meant young men would flock to his banner, bringing their wives and sweethearts with them. Everyone who was anyone would be in Brussels this year. It was an appealing notion and deserved serious consideration. Once she wouldn't have hesitated to follow it up and send a letter to her friend affirming her intention to come. However, now things weren't so simple. Now there was Anthony to contend with. Everything came back to him in the end. If he gave his permission she might go to Brussels. If not...She crumpled the letter in her hand.

'Damn it!'

For a minute or two she paced the rug, trying to put her thoughts in order. What was happening to her? She hardly recognised the woman she was becoming. No, she amended; she didn't recognise the woman she was allowing herself to become. Once upon a time she wouldn't have tolerated this. Why was she doing it now? Their marriage was a sham. Indeed Anthony had just voted with his feet. She didn't need his permission to go to Brussels or anywhere else; she had only deluded herself into thinking she did. In short, she had let him assume control. *Genet will not approach you again.* Perhaps not, but that didn't mean she could not approach Genet.

Now that matters abroad were coming to a head, the Intelligence services must be stretched to the limits. He had once thought highly of her abilities; it shouldn't be too hard to persuade him that he could still utilise them. She would go to London tomorrow. It was an easy journey and she could be there and back in forty-eight hours. If Genet was taken by surprise he would be more likely to accede to her request. When he did she would reclaim her independence.

However, that wasn't enough. Before she could truly be herself again she needed to regain emotional independence, to be out of Anthony's sphere and free of his influence. To do that she had to face facts and stop pretending that he held no attraction for her. It had been there ever since that fateful meeting in Paris. Instead of denying it she needed to admit it and then, having identified the real problem, overcome it. Only then would she be able to regain the focus she had temporarily lost.

Chapter Eleven

Genet surveyed her from across the desk. 'Ordinarily I would be delighted to offer you another posting, my dear, but as things stand I cannot.'

Claudia met his gaze and held it. 'As things stand?'

'You had a lucky escape from Paris. Only two others got out in time.'

'I heard as much. They fled to Antwerp, I believe.'

He nodded. 'Initially. From there they made their way to Brussels and reported in again.'

'Then they're still in the employ of the service.'

'Yes, I'm glad to say. They're good men. I could ill afford to lose any more. I have since heard that Poiret is dead, along with five others.'

'Do you know who betrayed them?'

'Not yet, but I mean to find out.'

'Let me help you.'

'I already have experienced operatives in place.'

He paused. 'Besides, your husband has made his views quite clear.'

Claudia's fingers tightened on the reticule in her lap. 'He has made his views clear with regard to my taking on any dangerous missions. What I seek is something quite different; something useful but low key.'

'My lady, I cannot…'

'The situation in Europe is escalating. The department must be stretched to the limits. You need good people to work for you.'

'That is true and, as I said, ordinarily I'd be grateful for your offer, but…'

'You fear my husband's response.'

'To be frank, yes. Not only is he a forceful character, he is also wealthy and powerful. I should not care to incur his further displeasure.'

She nodded and summoned a sympathetic smile. 'I understand your predicament, sir.'

'I wonder if you do.'

'I don't quite…'

'Did you know that, at his insistence, one of my men has been watching Oakley Court since your return?'

Suddenly she remembered the man she had seen in the park, the one she had taken for a poacher. 'My husband did that?'

'Since we did not know how far the rot had spread through the service, he saw it as a necessary precaution. I was inclined to agree.'

The revelation took her aback. She'd had no idea that Anthony had taken the matter so seriously. It was disturbing on many levels. 'And has there been any evidence of a threat?'

'None so far, but it was better to be safe than sorry.'

'Of course.'

'In consequence, I'm sure you can understand my reluctance to involve you any further in the business of the service.'

Claudia hesitated, thinking furiously. Clearly direct confrontation wouldn't work here. A more subtle approach would be required.

'Would it help you to know that we were intending to go to Brussels anyway?' It was a partial truth only since the last pronoun was incorrect, but that couldn't be helped.

'May I ask why?'

She raised an eyebrow. 'My dear Monsieur Genet, the whole of fashionable society will be there this year, along with every military commander of note and most of the crowned heads of Europe. It promises to be a Season like no other.'

'Yes, I see.'

'Since I am to be there anyway, it seems a pity not to make use of my skills.'

He hesitated. 'Well, since you put it like that...'

Scenting victory, Claudia held his gaze. 'I want to do something for the war effort, no matter how small, for Alain Poiret's sake if for no other reason.'

'There is something you could do. It carries little risk but it would be useful.'

'Name it.'

'Poiret had a mistress, a woman called Madeleine Fournier. She fled Paris following his arrest and is now residing in Brussels. It is just possible that she knows something.'

'But surely your operatives there have already spoken to her.'

'They have tried. However, Mademoiselle Fournier asserts categorically that she knows nothing, and refuses to say any more.'

'Then how can I be of use?'

'She may be more willing to speak to a woman.' He paused. 'If you learn anything you will report it at once.'

'How shall I find my contact?'

'He will find you. In the meantime, I'll give you Madeleine Fournier's address.'

Claudia returned to Oakley Court in a mood of quiet exultation. Even the deteriorating weather could not dampen her spirits. By dint of keeping herself busy she passed the rest of the week tolerably well. It was only the evenings that she found difficult when the empty place at the end of the table reminded her that she had grown more accustomed to Anthony's presence than was good for her peace of mind. In spite of her best efforts she had missed him, and she needed to break the habit before it became too deeply ingrained.

After she had eaten she retired to the drawing room and played the pianoforte for a while, but the music failed to soothe. In the end she gave it up and turned to her book instead. Yet even the pages of *Camilla* could not hold her attention for long. It was one of her favourite stories, but somehow Edgar Mandelbert no longer seemed such a dashing hero. Her thoughts were preoccupied with a very different man. She sighed. It was ridiculous to compare them. No-one could be further removed from the heroic ideal than Anthony Brudenell; and yet somehow, in a matter of a few weeks, he had made an indelible impression. Not even weeks, she amended. He'd made an indelible impression immediately. Ten minutes in bed with him put paid to any thoughts of Edgar Mandelbert and his ilk for all time. The recollection was enough to set her blood tingling. That of itself was humiliating. In effect it was as though she had learned nothing from the past, from her parents' marriage or from the family she had married into. Not only that, she had allowed physical attraction to distract her from the promise she had made to Henry.

Outside, a squall of wind flung rain at the window. Occasional droplets came down the chimney and hissed into the fire. Far off she heard the rumbling growl of thunder. The sound reinforced the unwonted sensations of isolation and loneliness.

A glance at the clock revealed that it was only just nine. In spite of that she felt unusually weary. An early night wouldn't come amiss.

Her bed chamber with its cheerful fire and drawn curtains felt cosy compared to the other rooms. Having undressed and brushed her hair she slid into bed and glanced at the bedside table for her book. In spite of his shortcomings, Edgar Mandelbert would have to do this evening. Then she remembered she'd left him in the salon. The thought of a chilly walk downstairs to fetch him had no appeal so she snuggled under the covers and closed her eyes.

However, sleep proved elusive and it was half an hour before she sank into a restless doze. There, the fictional hero was displaced by another man whose touch ignited desire and whose kiss overrode the fear of intimacy. In moments she was back in Paris, cocooned in velvet darkness, her nakedness pressed to his while his hands explored her body, awakening delicious and forbidden sensations that left her longing for more. She ceased to resist and returned his embrace, but in the street below she heard the sound of hooves and then voices. The police had arrived. Then there was a deafening thunderclap.

She woke with a start, heart hammering. Another thunderclap sounded overhead. Realising then where she was, she let out a long breath and with it some of her former tension faded. Her gaze went to the bedside table again. Sleep would be impossible for a while; she was going to have to fetch her book.

Throwing a shawl around her shoulders, she slid her feet into slippers. Then she relit a candle from the fire and set out for the salon. The corridor and the stairs were every bit as chilly as she had anticipated; the darkness more profound. Lightning illuminated the hallway with flashes of eldritch blue, and shadows swayed in the light of the candle flame. It was, she thought, like a scene straight out of a story by Mrs Radcliffe or Monk Lewis. All it lacked was a ghost. Drawing her shawl closer, she hurried into the salon.

The glow of the dying fire revealed the couch and the forgotten novel. Breathing a sigh of relief she retrieved it and turned to retrace her steps. She had almost reached the door when the next flash of lightning revealed the tall dark figure standing on the threshold. Claudia shrieked and dropped the book.

The figure advanced into the room. 'I'm sorry. I didn't mean to startle you.'

Her heart leapt towards her throat. 'Anthony.' With shaking hand she set the candle holder down and tried to gather her wits. 'What are you doing here? I thought you were at Ulverdale.'

'I was, but business concluded sooner than I'd anticipated.'

'Oh.' Her recent fright and his nearness now made it difficult to think. 'When did you arrive?'

'About half an hour ago.'

'Have you eaten?'

'I dined on the way.'

'I see.'

The effect of light and shadow rendered that handsome face more striking, more disturbing in every way, like the aura of virile power he wore so effortlessly. Its attention was focused entirely on her. Belatedly she realised that her shawl was no longer round her shoulders but reposing across her arms instead; that her nightgown was now on open view and that the thin fabric revealed every line and curve beneath it. He stepped closer and suddenly all sensation of chill vanished.

'There is no need for me to ask if you are well. The evidence is overwhelming.'

'I could say the same of you.'

'How have you occupied yourself in my absence?'

'With all the usual things.' It wasn't a subject she wanted to dwell on. 'Was Ulverdale as you expected?'

'Ulverdale remains as it always was,' he replied, 'although the atmosphere is somewhat lighter these days.'

She could well believe it. The demise of the old Earl would have seen to that. Again it wasn't a topic to dwell on so she made no reply. Then it was hard to know what to say and so the silence stretched out, a silence charged with awareness. Dreams of Anthony's physical presence had fallen far short of reality.

'Has anything of note happened here?'

'No, there's nothing exciting to report.'

'I see.' He hesitated. 'Did you miss me, Claudia?'

The answer to that was undeniable. She had missed him; if he ever guessed how much his triumph would be complete. She couldn't make it that easy.

'Fishing for compliments, Anthony?'

His lips twitched. 'Needs must since I cannot suppose you would offer one.'

'No, for then you would take it as flattery.'

'That is the very last thing I would expect from you.'

'Do you want flattery?'

'Not in the least. Besides, I have grown used to your incisive wit. It has the merit of being truthful and is therefore more appealing. Indeed, it's part of your very considerable charm.'

'A backhanded compliment if ever I heard one.'

'Not in the least, though perhaps bewitching would have been a more apt expression, particularly when you're wearing such a very seductive nightgown.'

The focus of his attention shifted. Lifting a hand he slid one finger under the lacy neckline, slowly tracing a path from her collarbone to the plunging v between her breasts. The touch sent a tremor through the length of her. Her breathing quickened. She was far from being the seductress that his words implied but it didn't stop her from wanting him, from wanting this. She ought not to. It was playing with fire and she knew it, knew and didn't care. She lowered her gaze.

'At the risk of making you conceited, I admit that I did miss you.'

'Now I *am* flattered.'

'I will not ask if you missed me,' she continued, 'since I know that you were much too busy.'

'It would never be possible to be that busy.'

'So you did think of me sometimes.'

'How could I not?' he replied.

'It's just that you seemed so keen to get away.'

'Not at all. Rather, my absence was necessary.'

The statement was ambiguous, perhaps deliberately so. As ambiguous as her own feelings at that moment.

'Of course,' she said.

The steady gaze never left her. 'I thought you'd have been abed long since.'

'I was, but the storm woke me. I came down for my book.'

'A happy chance then.'

'Is it?'

'I think so.'

His hand moved a little, the thumb brushing

across the peak of her breast. All ambiguity disappeared. The thumb continued to stroke, eliciting a sharp indrawn breath. He heard it. Locking an arm around her waist, he pulled her into a more intimate embrace. She made no attempt to resist him, or the tide of heat inexorably flooding through her veins. Her mouth yielded to the coaxing pressure, her tongue tentatively exploring and flirting with his. In response he crushed her closer and the kiss grew deeper.

Claudia rose on tiptoe and slid her arms around his neck, pressing her body against his. Through the thin stuff of her gown she could feel the beginning of his arousal, but what she felt now was not trepidation only mounting excitement. His finger slid the gown off her shoulder. Then he pressed kisses to her neck and throat, moving thence to her breast. He took the soft peak in his mouth, sucking gently, teasing the nipple with his tongue. The result was a jolt of electricity through the length of her body. She gasped, arching against him, pressing closer, throwing caution to the wind. She no longer cared if this was unwise or dangerous; danger had just become irresistible and she craved it as a starving man craves food.

He lifted her off the floor, carried her slowly backwards until her legs connected with something solid. Moments later she was tipped onto the couch. He shrugged off his coat and then followed her down, pressing her against the cushions. She felt his breath feathering along her neck and then his tongue gently probing her ear. It sent a delicious shiver through her entire being. The tongue teased the lobe and moved on, tracing a line along her neck to her throat, and thence lower. He slid the gown off her shoulders and drew it down until her upper body was naked, and then his mouth gently resumed where it had left off, triggering other exquisite sensations and sending pooling warmth to the centre of her pelvis.

Sliding her arms around him, she drew him closer, exploring the planes of his back and shoulders, feeling the play of the muscles beneath her fingers. Tugging the shirt out of the way she slid her hands along his skin. Its musky scent was erotic and exciting turning her thoughts in hitherto unsuspected directions.

She felt his weight shift a little and then the skirt of her gown was up around her hips and his hand caressing the bare skin of her belly and thigh. Warmth coiled deeper in her pelvis as the caress became more intimate, more arousing, like his hardening response and the thought of him inside her. His kisses moved lower. Instinctively she reached out to touch his face, her fingers brushing across his brow and the deep furrow there.

Anthony froze and looked up, trying to discern her expression but, since the couch was outside the circle of candlelight, everything was concealed in shadow. He grimaced. Whenever the barriers came down between them it was always in shadow. He had thought of this moment many times since that night in Paris; had tried to imagine the circumstances in which it might happen. He wanted her so badly it hurt. He wanted to possess her, wanted to hear her cry out, wanted to take her to a climax so intense that she'd faint. He wanted to monopolise her thoughts so that no other man would exist for her. He wanted her to yield herself completely, to want him in the same way, for his appearance not to matter. Clearly though it did matter.

It had always mattered, from that first horrifying look in the mirror when the bandages came off and he realised how drastically his appearance was altered. He had not thought himself vain—until then. Having always taken his face for granted he hardly recognised the gargoyle he had become. The surgeon's careful lack of expression was more eloquent than any words. Eloquent too were the looks of pity and disgust from others. And so he hid the ravaged flesh behind a mask, and the attendant emotions with it. Having done that, he assumed a different persona. As Antoine Duval it was easy to avoid intimacy; as Anthony Brudenell it was another matter. He'd hoped that Claudia might look beyond the physical to see the man he really was, but the hope was a chimera. Even in the dark the scars made their presence felt. Had it not been for his unexpected return tonight this apparently romantic interlude would not have happened, and he knew it.

She felt him draw back, then slowly pull up the displaced fabric to cover her breasts, and slide the nightgown back over her shoulders. Then the skirt was drawn down over her bare legs. With that his weight shifted and he moved away from her to sit on the edge of the couch. Claudia swallowed hard.

'Anthony? What is it? What's wrong?'

'Nothing. Or rather, nothing for which you are to blame.'

'What do you mean?'

'I mean it won't do, my sweet.'

'What won't do?'

'This entire situation.' He bent to retrieve his coat and then stood, looking down at her. 'I'm sorry.'

With that he turned and headed for the door. He paused on the threshold for one backward glance. Then he was gone. Claudia stared after him in bewildered and heart-thumping disbelief, wondering if she had somehow dreamed the last ten minutes. Yet her flesh still burned from his touch. She lifted a hand to her lips. It had been real all right. He had wanted her, or seemed to, only to reject her a few moments later. Nor was this the first time. Humiliation replaced bewilderment, and then a sense of chill. Shivering now, she rose from the couch and sought her shawl, wrapping it protectively around her. Then, lifting the candleholder, she retraced her steps to her room.

She reached it unhindered. There was no sound from Anthony's chamber although a faint line of light below the door suggested he was there. Just for a moment she contemplated the possibility of knocking and then of having this out with him. Almost as quickly she dismissed the notion. How could she run after him now? What was there to say? She had stopped pretending indifference; acknowledged that she wanted him and made her willingness apparent. *No respectable woman enjoys intimacy.* What nonsense that had turned out to be. She had not only enjoyed it, but had craved more. Surely that could not be wrong between husband and wife.

In any event, one humiliation was quite enough for one night. It was quite enough, full stop. Of course, it served her right. If you played with fire you got burned. When she thought of how badly she might have got burned she felt saddened. That casual encounter might have led to far more serious consequences, and all for a man who didn't love her. The entire scenario should never have happened; it was embarrassing and degrading and it demonstrated how far she had lost direction. She had to put that right, take back control of her life before it happened again. Next time she might not escape so lightly. Taking a last glance along the corridor, she let herself into her room and locked the door behind her.

Chapter Twelve

Anthony leaned on the mantel, staring down into the fire, his thoughts in chaos. He could no longer see his way forward. All he did know was that he couldn't leave things as they were. More rational thinking made him realise he'd over-reacted and badly too; allowing morbid sensitivity to cloud his judgement. A casual touch was exactly that. He shouldn't have refined upon it so, but old habits were hard to break. He also realised he had to talk to Claudia and try to explain. Heaven knew it wasn't going to be easy, and yet so much remained unsaid. He sighed. After what had just occurred she might be in no mood to listen. All the same, he had to try. Taking a deep breath, he made his way to her room and tapped lightly on the door.

'Claudia?'

When he received no answer he tried again but with no more success.

'Claudia, please talk to me.'

There was no answer and no sound from within.

He tried the handle but the door was locked. He sighed. Short of forcing his way in there was no way to resolve this. While breaking the door down would have been quite easy, and provided a release for pent up emotion into the bargain, he could not suppose it would advance his cause in the least. Admitting temporary defeat he retired to his chamber once more.

In spite of his weariness sleep was a long time in coming that night; the memory of her was too sharp, too immediate to banish. The scent of her was in the air he breathed, subtle, sensual, exciting like the woman herself. That wonderful brief liaison had not dulled desire in the least; rather it had sharpened it. He wanted her more than anything in his life before. He wanted to hold her, to protect her, to tell her the secrets of his heart. He wanted to make up somehow for all the wasted years. Consequently it was not until the early hours that he finally dropped off into an uneasy doze and then a much deeper sleep.

As a result he awoke later than usual and it was ten o'clock before he went downstairs next morning. There was no sign of Claudia, although that did not entirely surprise him. He partook of a light breakfast and read some correspondence. When, an hour later, there was still no sign of her he went to her room and tapped lightly on the door. His knock elicited no answer. He tried the door, expecting to find it still locked, but instead it opened easily. He stepped into the room.

'Claudia?'

The chamber was quite still and also chill. He frowned, looking swiftly around. The bed had been remade but the fire was a pile of grey ash. There was no evidence of any clothing at all; not so much as a handkerchief. The dressing table was bare of brushes and combs and jars. An unpleasant suspicion began to form in his mind. Striding across to the chest of drawers he pulled it open. Every drawer was empty; likewise the closet. His jaw tightened. Things were much worse than he'd imagined. For a moment or two he surveyed the empty room with a mounting sense of dread. Then, turning on heel, he retraced his steps and summoned the butler.

'Where is Lady Claudia?'

'She left first thing this morning, my lord.'

'I see.' He did see, only too well, as every moment of the previous night's events returned to haunt him. With an effort he gathered his wits. 'She has gone to London, I collect.'

'Yes, my lord.'

'Did she go alone?'

'No, her maid went with her.'

That at least was something. Her present state of mind he could only guess at. 'Find Matthew and tell him I want to speak to him at once.'

An hour later the Earl was on the road. He had

plenty of leisure to regret his folly now. He should have talked to her last night; should have broken the door down, taken her in his arms, begged her forgiveness. Instead he had listened to his doubts and let the gulf widen. He had no idea how he was going to repair the damage, only that he had to try. To do that, he had first to find her.

Claudia saw little of the passing countryside beyond the carriage window, or of the busy quayside inn or indeed of the packet boat later. Her thoughts were otherwise engaged. She had slept little and risen at dawn. Her body still throbbed with the recollection of that brief passionate interlude with the Earl. She had never anticipated that a man could make her feel like that. Recent events should have killed all desire, but to her shame they left sensation heightened. Just thinking about it caused her pulse to race. The memory of his caresses was imprinted all over her skin like a brand. It had been so tempting to open the door last night and let him in, but if she had there could only have been one outcome. She would never have had the strength to refuse him once he touched her again. She would have given herself to a man who took her only because he could, because it was his right and because he needed an heir. And yet if that were so, why had he pulled away at the last moment? Surely he would have taken her, regardless? Confusion mounted. To have opened her door after that would have been to forfeit all self-respect and, ultimately perhaps, a lot more besides. Instead she had lain quite still and listened as he walked away. At dawn she summoned Lucy and told her to pack.

Brussels would provide a powerful antidote to the malaise that gripped her now. Quite apart from her new mission, the change of scene, reunion with friends, the social round of parties and balls would help her to forget. It would be some time before Anthony discovered where she was; she had left no note, no clue as to her destination. If she had to talk to him now she suspected that she wouldn't be strong enough to see her plan through. As it was, by the time he did find her, she would be over this. No doubt he would be angry but she no longer cared about that. Nor would she allow herself to be dominated. If it came to a confrontation she would face it. Then they could go back to living the separate lives they had always lived.

For the majority of the crossing Claudia remained on deck, feeling disinclined for company. The fair weather was an added inducement. The sea was all sun-shot greens and blues and the breeze kind. She could not but reflect how different it was from the last time she had travelled by boat. Of course, Anthony had been with her, a strong bulwark between her and disaster. He had known the truth by then, but he could never have guessed how that revelation would mire them both in more trouble. Perhaps it would have been better if he had never spoken; had let her continue to think he was an adventurer called Antoine Duval. To think she had once believed that bedroom scene in Paris to be disturbing. How naïve and foolish that had been.

The Earl arrived in Grosvenor Square to find the house empty apart from a skeleton staff. The rooms were shuttered, the furniture still under Holland covers. Of Claudia there was no sign whatever, nor any indication that she had ever intended to come. His questioning of the servants drew a complete blank too. He realised then that she must have laid a false trail to throw him off the scent. She could be anywhere. Concern became tinged with anger that she could have acted with so little thought for safety.

Rather than remain in the dreary mausoleum in Grosvenor Square, he put up at an inn and ordered dinner. It gave him time to think. He was quite sure that his wife had friends in town but he had no idea who they might be. Moreover, she must have guessed that London was the first place he would look and that, in the relatively small exclusive circle of Society, it would only be a matter of time before they met. Then, unless she wanted to be food for a Season's gossip, she would be compelled to live under the same roof with him again. With the insight he now possessed into Claudia's character, he knew that wasn't part of her plans. If he guessed aright, she meant to reclaim her independence. For the time he felt the prickling of real apprehension. This flight of hers was not a ruse to test his interest and see if he would follow her; his wife did not wish to be found.

Lady Anne Harrington's house was in the Rue Royale overlooking the park. The street with its imposing buildings and prime location was among the most sought after addresses in Brussels. Claudia glanced up at the pillared entrance and smiled to herself, hazarding a guess that the rental must be costing a pretty penny. Not that that would trouble Anne for a minute. Her tastes were extravagant and she had married a man rich enough to indulge them. Sir Quentin was twenty years older than his wife but he doted on her and their two children. Claudia had spoken to him on only a few occasions, but he was a kindly man, easily disposed to like his wife's friend.

When the footman showed her into the drawing room Lady Anne rose to greet her. Two years older than her guest, she was a pretty young woman with fair curls and sparkling blue eyes. Her face was wreathed in smiles.

'Claudia, what a delightful surprise it was to receive your note yesterday. I had no idea you were coming to Brussels.'

'Nor did I until recently, but I needed a change of scene.'

'You've come to the right place. Quite apart from the officers, most of the *ton* is here. There are balls and parties every night, and the theatre and the opera of course. The local countryside is beautiful too.'

'In that case I'm glad I came.'

'When did you arrive?'

'Two days ago.'

'You look tired my dear. Was the journey dreadful?'

'Not so bad. A good night's sleep is all I need.'

'Where are you staying?'

'I am putting up at an hotel, until I move into permanent accommodation.'

'My dear, you should have come here. We have room and to spare.'

'I would not put you to the inconvenience. Besides, my new house will be ready on the morrow.'

'You must give me the address.' Lady Anne smiled. 'In the meantime we shall have some tea and you can tell me all your news.'

What she received was a highly censored version of events, omitting all mention of Paris and intelligence work. However, the news of the Earl's return was sufficient to hold her friend's attention since she knew, broadly, of the circumstances surrounding the marriage.

'It must be very strange to meet a husband one has not seen for so long.'

'Yes, it was.'

'Well, Brussels may help to pave the way; it will give you the chance to get to know each other again. A second courtship as it were.'

Claudia laughed. 'Hardly, since there was no first. Besides, my husband is not with me.'

'Oh. Oh, I see.' Anne was momentarily taken aback. 'No doubt he has much to attend to at present and will join you later.'

'He has his life, Anne, and I have mine. That's the way it has always been.'

'Forgive me, I do not mean to be presumptuous, but might you not…I mean, might there not be a reconciliation?'

'I think it highly unlikely.'

'Then I am sorry. I would so like to see you in a warm and loving relationship.'

For no good reason Claudia's throat tightened. 'Not everyone is as fortunate as you. I shall have to make do with the social round.'

'That cannot sustain you for ever.'

'It must, since there is nothing else.'

Anne regarded her thoughtfully for a moment. 'Well then, join us for the opera tomorrow evening. Catalani is singing. I feel sure you will enjoy it, and it will be a good way to announce your arrival to the rest of your friends and acquaintance.'

Claudia mustered a smile. 'Thank you. That would be delightful.'

* * *

Anthony returned to Oakley Court the following day to consider his next move. Having drawn a blank in the capital, he had to hope that there might be some clue in the house as to her present whereabouts. Not that he thought Claudia would make it easy. He could only guess at her present mental turmoil, at the unhappiness and desperation she must have felt. Knowing himself to be its author only made it worse. Mingled with guilt and remorse was increasing concern for her safety. That she had taken her maid with her gave him small comfort. A maid might provide a veneer of respectability but would be unlikely to provide any real protection should the need arise. He prayed that Claudia was staying with friends somewhere, and that her desire for independence hadn't caused her to strike out alone. All manner of perils attached to that, and they loomed larger in his imagination by the day.

The house seemed strangely quiet on his return, and somehow devoid of life. As he stood in the hallway he found himself listening for the rustle of a gown or a light step on the floor or the sound of music drifting from the drawing room, anything that would indicate that she had changed her mind and come home. However, none of those things happened. Instead, the silence rose up to mock him.

Putting sentimental thoughts aside he bent his mind to the task of finding the information he needed. A more thorough search of Claudia's chamber provided no clue as to her whereabouts; nor did the library or the study. Eventually he wandered into the salon and stood by the hearth, trying to think. As he glanced round, his eye fell on the bureau and then his heartbeat quickened.

A swift search of various drawers produced a pile of papers: invitations, bills, lists, inventories. He glanced at them and tossed them aside. The last drawer revealed a bundle of letters tied with red ribbon. He unfastened it and leafed through the contents. There were several from a Lady Anne Harrington. Ordinarily he wouldn't have dreamed of reading anyone else's correspondence, but this was no ordinary situation. He scanned the sheets swiftly. They revealed nothing of significance; references to bygone social events, family matters, entertaining scraps of gossip, the intention of travelling to Brussels…

As he read that last detail he was suddenly very still, experiencing a moment of quiet revelation. That had to be it. How on earth had he missed something so obvious? With Napoleon at large and raising an army, Wellington had been recalled from Vienna to muster the Coalition forces. Brussels would be full of officers of every nationality. Half of the crowned heads of Europe would be there and most of the *ton* with them, including Claudia's friend. He smiled grimly, knowing now with absolute certainty where his wife had gone.

* * *

As Lady Anne had said, Claudia's appearance at the opera had reunited her with different friends and acquaintance. It had also caused ripples of interest among the military men present; several of whom had asked to be introduced. The result of all this was a flurry of invitations. For several days she lost herself in a whirl of shopping and visiting and soirées.

In between times she familiarised herself with the rented house in the Rue de Namur. It was a pleasant thoroughfare close to the park in the fashionable area of the city. The house with its pale pink frontage and green shutters looked pretty enough from the outside, and indoors had about it a look of faded grandeur that chimed with her mood. The property suited her purposes very well. She also set about hiring some local servants.

With so much to do she managed to avoid thinking about Anthony very much during the day. It was at night, when she lay alone in her room that the memories came flooding back. The bed seemed too big. Each time she closed her eyes she saw his face, felt his body pressed close to hers. No matter how hard she tried to blot him out, the image refused to be banished. If only things had been different between them. If only physical attraction had been allied to sincere affection, but his heart was as untouched as it had ever been. Anne had spoken of wanting her to enjoy a warm and loving relationship, but her friend had no way of knowing how futile a hope it was. If love existed in marriage it was completely outside Claudia's experience.

Chapter Thirteen

'I'll see you at the ball this evening then,' said Lady Anne as Claudia stepped out of the chaise.

'Yes, you will. I cannot tell you how much I'm looking forward to it.' It was perfectly true, she thought. She would dance all night. The event wouldn't end until the early hours by which time she'd be too tired to do anything more than fall into a deep and dreamless sleep. How appealing that was.

Claudia waved her friend farewell and then went into the house. It would take her hours to get ready for the evening, her mind occupied with trivia and not with her disastrous private life. In order to be able to stay the course, she had a nap in the early part of the afternoon and then, with Lucy's help, began her preparations. These began with a leisurely bath and the softening of her skin with sweet oils, and then went on to the arranging of her hair, dressed high in a knot from which fell in a profusion of glossy curls. The lightest touch of powder and rouge highlighted her cheekbones and lips.

She had purchased a new gown for this occasion, a confection of exquisite, gossamer-fine Indian muslin with an overskirt spangled with tiny faceted crystals that caught the light with every movement. Diamond drops sparkled in her ears and echoed the matching pendant round her neck. A diamond clasp nestled among her curls. White gloves and slippers completed the ensemble. Lucy surveyed her mistress critically.

'You look wonderful, my lady.'

'Thank you.'

'A touch of perfume perhaps?'

'Yes, of course.'

It was her favourite scent, made up for her in Paris, a special blend of white musk and attar of rose. Finally she threw a light silken cloak about her shoulders.

'I expect to be back very late, Lucy, so don't wait up.' With that she was gone.

The ball had been in progress for about an hour when she arrived. As her gaze swept the assembled crowd she smiled, feeling a familiar tingle of anticipation. Tonight she was going to dance and forget.

'It looks as though just about everyone is here this evening,' said a voice beside her.

She looked round and smiled to see Lady

Anne. 'It's a crush, isn't it? Our hostess must be delighted.'

'I'm sure she is.'

'Rumour has it that Wellington will be here later.'

'That would be the ultimate social accolade,' replied Claudia.

'It's exciting, isn't it? There are so many handsome officers here tonight. I confess I always had a soft spot for a man in regimentals.'

'Well, then, you may flirt to your heart's content this evening.'

Anne laughed. 'I have a feeling that there are several officers keen to flirt with you, if their expressions are anything to go by.'

In this respect she was quite right and in a very short space of time Claudia was surrounded. She accepted all invitations to the ballroom floor, determined to put everything else out of her head. The music and the candlelight and banks of flowers were beautiful. The scent was wonderful. Two glasses of champagne added to her natural vivacity and wit ensured the attention of a crowd of admirers, all vying with each other to be the most entertaining. Many of the officers were striking figures. Their ardent expressions left her in no doubt of their thoughts; any encouragement from her would be eagerly received. *You could always take a lover.* It would be easy, she thought. Such things were commonplace and well understood in fashionable circles, especially here on the Continent. Provided that one used discretion there was no reason not to enjoy a secret liaison. *I knew I was right.* Madame Renaud's mocking smile returned with force.

'Are you all right, Lady Claudia?'

She looked up quickly and saw concern on the face of the captain of hussars by her side. 'Oh, yes, perfectly. It's just that I'm a little thirsty, that's all.'

'Then allow me to fetch you some refreshment.'

'That would be most kind.'

She watched the tall, broad shouldered figure depart and turned back to the dancing, but this time saw nothing. How was it that a man she would have considered deeply attractive only a month ago should suddenly seem lacking? His attention was flattering but it did not set her heart beating faster; the thought of his kiss did not set her alight. Only one man had ever done that, but to him it had meant nothing. He had never loved her and never would. In spite of other masculine adulation, the rejection still stung. She had to put him out of her mind and move on.

Presently the captain returned with a glass of fruit punch. She thanked him with a smile. In fact, she hadn't been untruthful when she'd said she was thirsty. With its numerous candles and the press of people the heat in the room was considerable.

'I wonder, do you like to ride, Lady Claudia?' her companion inquired.

She nodded absently. 'Yes, when I can.'

'Then would you do me the honour of accompanying me tomorrow? The countryside hereabouts is very fine.'

There it was, she thought, a casual prelude to a possible *affaire*. If she accepted his invitation and rode alone with him, he would take it as encouragement of a very particular kind. She could see it unfolding in front of her; the ride, the excuse to stop awhile, the first passionate kiss...

'I'm afraid I have no mount,' she replied, 'and I have other engagements tomorrow.'

He concealed disappointment beneath a polite smile. 'Some other time perhaps.'

She returned a non-commital smile of her own, and took another sip of her drink, her thoughts in turmoil. What was wrong with her? He was well-connected, good looking, good company...he clearly admired her. Why not enjoy his company for a while? And then Anthony's face floated into her mind and she knew why.

Making a polite excuse she left the captain and went into the adjoining salon. It was cooler here and she took a few deep breaths to recover her equilibrium. She could see Anne in a group across the room and made her way over to join them. The group opened to admit her and then the conversation continued.

Anthony paused in the lighted hallway, letting his gaze travel up the staircase in front of him, already aware of the covert looks he was attracting from the guests on the landing above. His jaw tightened. Since Vittoria he had eschewed fashionable society, and in particular all occasions such as this, knowing that his appearance would inevitably mark him out. While he didn't imagine that the men would be overly concerned, he dreaded the reactions of women. In the persona of Antoine Duval it hadn't mattered; his work rarely brought him into contact with them, and never in a social setting. As Anthony Brudenell things were different and it mattered very much. Yet somewhere among the scented, candlelit chambers above was the fugitive he had come to find. No matter what the obstacles, he did intend to find her, but first he was going to have face down a demon. Squaring his shoulders he took a deep breath. Then, slowly, he began to climb the stairs.

Claudia listened to the conversation with only half an ear. Once she would have been entertained by the latest society news or whispered scandal, but now could summon little enthusiasm for it. However, good manners decreed that she should make an effort so she smiled and assumed an expression of rapt interest. And then, without warning, the conversation faltered and ceased and the ladies around her were no longer looking at each other but across the room instead.

'Lord, who's that?' murmured Anne.

Claudia glanced round in idle curiosity, and then her heart leapt towards her mouth as she recognised the tall, elegant figure in the doorway. Anthony had always been physically imposing, but the austere black and white evening dress only strengthened that impression. However, it was his face that commanded attention; the handsome chiselled features lent added distinction by the scarred brow and the black mask beneath. Moreover, there was in his upright bearing just the faintest touch of arrogance, and it lent blatant virility a sombre and dangerous edge that was both forbidding and exciting—as though an eagle had suddenly appeared among a flock of gaudy parakeets.

The Earl scanned the room for a moment or two, apparently oblivious to the heads turned in his direction, or the excited, whispered conjecture that rippled outwards from behind myriad fans. Then he saw her. The blue gaze locked with hers, steely and quietly intent. Its expression sent a *frisson* down her spine. In that look she read many things, none of them in the least bit reassuring. He had found her and there would be a reckoning. There was no way of knowing what form it might take, but suddenly it was much harder to breathe and a rabble of butterflies took wing in her stomach. For a moment she stood transfixed as he made his way unhurriedly but inexorably through the throng towards her. It was effortless too; a word here, a touch there and the company parted to allow his advance. Claudia swallowed hard. Then, recovering some of her wits, she excused herself from the group and moved a few paces away, waiting.

And then he was in front of her, his gaze coolly appraising, taking in every last detail of her costume. In heart-thumping silence she watched him bow, then possess himself of her hand and lift it to his lips. The touch seemed to scorch.

'I believe the next dance is mine, my lady.'

Strong fingers retained their hold as he led her away. Claudia lowered her voice. 'What are you doing here?'

'Looking for you.' He glanced down at her. 'That dress becomes you very well, by the way.'

'You didn't come here to compliment me on my dress,' she retorted. 'What are you about, Anthony?'

'Let's just say your departure left many things unsaid.'

'There's nothing more to be said.'

'I think there is.'

Their arrival in the ballroom precluded an immediate reply. He led her on to the floor as the orchestra struck up a waltz. Claudia had only performed the dance a handful of times since in England it was still regarded as rather shocking. The thought of performing it now filled her with apprehension that had nothing to do with remembering the steps.

'Anthony, I'm not going to…'

He drew her closer. 'Oh, yes, you are.'

And then they were gliding into the opening steps. It was the first time they ever danced together. However, it was certainly not the first time he'd ever danced a waltz. He moved with effortless assurance, leading her deeper into the whirling pairs around them. Claudia surrendered to the music and tried not to think about the strong fingers clasping hers or the firm hand on her waist or the fact that only inches separated them. Her heart raced, but not with fear.

'How did you find me?'

'A little detective work, my sweet.'

'To what end?'

'I think you know that.'

The implications were infinitely disturbing, but not as disturbing as the treacherous knowledge in her heart. In confusion she looked away.

'What are you afraid of?'

'Nothing.'

'Then why did you run?' he demanded.

Her gaze met his again. 'I didn't run. I left. There's a difference.'

'Is there?'

Unwilling to go further down that road, she changed the subject. 'Where are you staying at present?'

'In the Rue de Namur, my sweet. Where else?'

The dark eyes flashed indignation. 'Oh, no, you're not.'

'I beg to differ.' He paused. 'Besides, if you think about it, there is no other possibility unless you wish to become the talk of Brussels.'

Her jaw tightened but she knew he was right. For a husband and wife to live apart would occasion endless gossip and speculation. 'You think you have it all worked out, don't you?'

'Far from it. However, private matters should remain exactly that.'

She nodded reluctantly. 'All right, I suppose a little more hypocrisy won't make any difference.'

'Hypocrisy? For a husband to live with his wife? Hardly.'

'You know what I mean.'

'No, I'm not sure I do. You can explain it to me later. In the meantime, let's enjoy this waltz.'

They whirled on around the floor. Claudia stopped trying to rationalise any more, and just gave herself up to the dance. She was enjoying it and despised herself for it; for wanting to be with a man who didn't care for her. She wished she could feel as indifferently towards him, but she did not. That was the awful truth. His power over her had nothing to do with a marriage certificate or what the law said; it was about the way he made her feel now, about the memory of lying naked in his arms, about wanting to do that again.

Eventually the dance ended. She dropped a curtsey and turned away, anxious to be gone now before he read in her face what was written on her heart. A hand closed on her elbow, arresting her abruptly.

'Where are you going, Claudia?'

'I…this dance is taken.'

'Not any more.'

'Anthony, you can't just…'

He evinced polite interest. 'Can't what?'

'You can't do this.'

As her next partner approached, the Earl stood his ground and fixed the intruder with a cool, quizzical stare. The younger man reddened a little, hesitated, then bowed and, stammering something inaudible, backed away. The Earl turned back to his wife.

'Shall we?'

Torn between amusement and annoyance, Claudia surveyed him steadily. 'That was outrageous.'

'Yes, I suppose it was.'

'You had no right…'

'There I disagree.'

'What justification can you offer?'

'The right of a husband.'

Her chin came up at that. 'You are quite shameless.'

'You realise it, then.'

With that he took her in his arms and swept her into the next dance, and the next. Again she gave herself up to the music and the moment and the man, forgetting everything else, exhilarated by his nearness, aware of him to her fingertips. When at length the dance ended she felt sure that he would relinquish his claim on her. Instead he kept a firm hold on her elbow.

'It's warm in here. Let's get some air.'

He steered her towards the French windows that gave on to the terrace. The latter was presently occupied by two other couples who had retired to talk, away from the heat of the ballroom. The Earl ignored them and drew her further off where there was no possibility of their conversation being overheard. Then he turned her round to face him. Her heartbeat accelerated dangerously.

'Why have you brought me out here, Anthony?'

'I wish to refute the charge of hypocrisy that you laid at my door earlier.'

'And just how do you propose to…'

The sentence was never finished because she was drawn firmly against him and then his mouth was on hers making speech impossible. All attempts at resistance were ignored until resistance was abandoned, and then the kiss became gentle and lingering and infinitely persuasive, reviving the memory of their last encounter. The familiar spark leapt and became flame, filling her with shameful desires.

Eventually he drew back a little to allow breath, but his hold remained inflexible, his face only inches from hers. His expression was sufficient indication of his inner thoughts to send a *frisson* down her back. Recognising the danger she made an unsuccessful attempt to free herself, to get away before it was too late and weakness triumphed.

'Please, Anthony, I...'

'It's no good, Claudia. You can't run from me.'

'All right. You've found me. Isn't that enough?'

'Not by a long way. We're going to finish what we began, my sweet.'

Her heart turned over. 'But...'

'No buts. Fetch your wrap: we're leaving.'

The journey home was short but for Claudia, trying to marshal her thoughts, it passed all too quickly. Every particle of her being was attuned to the man sitting opposite but the events of the last hour had not entirely seduced her mind. His presence tonight might have taken her unawares, like that calculatedly sensual scene on the terrace, but that didn't mean he could take the outcome for granted. It would be all too easy to let the force of his personality sweep her away again; to succumb to the charisma he wore so effortlessly. To allow that would be to risk everything.

Sensing her unease, Anthony waited until they were within doors before he broached the subject. He followed her into the salon, closing the door behind them. For a moment they faced each other in silence.

'Now, tell me. What is it, Claudia?'

'Just what I was going to ask you? What is this really about?'

'You leave without a note, or even a word, and you ask me that?' His gaze bored into hers. 'Did it ever occur to you that I might have been sick with worry?'

'I could hardly be expected to think that, could I?'

'Well, believe it now. You have caused me several sleepless nights.'

The intensity of his expression took her aback. 'Anthony, I…'

'No, you're going to hear me out.' He advanced until only a foot separated them. 'I know how far I am to blame for the past. There are no recriminations you can heap on my head that I have not deserved, or any that I have not already accused myself of a hundred times over. I know that my actions have hurt you and, God knows, if I could undo them I would.' He paused. 'When I discovered that you were the wife I'd left all those years ago, I didn't know if there could ever be a chance for us; all I had was a faint hope. I did not imagine the spark between us that night in Paris. More than anything I wanted to rekindle it.'

Claudia's heart thumped uncomfortably hard. 'You are the one who walked away, remember?'

'I've thought of nothing else since.'

'Why? You didn't want me that night. You have never wanted me.'

'That isn't true.'

'It is true. Why don't you admit it? You think

me a whore and you've thought so since Paris.' Tears pricked behind her eyelids. 'You as good as accused me of infidelity. That's why you walked away. You couldn't overcome your disgust.'

He paled. 'Dear God, is that really what you thought? You couldn't be more wrong.'

'If I'm wrong why did you do it?'

'After Paris, after I'd tasted just a fraction of your passion, I knew that nothing else would do. So I waited and hoped, and then, one night, it seemed to happen.'

Her chin lifted. 'Seemed?'

'It did happen, but I allowed doubt to persuade me otherwise.' He made a vague gesture with his hand. 'I feared you had only yielded in the heat of the moment because my return had taken you by surprise.'

'What!'

'Well, I could not suppose you were attracted by my looks, could I?'

Claudia stared at him, dumbfounded. 'I beg your pardon?'

'I am well aware that my appearance is not calculated to inspire romantic thoughts.'

'Oh, so you thought that it was just a casual liaison perhaps; that I would allow myself to be seduced in such a way?'

'No, of course not, but…'

'But you couldn't help remembering Paris.'

'That's not what I meant.'

'Isn't it?'

'God knows what I was thinking that night.' He paused. 'I wanted to talk to you afterwards, to apologise and to explain, but you wouldn't let me in. I cannot blame you for that, but you should not have left without a word.'

'There seemed to be nothing to say.'

'Once you were away from Oakley Court I could not protect you, Claudia. Anything might have happened.'

'If you had not walked away that night I would not have gone.'

'I know.' He took her by the shoulders. 'Believe me, it's not a mistake I intend to repeat.'

'So you intend to claim your rights after all.'

His grip tightened a fraction. 'If that was all I wanted I'd have done it long since.'

She tried unsuccessfully to free herself. 'Do you think so?'

'Do you think you could have prevented it?' he growled. 'I could have taken you the first night I returned to Oakley Court, and every night since if I'd wanted to.'

'Why didn't you?'

'Don't think I wasn't tempted. However, I've never forced a woman and I won't start with you.'

'What do you want then?'

'I told you: to finish what we started.' His expression was implacable. 'But, if that happens, it'll be of your own free will.' He drew her against him, looking down into her face. 'Tell me you don't want this, Claudia, and I'll let you go.'

Her heart lurched dangerously, but not with fear. Rather it was in recognition of the desires she had tried to bury and which now refused to be denied.

'I cannot tell you that,' she replied.

He crushed her against him for a deep and lingering kiss that set every nerve alight. It was madness and she knew it, but now couldn't help herself. Her arms slid up round his neck and she pressed closer, first yielding to the embrace and then returning it, every part of her wanting him, unable to deny the fierce and growing need for him.

Eventually he drew back a little, just long enough to lift her in his arms and then head for the stairs. What followed was a sense of disorientation, but when next she got her bearings she realised that they were in his room, not hers. He laid her on the bed and then, without taking his gaze off her, began to divest himself of clothing. Firelight played on the muscles of his arms and shoulders and lent a ruddy hue to his skin. She could see the lines of the scars and the gold brown hair on his chest, leading the eye to the narrow waist. The close-fitting breeches accentuated lean hard flanks and long muscular legs. His arousal was evident. With thumping heart she saw him cross to the bed. Taking her hands in his he drew her to her feet and proceeded to undress her, slowly removing each layer of clothing until every last stitch was gone.

Then drawing aside the coverlet he lifted her into bed. As she slid between the sheets he unfastened the breeches and removed them. Then he came to join her. Strong hands closed on her waist, drawing her body against his, warming her. She felt his breath feathering along her neck and then his tongue gently probing her ear. It sent a delicious shiver through her entire being. The tongue teased the lobe and moved on, the tip tracing a line along her neck to her throat to her breast. Then his mouth gently resumed where it had left off, triggering other exquisite sensations.

His hands slid from her waist to explore her back and the curve of her hips. Instinctively she followed his lead, caressing him in return, exploring him slowly, learning the planes of his muscles and the deep lines of the scars along his shoulder and arm; her fingertips stroking the hard nipples and the wiry hair on his breast and abdomen, nostrils breathing in the erotic musky scent of his skin. Her hand moved lower and closed around him, gently stroking the velvety shaft. The result was a sharp indrawn breath.

She felt him stroke the secret place between her legs, gently drawing a finger through the soft flesh, seeking the harder nub hidden there. Her breathing quickened. He heard it and continued. The throbbing tautness in her loins increased, building slowly. Claudia gasped as the first tremor shook her in a sudden rush of liquid heat. Her eyes widened as successive shock waves of pleasure flooded her body sweeping her inexorably towards the edge of a precipice.

Anthony looked down into her face. No trace remained of the snow queen now; only the fiery, sensual creature in his arms, her velvety eyes dark with passion, her lips swollen with his kisses, skin sheened with sweat and flushed with desire. He felt her writhe beneath him. She was more than ready now but he continued to make her wait, using every ounce of self-restraint he possessed not to follow the primal urging of his baser nature and satisfy his own desires. Hurting her had no place in his plans; nor did haste. He wanted her to enjoy this, wanted her to crave more. It wasn't enough just to take her body. By the time he was done she was going to be his completely.

'Anthony, please...'

He flung off the restricting bedclothes and rolled, pinning her beneath him, parting her thighs. She felt his erection push into her, push into her and then meet resistance. She saw him frown. Before he could fully assimilate the implications her hands clutched his back, pulling him closer, deeper.

'Don't stop. Whatever you do, don't stop.'

She felt him thrust into her again and stifled a cry as the momentary burning pain took her by surprise. Then he was inside her, the whole length of him moving in a slow delicious rhythm that turned her blood to fire. The rhythm gradually increased, the thrusts growing deeper, stronger. Her body shuddered as he took her closer to the brink. And then she was over the edge and he followed her, crying out in the hot rush of release.

She closed her eyes, deliciously sated, steeped in dreamy inertia. While she had always known what happened between men and women, she had never imagined it might be like this. In spite of her inexperience she knew he had been considerate, that he had restrained his desire to increase hers. And it had. The recollection left a banked fire waiting to be rekindled.

He lowered his weight on to his elbows, breathing hard, his gaze on her face. The expression in the dark eyes was unreadable though he saw her smile. He smiled too and rolled aside, letting his body relax, waiting for the wild thumping of his heart to slow. He had expected to enjoy this but nothing had prepared him for the incredible soul-singing joy of the experience. His gaze returned to her naked body, tracing every line and curve. It was lovely and inherently sensual. He could have looked all night but, now that the heat of passion had temporarily died down, the cool air was making itself felt and he didn't want her to get cold. He sat up, about to reach for the covers when he noticed the blood on the sheet. He frowned. Then, gradually, other details began to impinge on his consciousness and the implications put aside before returned with force.

For a moment his mind reeled. Then initial surprise gave way to deep and fierce satisfaction. Claudia had never taken any lovers before tonight. Now she truly belonged to him and, while he lived, he would be the only man she ever knew. With an effort he found his voice.

'Why didn't you tell me, darling?'

Her throat tightened. 'I did tell you. Don't you remember?'

'I can't quite...'

'It was just after we'd left Paris and you suggested I might take a lover. I said I had no intention of doing so. I knew then that you did not believe me, that perhaps...perhaps you were thinking of yourself in that role.' She took a deep breath. 'I suppose, after what occurred in Paris, it was hardly surprising.'

He paled as the details of that conversation returned with sickening clarity. 'I should not have said that.'

'You were speaking as Antoine Duval. I thought that, since our association would be of short duration, his opinion didn't matter. I certainly wasn't about to argue the point.'

'Neither should you. He...I...had no right to make such an assumption.'

'When I discovered that you and Duval were one it suddenly mattered very much. I didn't want you to think of me in that way. Yet what man would not, in the light of what had occurred?'

'When I finally realised who you were, it seemed quite unrealistic to think that you had not taken a lover—especially after the way I'd behaved.' He paused. 'There cannot have been any shortage of candidates.'

'There wasn't, only I never wanted to play the whore.'

'It's more than I deserve.' He sighed. 'I've been a damned fool, Claudia, allowing my personal devils to come between us.'

She turned to look at him. 'Personal devils?'

'My appearance, I mean.'

'I don't follow.'

In anyone else he would have suspected duplicity but her expression made it evident that she really meant it. The realisation both gladdened him and enhanced the sense of his former folly.

'After Vittoria it took a while to come to terms with what had happened. Even now there are times when I over-react; like that night at Oakley Court. I wanted to explain, but I left it too late. The blame rests with me.'

Claudia made no reply, being temporarily stunned by the revelation. It offered her the first real insight into his mind; to understanding just how deeply the aftermath of Vittoria had affected him. For the first time too she glimpsed his vulnerability and his need, and they touched her in ways she could never have anticipated.

'I do mean to make it up to you,' he said then.

She smiled. 'You already have.'

He gathered her in his arms. She felt his body curve around hers, warm, strong protective. Yet, now, in the languid aftermath of passion, other disquieting thoughts returned. Involuntarily her hand went to her belly. Had his seed already taken root in her? Even if it had not, on this occasion, it could only be a matter of time before it did. She knew beyond doubt that Anthony would expect this scenario to be oft repeated; now that hunger had been awakened it would be fed. He had been tender and considerate and no doubt would be again, but he had not said he loved her. Quite apart from desire, there was the more practical aspect of the whole matter—he needed an heir. Now that she was truly a wife, the next logical step was motherhood. Yet the thought persisted that a child should be conceived in an act of love. How much easier to accept it then. Deep inside, part of her wanted that. How was it possible to want and to fear at the same time?

Then there was the other matter, the real reason for her coming to Brussels. Anthony would have to know the truth eventually, but goodness alone knew what would happen when he found out.

Chapter Fourteen

When Anthony woke later the sun was high. For a moment or two he wondered if he had dreamed the events of the previous night, until he turned his head and saw the woman lying beside him. Carefully, so as not to disturb her, he propped himself on one elbow and watched her sleeping, his gaze exploring all the delicate lines and curves of her body. It was made for a man's caresses; his caresses. Possession had not satisfied desire, rather it had increased it. Allied to that was aching need. Both had been there since Paris although, initially, he had failed to recognise that. It had required longer proximity to reveal what his deeper feelings were. He smiled and traced a finger lightly down her side.

Claudia stirred and turned on to her back. Then she opened her eyes. He bent to kiss her naked shoulder.

'Good morning.'

She smiled. 'Good morning yourself.' Then,

squinting at the clock on the mantel, she added, 'Although there's not much of the morning left.'

'There's time enough. What would you like to do today?'

'I should like to see something of the city.'

'In that case we might go for a drive.'

'I'd like that.'

'Very well.'

His hand caressed her lightly from shoulder to breast, letting his thumb brush the delicate skin. The response was immediate and electric. At the same time the need to talk to him and to tell him the truth was ever more pressing.

'Anthony?'

His lips nuzzled her neck. 'Mmm?'

It was suddenly much harder to concentrate. 'Anthony, I...'

'What is it, darling?'

She hesitated, dreading his anger, knowing that if she told him now the present mood would be destroyed. After all that had happened between them she was reluctant to do that. Besides, his touch was re-awakening all manner of delightful sensations. Love making was a risk, but, after last night, this could surely make no difference.

'No matter.'

'Something, surely?' His hand slid between her thighs and stroked gently.

Claudia drew a sharp breath and resolution faded. 'It'll keep for a while.'

'This won't,' he replied.

She felt his weight shift, pressing her down into the bed and then all other thoughts disappeared for some time.

Later they went out together for the promised drive. On so fine a day it was delightful to ride in an open carriage. The sunshine was warm, lifting the spirits, like the sight of new green on every bush and tree, and pink and white blossom in gardens. Everywhere the earth had thrown off the icy shroud of winter and was returning to life with renewed vigour. Claudia saw it all with quiet approbation. Moreover, Brussels was a fine city. It would be exciting to explore more of it. She glanced at her companion. It would be exciting to explore it with him. His presence added a different and exciting dimension to the entire situation. Moreover, the tension so evident earlier in their relationship was lacking now. Of course, he still didn't know about her visit to Genet. The thought of having to tell him, of spoiling this new-found harmony, was unappealing. She would have to eventually, but just then she wanted only to enjoy the moment.

The Earl too seemed relaxed, keeping up a light flow of conversation, pointing out places of interest, answering her questions about the military uniforms everywhere in evidence. It was hard not be dazzled by the sight of so many handsome officers, laughing and talking in groups or swag-

gering along the streets and smiling at the pretty
Bruxelloises as they passed. Scarlet jackets inter-
mingled with Riflemen's green and Dutch blue,
adorned with cross belts and epaulettes and gor-
gets and profusions of gold or silver lace. Everywhere she could see elegant shoulder capes and
polished and tasselled Hessian boots and myriad
military caps and shakoes and kepis. The very air
seemed charged by the dynamic and vibrant presence of these men.

'Wellington seems to have gathered a large force
already,' she observed.

'Yes, but there are precious few Peninsular veterans among them and those he has are mainly
infantrymen. Most of the cavalry have come out
from England and they're untried in battle. No-one
knows how they'll behave under fire.'

'Not like parades and drills then?'

'Decidedly not,' he replied. 'A few minutes
under heavy bombardment will demonstrate the
truth of the matter; that and a cavalry charge.'

She shot him a swift sideways glance. 'Was that
what happened at Vittoria?'

He hesitated, and for a moment she thought he
was going to brush the question off, but then he
seemed to change his mind.

'We'd come under heavy fire from the French
but, as their force advanced, some of their cavalry
broke through on our flank before we had time
to form square. Men on open ground have little

chance against a mounted attack otherwise. They were upon us in moments, sabres drawn. We accounted for a few of them though, before we were cut down.'

'Good Lord. You were lucky to survive.'

'Yes. Most of my companions did not.'

'What happened then?'

'I was left for dead. When I woke up I was in a field hospital. The surgeons couldn't save my eye, but they patched up the rest of me as best they could. For a while they thought I had lost the use of my arm as well, but it healed eventually and with regular exercise the use of the muscles returned.'

Beneath that matter-of-fact account she heard all the things he didn't say about pain and horror, and for the first time she glimpsed his loneliness. Forced to resign his commission, cast out from his friends and the life he loved and dreading the thought of home, he must have felt utterly lost—for a while at least. It must have been tempting to give up, to sink into self-pity or drink or both. Instead he had worked doggedly to get his strength back. She guessed it had taken months of determination and painful effort to do that. Having achieved it, he then let go of the past and Anthony Brudenell with it, to plunge into the strange shadow world of espionage; a world where one had contacts instead of friends and home was a series of rented rooms in different cities. Claudia shuddered inwardly. No wonder he wanted to reclaim his life.

'You could never have imagined then that Napoleon would one day be instrumental in restoring what he took from you,' she said.

'No, I could not.'

'It seems that both of you have returned from exile, doesn't it?' He regarded her in surprise, but there wasn't the least shade of mockery in her face, only quiet understanding.

'In truth it does feel a bit like that.'

'Then I'm glad of it.'

He saw a look in her eyes that he had never seen there before; a look that made his heartbeat quicken. Before he could reply he became aware of a voice calling his name. He looked round, saw a group of four officers on the pavement and then stared, his face lit by an incredulous smile.

'Good Lord! I don't believe it!'

Bidding Matthew to stop the carriage, he waited for the little group to catch up. The one who had hailed him was the first to arrive. Curiosity thoroughly roused now, Claudia surveyed the newcomer closely. He was dressed in scarlet regimentals; an officer's uniform, carrying the insignia of a Colonel. He was tall and he seemed to be of an age with Anthony. However, there the likeness stopped. The stranger had dark hair and grey eyes, his face remarkable for rugged good looks rather than classical beauty. He leaned over the carriage door and clasped the Earl's outstretched hand in a hearty grip.

'Brudenell! I knew I was right. By heaven, it's good to see you.'

The Earl grinned, an expression of open-hearted, almost boyish delight that wrung Claudia's heart.

'It's good to see you too, Falconbridge,' he replied.

'It's been a long time.'

'Too damned long.'

Just then the other three officers arrived. Falconbridge grinned. 'You've met Fitzroy, I believe.'

The two shook hands. Fitzroy smiled. 'Falconbridge said it was you but I could scarce believe it. I'm so glad he was right.' He turned to his companions. 'May I introduce Major Channing and Colonel Maynard?'

The Earl inclined his head. 'My pleasure, gentlemen.'

They professed themselves delighted. However, he became aware that their attention had shifted past him and was riveted elsewhere. He smiled wryly, aware of conflicting emotions, not least of which was pride. He'd have been less than human if he hadn't enjoyed seeing their expressions just then.

'May I introduce my wife, Claudia?'

They made their bows with the kind of flourish that made the Earl want to laugh out loud. He might have done had it not been extremely ill-mannered.

Falconbridge's grey eyes registered admiration. 'Delighted to make your acquaintance, my lady.'

A chorus of agreement followed.

She inclined her head graciously. 'And I yours, gentlemen.'

Falconbridge turned back to the Earl. 'What brings you to Brussels?'

'The same thing as you, I imagine.'

Falconbridge laughed. 'Well, it's the best news I've heard for weeks.'

'In truth it's good to be back.'

'Sabrina will be thrilled when I tell her.'

'Is she here with you then?'

'Of course. She would never have consented to be left behind.'

'I rather think she would not.'

'There is so much to tell you. Believe it or not, I became a father last year.'

'Good Lord! Congratulations, Robert. A boy or a girl?'

'A boy; John. We named him for Sabrina's father.'

Anthony grinned. 'That's wonderful. Is the child with you?'

'Yes, he is.'

'I look forward to meeting him.'

'So you shall. I know Sabrina would like to see you again, and to meet your beautiful wife. The problem is that I'm tied up with duties for the next few days. It's a confounded nuisance.' He paused, but then an idea dawned. 'Do you attend the Somersets' ball?'

'Yes, we do.'

'Excellent. We shall see you there. Then we can organise something properly.'

'We'll look forward to it,' said the Earl.

'Until then.' Falconbridge stepped back and lifted a hand in token of farewell. His friends added their goodbyes and then moved aside.

As the carriage pulled away, Claudia regarded her companion with close interest. 'A good friend of yours, I take it.'

'Yes. We served together during the Peninsular Campaign. Fitzroy was there too, but I didn't know him as well as Falconbridge.'

'Was Colonel Falconbridge already married then?'

'He met his wife while he was out in Spain. They went on a secret mission together and fell in love in the process.'

Claudia smiled. 'How very romantic.'

'Yes, I suppose it was.'

'Was she working for the Intelligence Service as well?'

'In a minor capacity, initially. Her father was a cartographer and he was captured by the French. Sabrina…Mrs Falconbridge…was offered a chance to obtain his release in exchange for her help on the mission I just mentioned.' He shook his head. 'It was exceedingly dangerous but she went anyway.'

'She must be a very brave woman.'

'She's a very remarkable woman.'

The warmth and admiration in his voice caused an unexpected pang. It was evident that he wasn't entirely indifferent to Sabrina Falconbridge. Had he once been a rival for her affections? There had been no sign of any tension between the two men that might indicate such a thing, but even so the lady had made a lasting impression. Once again Claudia was reminded how little she really knew about his past.

'At one point she and Robert got caught and interrogated by the French,' he went on. 'It was tight spot and no mistake. They escaped by the skin of their teeth.'

Claudia recovered herself quickly. 'Goodness, how exciting. I can't wait to meet her.'

'I think you'll get on very well.' He grinned. 'After all, you have a lot in common.'

'I think my feeble exploits can hardly compare to that.'

'There's nothing feeble about you or your exploits.'

'How am I to take that?'

'As a compliment, my sweet. Very much so.'

The accompanying look was as unmistakeably sincere as the tone. Both warmed her immeasurably. They also increased the feeling of guilt that she was not being entirely sincere with him. She had to find the right moment and tell him the truth.

Yet the thought of his anger filled her with dismay. Their marriage had been a battleground for too long and they needed to put conflict behind them. Their recent conversations had given her a glimpse of something different, something that, suddenly, she wanted very much. Now it looked as though the obstacles in the path were of her making.

She was drawn out of thought by the sound of galloping hooves and the rumbling of iron wheels' rims on stone, and looking up, saw the horse and cart thundering down the road towards them. Flattened ears, outstretched neck and white-rimmed eyes told of a frightened animal in headlong career. Behind it the cart swayed wildly, but there was no driver. As the vehicle bore down on them Matthew reined his horses over as far as he could, but in the narrow thoroughfare it was impossible to avoid collision.

Anthony swore softly and grabbed hold of Claudia, throwing her against the far side of the carriage, shielding her with his body. The thunder of hooves grew louder. Moments later the air was filled with flailing hooves and splintering wood and horses screaming. The carriage lurched, flinging them hard against the side. Claudia gasped, her startled gaze taking in leather upholstery and door and sky and the fabric of Anthony's coat. Eventually the movement stopped, and for the space of a few heartbeats it was unnaturally quiet. Then, as from a distance, she could hear people shouting and the sound of running feet. She tried to sit up but the carriage was leaning at a drunken angle and she was pinned by Anthony's weight. He eased himself back a little and looked down at her.

'Claudia! Are you all right, darling?'

She managed a shaky smile. 'I think so.'

'Thank heaven for that.' He leaned across to open the door and then took hold of her hand. 'Let's get you out of this.'

He jumped down and lifted her after him. They were joined by a white-faced Matthew.

'Are you hurt, my lord? My lady?'

The Earl shook his head. 'No, we're all right.'

'I'm so sorry…'

'There was nothing you could have done, man. If you hadn't pulled over so fast it would have been a damn sight worse.'

'It's bad enough, my lord.'

The impact had torn off the near-side rear wheel and done the same to other vehicle. However, the horses, though frightened, were unscathed. Claudia swallowed hard. They'd been lucky and no mistake. The Earl looked around at the group of people gathering nearby.

'Whose cart is this?'

The men exchanged blank looks; then one stepped forward. 'No-one knows, monsieur.'

The Earl turned back to Matthew. 'No doubt the owner will be along soon. In the meantime, have a couple of these men help you to cut the horses free. I'm going to take Her Ladyship home.'

Claudia had little recollection of the journey in the hired fiacre. Neither she nor Anthony spoke. Reaction had set in and she was trembling, as much with the horror of the aftermath as with the knowledge of what might have happened. It was good to feel his arm around her and comforting to share his warmth, to feel protected. She remembered that he had protected her earlier too, using his body as a shield just before the impact. There had been no time to think; only for the swift, spontaneous act that put himself between her and danger. Not so long ago she would have found that to be inconceivable. Now it seemed only natural and right.

When they reached the house he suggested that she might like to go and lie down, but she refused.

'I'm all right, Anthony, really.'

'Are you sure? You still look very pale.'

'Some hot tea will be a perfect restorative.'

He looked sceptical but didn't argue. Having sat her by the fire in the salon he sent a servant to fetch some tea. In the meantime he poured two glasses of brandy and handed her one.

'Here. This will help.'

In fact it did steady her and, along with the tea, helped to banish the sick sensation in her stomach. Anthony sat with her, quietly attentive, watching with relief as some of the colour returned to her face. They'd had a narrow escape. Had it been any other woman he knew he would likely have been treated to a fit of hysterics, or the vapours at least. Claudia had not only spared him that, she had behaved with a kind of courage that touched him far more deeply. It also filled him with pride. Only her eyes betrayed any sign of inner anguish.

He squeezed her hand gently. 'It was a horrible experience but it's past now. You must try not to dwell on it, my sweet.'

'I know, but it won't be easy. We came so near to disaster, Anthony.'

'Too near.'

'It all happened so quickly. It seems unreal even now.'

'It's the effect of shock.'

'I know.' She shuddered. 'After experiencing all the dangers of Paris I ought to show more courage.'

'You have courage and to spare.'

Something in his look caused her pulse to quicken. She had not thought before that a man's approval could matter so much.

It was more than an hour later before Matthew returned. Claudia had retired to her room to change for dinner by then so Anthony was afforded the opportunity for private speech.

'Did you find the owner of the cart?' he asked.

'No, my lord, I regret that I did not. I made numerous inquiries but no-one seemed to know anything about it or even to have set eyes on it before today.'

The Earl frowned. 'Perhaps the fellow ran off when he saw what had happened, fearing to get into trouble.'

'I wondered the same thing, my lord...until I had a closer look at the vehicle that hit us.'

'What do you mean?'

'The horse must have been badly spooked to run blind like that, which argued that it had either been frightened or it was in pain. So I checked the harness over and found these stuck through the leather.' He held out his hand to reveal a half a dozen tacks.

'Good Lord!'

'This is just a sample,' Matthew went on. 'There were plenty more. Every movement would have caused pain. The poor brute must have been beside itself.'

'Then what happened today was no accident.'

'I think not, my lord.'

'Keep this to yourself for the time being,' said the Earl. 'My wife has had enough unpleasantness for one day.'

'Very good, my lord.' Matthew paused. 'I hope Her Ladyship is recovering from the shock.'

'Tolerably well, all things considered.'

'I'm glad to hear it, my lord.'

'Thank you, Matthew, and for what you did today. Without your quick thinking it might have been very much worse. We have no way of knowing whether there was one intended victim or three. Nor do we know who was responsible.'

'No, but unfortunately they know us. There may be another attempt.'

'We'll need to be much more careful from now on, that's all.'

'My thought exactly, my lord.'

Chapter Fifteen

When Claudia rejoined him for dinner that night he could detect no sign of their earlier misadventure in her countenance or bearing. Only her appetite was less than usual, a circumstance that did not surprise him in the least. However, she kept up her part in the conversation which he deliberately steered towards safe topics.

Claudia knew what he was doing and why, but at the same time the need for a frank conversation had become more pressing. He had put himself at risk for her yet again, and the least she could do was to be honest with him. Thus she went along with casual discussion and bided her time until they should retire to the salon.

By then her stomach was fluttering. She poured herself some tea from the tray that the servants had left and watched Anthony help himself to cognac. Then he strolled across to the pianoforte.

'Will you play some music for me?'

She set down her cup and rose from the chair.

'If you wish it, I will play for you later. First I need to tell you something.'

He smiled. 'I'm all attention.'

Claudia swallowed hard, dreading to speak but knowing she must. 'It concerns my reason for coming to Brussels.'

'The fault for that was mine. You have nothing to reproach yourself with.'

'But I do.'

'How so?'

'I didn't just come here for the social round, Anthony.'

'I don't think I follow.'

'While you were at Ulverdale I went to London.'

'London?'

'Yes, I...I went to see Genet.'

His gaze never left her. 'Why did you do that, Claudia?'

The velvety tone caused a distinct tremor and her mouth dried. However, she had gone too far to retreat now. 'I asked for another assignment.'

'I thought I had made my views quite clear on that score, to both of you.'

'Genet refused at first...'

He took a pace towards her. 'At first?'

Claudia stood her ground. 'I gave him to understand that we intended to come here anyway, and that there could be no harm in my undertaking a low-key assignment.'

'And he refused.'

'No, he agreed.'

His expression then raised goose bumps along her arms. 'Then Monsieur Genet will rue the day. As for you, my girl...'

This time she did take a step back. 'It's not a dangerous mission, truly. It's only to talk to someone and...' She broke off with a gasp as his hands closed around her arms, dragging her very much closer.

'I don't give a damn what kind of mission it is. You won't be taking it up.' He glowered down at her. 'I don't know what tale you told Genet or how you managed to wheedle your way around him, but now you have me to deal with.'

Her heart thumped against her ribs. 'Anthony, I didn't mean...'

'I know what you meant. You bided your time, didn't you? Then you went behind my back.'

'It wasn't like that.'

'It was exactly like that. Then you connived with Genet even though you knew I had expressly forbidden it.'

'You had no right to forbid it.'

'I have every right. I am your husband, and you've disobeyed me for the last time.'

'What are you going to do?'

'Tomorrow I take you back to England, and this time I'm going to take steps to ensure that you stay there.'

Claudia paled. 'I won't go back and you can't make me.'

'Oh, can't I?'

She began to feel seriously alarmed. For all her bold words she had a terrible suspicion that he not only could but would. Moreover, feeling physically and emotionally drained by the events of the day, she didn't even feel able to challenge the assertion, much less fight.

'Why won't you listen to me?'

'I think I've heard quite enough.'

To her horror her eyes filled with tears. She tried desperately to blink them back but they overflowed anyway. Mortified, she tried to turn away but as he still had hold of her it proved impossible.

Anthony was appalled, his anger temporarily displaced by something quite different. He let out a long breath. 'Claudia, please. There's no need to cry.'

The sudden gentleness in his tone had the opposite effect to the one he intended, and the tears flowed faster. She tried in vain to dash them away with her hands. 'I'm s..sorry. I didn't m..mean to.'

'Come here.' He drew her against him and folded his arms around her.

Completely overwrought she began to sob. Had it been a case of a few sparkling tears and a play with wet eyelashes, he'd have known exactly how to act. As it was, the shuddering sobs left him completely at a loss. Nor would he have expected the sound to hurt so much. He let her have her cry out, waiting until she quieted a little. Then he reached in his pocket for a handkerchief.

'Here. Take this, before you ruin my coat entirely.'

The words were greeted by a watery and embarrassed smile. 'I b..beg your pardon. I d..don't know what came over me.' She drew a deep breath. 'I d..don't usually d..do this sort of thing.'

'I know.' That, more than anything else, gave him pause. He glanced down at her. 'Better now?'

She nodded and wiped away the last of the tears. 'I m..must look a p..perfect fright now.'

'Hideous,' he agreed. Privately, her pallor alarmed him, and his conscience smote him for losing his temper and behaving like a brute, especially after so terrible a day. He led her to the couch and drew her down to sit beside him. 'Now, tell me.'

She took another deep breath. 'I am sorry that I went behind your back, but I have to take this mission, Anthony. If I do, it may help to identify the man who betrayed Alain Poiret and the others in Paris.'

'Poiret?'

She nodded and then proceeded to outline the substance of her talk with Genet. The Earl listened intently, torn now between the need to protect her and wanting to discover the truth. Sensing his hesitation Claudia laid a hand on his sleeve.

'I cannot bear to think that Alain and the others died for nothing. If the traitor is not apprehended who knows what he may do next. Napoleon's agents will stop at nothing.' She paused, her gaze searching his face. 'There can be no danger in my speaking to Madeleine Fournier. She may even refuse to see me. All the same, I have to try. I made a promise to Henry...please don't force me to break it.'

His jaw tightened. As her husband and her protector he ought to stand firm over this. His instinct was to forbid it, to take her home immediately, put armed guards at every ten paces around Oakley Court and then go and run Genet through so he couldn't endanger her again. Thought of the latter gave the Earl particular satisfaction. However, Claudia's words gave him pause. It was clear now that she had other motives for her actions which had nothing to do with defiance of him. Could he criticise her for loyalty; for wanting to keep faith with others? Could he refuse to listen; ignore the earnest plea that he saw in her eyes? If he did that she would never forgive him, and any chance he might have had to build bridges would be gone. In spite of his anger, in spite of everything, he knew in his heart that he did want to build bridges. It was weakness but he couldn't help himself. Somehow Claudia always found the chinks in his armour.

'Very well. You may speak to Madeleine Fournier but that is all, do you understand?'

Relief found expression in a tremulous smile that was reflected in her eyes. 'I understand. Thank you.'

'You will not go alone either.'

'If I do not she may well refuse to speak.'

'I'll wait outside.'

'Then you…you mean come with me?'

'Yes, I do mean to,' he said, 'and the point is not negotiable.'

Claudia lowered her gaze. 'Of course. Whatever you say, Anthony.'

If he hadn't known better he might have thought her demeanour just then to be the epitome of meek wifely obedience. However, meek, obedient and Claudia never came together in the same sentence. He reached for her chin and tilted her face towards his.

'Look at me.'

The dark eyes met his unswervingly. 'I will keep my word.'

'Your life may depend on it,' he replied.

'What do you mean?'

It hadn't been his intention to worry her with his earlier discoveries but, as things stood, she needed to know the truth, so he gave her a précis of his conversation with Matthew. Claudia paled a little.

'Then what happened today wasn't an accident.'

'No, it wasn't. Nor do we know who our enemy is. That makes things doubly dangerous.'

'You think that whoever was responsible will try again.'

'It seems likely. For that reason we can't afford to take any chances.'

'I understand.' Suddenly she really did, and it put an entirely different slant on his earlier anger. Far from being merely dictatorial it suggested that he really did care. 'I won't take any foolish chances, Anthony, but, by the same token, nor should you.'

'I'll be careful.'

'I'll hold you to that.'

She smiled; an expression that held a familiar trace of mischief and something deeper that set his heart to beating a little quicker. At the same time it somehow enhanced the notion of her vulnerability. He wondered whether he had done the right thing in acceding to her request, but his word was given now. To go back on it would be unthinkable because it would break her heart, and he could no more do that than he could fly to the moon. All the same he intended to take every possible measure to ensure her safety, whether she liked it or not.

'Can we go and see Mademoiselle Fournier tomorrow?' she asked then.

'The sooner the better,' he replied. 'Then you'll be done with the wretched business once and for all.'

The address that Genet had given her took them across town to a narrow and dirty street lined with old half-timbered houses whose weathered and dilapidated frontages were testimony to many years of neglect. Like most of its neighbours, the house in question had been subdivided into smaller apartments, reached by a narrow wooden staircase. Stale cooking smells pervaded the dingy hallway. Claudia paused and turned to Anthony.

'I hope Mademoiselle Fournier still lives here.'

'Well, we'll soon find out, won't we?'

'I think I should go up alone.'

He hesitated a moment, then nodded reluctantly. 'All right. I'll wait for you here.'

'I won't be long.'

She climbed the stairs and reached a landing. Four doors led off it, none of which bore any indication of who the occupants might be. Claudia sighed. She had hoped not to draw attention to her arrival but now there was no choice but to ask. A knock on the first door elicited no reply. The second was opened by an old woman. Strands of grey hair straggled from beneath a dirty mob cap. A frayed woollen shawl was wrapped over a shabby brown dress. A strong smell of liquor clung to both. She regarded her visitor with ill-concealed suspicion.

'What do you want?'

'Do you know where I might find Mademoiselle Fournier?'

'Maybe I do and maybe I don't.'

Claudia took a coin from her reticule. A clawed

hand took the offering and the woman jerked her head towards the apartment opposite.

'Over there. Only she isn't in. She works during the day.'

'Works where?'

'Laundry. Down by the canal.'

With that the old woman shut the door in her face. Claudia sighed and retraced her steps. Hearing her descent, Anthony looked up.

'Well?'

'No luck, I'm afraid.' Briefly she recounted what she had learned.

'Well, we have two choices. Either we come back later or we visit the laundry.'

'Let's try the laundry.'

He smiled wryly. 'I had a feeling you were going to say that.'

In fact the premises weren't hard to find being only two streets away. The strong smell of lye soap and festoons of wet linen would have given it away in any case. A discreet inquiry of the stout matron by the door elicited the intelligence that Madeleine Fournier did indeed work there.

'I need to speak with her for a moment.'

'She's busy. Besides, the boss won't be pleased if he finds out.'

Claudia returned a conspiratorial smile. 'I won't tell if you don't.'

The woman shrugged. 'I'll fetch her.'

A few minutes later another figure emerged

from the courtyard. Claudia had an impression of a woman in her late twenties. She was of average height and build, and her face might have been pretty, save for its gaunt lines. It was framed by untidy brown hair. She halted several feet away, regarding the visitor warily.

Claudia smiled. 'Mademoiselle Fournier?'

'Who are you? Why have you come here?'

'My name is Claudia Brudenell. I need to speak to you about Alain Poiret.'

The blue eyes registered suspicion and unease. 'What do you know of Alain?'

'I know that he's dead and that he was betrayed.'

'I can't tell you anything.'

'Mademoiselle, I want to find out who was responsible, to bring a traitor to justice.'

'I told you, I don't know anything.'

'Even the smallest little detail may be significant. Whatever you can remember.'

'Alain never discussed his work and I never met any of his colleagues. I'm afraid I can't help you.'

'I see. Well, if you do think of anything, you can find me at this address.' Claudia handed her a small card.

'It won't be of any use.'

'Please take it. Just in case. One small detail might prevent others from sharing Alain's fate.'

After a small hesitation her companion took the card and slipped it into her pocket. Then she turned and walked away. She didn't look back.

Claudia sighed and then retracing her steps, rejoined Anthony in the street. He regarded her shrewdly.

'I take it that Mademoiselle Fournier was not forthcoming.'

'She was as tight-lipped as a clam.'

'You cannot be surprised.'

'She's scared, Anthony. I'd swear to it.'

'Probably she is, and with good reason.'

'I wish I could help her.'

He shot her a piercing look. 'You've done what Genet asked of you. That's the end of the matter, Claudia.'

She sighed. 'Yes, I suppose it is.'

They walked together back to the fiacre waiting at the end of the street. He handed her in and then took his place beside her. For a little while neither one spoke. Then she turned towards him.

'Thank you for coming today.'

It took him unawares, like the tone of her voice and the expression on her face just then. 'You're welcome.'

'All the same, I feel I've let the side down.'

'You have never let the side down,' he replied. 'Your brother would be rightly proud of you.'

She reddened a little. 'Thank you. I should like to think so.'

'You need not be in any doubt, Claudia.'

The sincerity in his voice was unmistakeable and it caused her pulse to quicken. Uncertain how to respond and keenly aware of that undivided attention, she lapsed into silence. The mission might have been a failure, but he had supported her beyond all expectation. When she thought of what he might have done instead she could only feel deeply thankful.

Just then another thought struck her, something so obvious she couldn't believe she had missed it. She shot her companion a sideways look.

'Anthony, I wonder…'

'What do you wonder?'

'Well, you remember the two agents who fled Paris.'

'Yes. What about them?'

'Would it not be a good idea to talk to them?'

'Don't even think about it, Claudia.'

'Oh, I didn't necessarily mean me, but you could speak to them.'

'And?'

She bit her lip. 'Then you could tell me what they said.'

In spite of himself he laughed. 'You artful little baggage.'

'Please, Anthony. It might be important. They might hold the clue as to who betrayed the group in Paris.'

'They might, but even if they did the matter would no longer involve you.'

'What matters is that the traitor should be discovered.' She laid a hand on his arm. 'Won't you please go and talk to them?'

'All right. I'll go, but you will remain at home.'

She hesitated. 'It wouldn't be dangerous for me to go along if I were with you.'

'You are not going along. I'll not have my wife frequenting gaming hells.'

Claudia shot him a sideways glance. 'What a pity it wasn't a bordello. I'd have been all right there.'

'You certainly would not.'

'Anyway, how did you know to find them in a gaming hell? You must already have made inquiries.'

He sighed. 'Yes, I made inquiries.'

'You were planning on going without saying anything to me, weren't you?'

'I would tell you if I learned anything significant.'

'Oh, really?'

'I swear it.'

'Let me come with you.'

'No.'

'Why not? I've been in gaming hells before.'

His expression became steely. 'You may have been before, you little jade, but you won't set foot in one again, under any circumstances. Is that clear?'

She lifted her chin. 'Quite clear.'

'I mean it, Claudia.'

For a moment she was silent. Then her expression grew contrite. 'You're right of course. A gaming hell would be quite inappropriate.'

'I'm glad you've seen sense at last.'

'We could arrange to meet them somewhere else. At an inn, say, or in the park, or...'

'Claudia, which part of *you're not going,* is still unclear to you?'

'You don't intend to give in, do you?'

'You realise it.'

'Well, I had to try.'

'I'd have expected no less, my sweet.'

'You know you can be utterly infuriating at times.'

'Only at times?' he asked.

It drew a reluctant smile. 'Most of the time, you odious man.'

While Claudia went shopping the following morning, accompanied by Lucy and Matthew, the Earl took himself off to see Jean Lebrun and Auguste Saunière. Having encountered them both in Paris on several occasions, he wanted to hear their side of the story. For that reason he arranged to meet them in a quiet tavern. It had a garden behind it where they could speak undisturbed.

Lebrun and Saunière were cousins but it was not evident from their appearance. Although both were of average height and build, Lebrun was dark and bearded, a distinct contrast with his companion's mousy brown hair and angular clean-shaven face. Both of them greeted Anthony courteously enough although their expressions gave little away.

'Weren't sure as we'd see you again, Duval,' said Lebrun. 'Thought you might have been arrested with the others.'

'It was a close-run thing,' replied the Earl. 'From what I hear you had a narrow escape yourselves.'

'Too damn narrow for my liking. While the police were breaking the doors down front and back, we were climbing on to the roof. It was the only other way out. Almost broke our necks half a dozen times before we got far enough away to risk coming down again.'

'And then?'

'We knew the roads out of Paris would be watched so we made our way down to the Seine and offered our services to a bargee in return for a ride. Then, when we were well clear of the city, we cut off across country and made our way to the border.'

'I'm impressed.'

'What about you, Duval?' asked Saunière.

'I got out by boat from St Malo.'

The other man nodded. 'Lucky, then.'

'Luckier than the poor bastards who ended up in police custody,' replied his cousin. Small dark eyes locked with Anthony's gaze. 'So what we want to know is who peached?'

'That's what I mean to find out,' said the Earl, 'but to do that I need to know what Poiret was on to.'

His two companions exchanged glances and some unspoken agreement passed between them. Lebrun leaned closer. 'We saw Poiret two days before the arrests, see. Said he'd got wind of a planned assassination; someone high up in the Coalition.'

'Who?'

'Dunno. That's what he was trying to find out. Said he couldn't do anything till he had a name.'

'I see.'

'Seems the plan is to make it look like the killer's linked to the Coalition in some way.'

Anthony's jaw tightened. 'And thus destabilise allied unity.'

'Looks like it.'

'With the Allies divided it would leave the way clear for Napoleon to march through Europe virtually unopposed.'

Lebrun spat into the dirt. 'That's about the size of it, I reckon.'

'Did Poiret say anything else?'

'No. That's it. We never saw him again.'

The Earl nodded, digesting what he had learned. Then, tossing some coins on the table to pay for the ale, he rose from the table. 'I'll be in touch.'

Saunière smiled, revealing stained brown teeth. 'You know where to find us.'

* * *

Since he had given his word to Claudia that he would keep her abreast of his findings, the Earl determined to do so as soon as might be. On returning home however, he discovered that she was still not back. It was another half an hour before she put in an appearance. He stood in the doorway of the salon, watching her divest herself of spencer and bonnet. Her excursion seemed to have agreed with her; she looked as relaxed as he'd ever seen her. Moreover, the sunshine and fresh air had enhanced the bloom on her cheeks and put a sparkle in her eyes. It was altogether a beguiling image.

Claudia turned and suddenly became aware of his presence. Under the power of that quiet scrutiny she felt her pulse quicken. 'Anthony. I didn't realise you were back yet. Did you have a fruitful morning?'

'Indeed. Would you like to hear about it?'

'Of course.'

She came to join him and he closed the salon door after them. Claudia sat down on the couch, clasping her hands in her lap, waiting expectantly. He stood by the hearth and leaned casually on the mantel, surveying her steadily.

'I went to see Lebrun and Saunière.'

Her eyes widened slightly. 'And?'

As he summarised what he had learned her expression grew more sombre. If Poiret's information were accurate, it had serious ramifications indeed.

'Someone became suspicious of Alain or of his informant,' she said, when Anthony had concluded his account.

'It would seem so.'

'What do you intend to do now?'

'Keep an ear to the ground, as always.'

She nodded and then sighed. 'I feel so useless.'

'You have no cause to. You have done your part and more.'

'I hate the thought that somewhere, perhaps not far away, is a traitor who threatens everything. If Napoleon is not stopped who knows where his ambition may take him next. England, perhaps?'

'I think you need have no fears on that score. He'd have to get past the British navy first.' He grinned. 'He'd also have to get past you, so I wouldn't rate his chances very highly.'

It drew an answering smile. 'I'd love a chance to get the horrid little man in my sights.'

'I'm sure you would.'

'Do you think Lebrun and Saunière are to be trusted?'

'Until we find out otherwise.'

She sighed. 'You're right of course. All the same, this whole business leaves a nasty taste.'

'Then let us speak of more pleasant things. Tell me about your shopping expedition.'

'It seems unexciting in comparison. All the same

I found a wonderful mercer's shop and they'd just received a new consignment of fabrics, including some exquisite Indian muslin in different shades. It was rather extravagant, but I bought enough for several gowns.'

'I look forward to seeing them.'

'I found some beautiful watered silk for a ball gown as well.'

'The Somersets' ball?'

'Yes. We shall see your friends there and I want to be a credit to you.'

'You are never anything less.' He possessed himself of her hands. 'Whatever you wear you'll be the most beautiful woman in the room.'

'Are you trying to turn my head with flattery?'

'I'd like to think it was in my power to do it, but I know better.' He drew her closer. 'I'll have to try something else.'

'Oh? What else?'

What else was a lingering kiss that set every nerve tingling. Claudia pressed closer, twining her arms around his neck, her entire being alive to him. The embrace went on for some time. Then she looked up at him.

'Will you waltz with me at the ball?'

'As often as you like.'

'Hmm. It will be regarded askance if you dance with me too often. You will be regarded as a jealous husband.'

'I am a jealous husband. Fiercely jealous.'

'It is unfashionable to be so. An air of indifference is the accepted norm.'

'To the devil with the accepted norm,' he replied.

Chapter Sixteen

The Somersets' ball was a grand affair and fashionably crowded to boot. She and Anthony had not long arrived before they met Falconbridge along with some of his fellow officers. Some of them evidently knew the Earl, among them Colonel Albermarle.

'Good to see you again, Brudenell. Didn't think we would after Vittoria. Bad do.'

'It's good to see you too, sir.'

'What have you been doing with yourself in the meantime?'

'Oh, this and that. Keeping myself busy.'

'Best way.' Albermarle glanced at Claudia and then fixed the Earl with a lofty stare. 'Well, aren't you going to introduce me?'

'I rather hope he's going to introduce all of us,' interjected a plaintive voice from the surrounding group.

'Forgive me.' The Earl performed the introductions, only to find his wife's hand solicited for several dances. He watched in silent chagrin as she went off on the arm of a dashing young grenadier guardsman.

Falconbridge read him correctly and grinned. 'These other fellows are a confounded nuisance, aren't they? I've just lost Sabrina to a colonel in the 52nd.'

His companions laughed and then Channing spoke up. 'We mean to see you quite cut out.'

'Just so,' said Fitzroy. 'You can't expect to keep your lovely wife to yourself, you know.'

Falconbridge sighed. 'In that case I shall have to go and drown my sorrows. Coming, Tony?'

'There's nothing else for it,' replied the Earl.

Claudia had two dances with the grenadier and then, as he led her from the floor, another man stepped into her line of vision. As her gaze took the narrow, angular face with its pale blue eyes, she experienced a jolt of recognition.

'Monsieur Viaud. What a surprise.'

His gaze swept her, lingering a moment on the low neckline of her gown. Then he bowed. 'A pleasure to see you again, my lady. It has been too long.'

The recollection of their last meeting returned with force. It had been at Oakley Court and they had discussed the use of the property's coastal access. She realised then that his presence here was not coincidental. *Your contact will find you.* He smiled and extended a gloved hand.

'May I have the honour of this dance?'

It was a waltz, a perfect opportunity to talk privately while in plain view of everyone else. While Gabriel Viaud certainly wouldn't have been her choice of partner for such an intimate dance, she had to acknowledge it was a clever ploy.

'You have spoken to Madeleine Fournier,' he said.

It was a statement, not a question. If he knew, then it suggested that she had been watched. The thought was not entirely comfortable.

'You are well-informed, monsieur.'

'It is my business to be well-informed.' He paused. 'May I ask what you spoke about?'

'I asked if she had any idea who betrayed Alain Poiret.'

'And?' The blue eyes watched her closely.

Claudia smiled ruefully. 'She said that she knew nothing of Alain's business. That he never discussed it with her.'

'Did you think she was telling the truth?'

'Perhaps.'

'Why perhaps?'

'I think that events in Paris frightened her very much. It's hardly surprising.'

'I suppose not.'

'She has also lost someone who had been very close to her.'

Viaud's lip curled. 'Alain Poiret wasn't her first lover.'

'That doesn't mean that she didn't sincerely care for him.'

'Women of that sort are concerned only with the money such liaisons bring.'

'Women only become that sort because of men, monsieur.'

He surveyed her steadily for a moment but Claudia held his gaze. Then he returned a mocking smile. 'I stand corrected, my lady.'

They lapsed into silence after this. Having delivered her message Claudia wanted to nothing more than to be out of his presence now. When at last the dance ended and he led her off the floor she could only feel a strong sense of relief.

The Earl had a glass of champagne with his friend and then, as other people broke into their conversation, he left them to it and moved on to mingle with the other guests. Without any appearance of deliberate intent he strolled into the ballroom and stood near the doorway, scanning the dancers. He saw Sabrina and the colonel, and then, further off, his own wife, dancing with Gabriel Viaud. The implication did not escape him and his brow creased for a moment. Then he reflected that it was probably a good thing. Once she had reported her findings her involvement was at an end.

When the dance concluded she parted company

with Viaud and her hand was immediately solicited for the next. She looked more relaxed now, laughing at something that her partner had said. Evidently a witty reply followed because he laughed in return. He happened to be a very handsome youth, his dark good looks set off by the dashing uniform he wore. They appeared to be getting along famously too, if smiles were anything to judge by. The puppy was getting a damned sight too familiar with her. Immediately, the Earl's annoyance turned inwards as he recognised his response for what it was. Until recently jealousy had been foreign to his nature. Claudia was naturally vivacious and blended effortlessly into the social scene, but she showed no sign whatever of favouring any one of her partners above the rest. He had no cause to be jealous. All the same, when the grenadier retained her hand for the third time, the Earl's tolerance wore thinner.

The dance seemed to go on for an interminably long time but when at last it ended and Claudia's partner led her from the floor, the Earl seized his chance.

She smiled and lifted one arched brow. 'I suppose it would make no difference if I told you that the next two dances are already taken?'

'Devil a bit,' was the cheerful reply.

'It's quite against the rules. You do realise that?'

'Of course I realise that.' He put his arm around her waist. 'It would be no fun otherwise.'

She made no further protest. It would have been a complete waste of time, and in any case there was no-one she would rather have danced with. He excited her as no other man ever had, but then no other man possessed the same magnetism, the same dangerous charisma. Every time he looked at her or touched her it only heightened the attraction. That other women watched them with envious eyes did nothing to diminish the sensation. She would have been less than human not to enjoy it.

After three more dances Claudia had to plead thirst. The room was hot and crowded and the thought of a refreshing drink was attractive. They went into the adjoining room where he found them some fruit punch. Just then a familiar figure joined them.

Claudia smiled, recognising Colonel Falconbridge. However, he wasn't alone.

'Lady Claudia, I should like you to meet my wife.'

Claudia looked curiously at the woman opposite. Sabrina Falconbridge was tall, willowy and blonde, her figure admirably shown off by a modish gown of spangled white sarsenet. She also had the most beautiful green eyes that Claudia had ever seen. They lit now in a warm smile.

'I am so pleased to meet you at last, Lady Claudia.'

'And I you. My husband has told me so much about you.'

'Oh dear, and I had so hoped to make a good impression.' The tone was friendly and ever so slightly mischievous.

Claudia smiled and relaxed a little. 'You need not be concerned. He spoke of you in the most glowing terms.'

'That was generous of him.'

'Not generous, sincere,' replied the Earl.

Sabrina gave him a smiling glance and then turned back to Claudia. 'I'll wager he didn't tell you that he once saved my life and Robert's too.'

'Indeed he did not.'

'It was a truly heroic deed.'

'It was no such thing,' said the Earl. 'I happened to be with the rescue party at the time, that's all.'

'Don't listen to him, Lady Claudia. He will only downplay his role in the affair.'

'I think I would rather hear your version of the story,' she said.

'You have my word on it.'

The Earl groaned, but his friend only laughed. 'It's no use. I'm afraid the truth will out.'

'I thought you were on my side.'

Falconbridge feigned surprise. 'Whatever gave you that idea?'

It drew a general laugh as he had intended, and the ice was well and truly broken. Sabrina looked at Claudia.

'Shall we leave the men to talk awhile and adjourn next door where it is a little cooler?'

Claudia seized her chance. 'That would be most pleasant. This heat is fatiguing, is it not?'

Having taking leave of their husbands for the time, they helped themselves to more fruit punch and then found an empty couch where they might talk in comfort. Sabrina was easy company and quite willing to recount some of her experiences in Spain. Claudia listened with rapt attention.

'It sounds so very exciting,' she said. 'I am quite envious.'

Sabrina grinned. 'It had its moments, your husband's rescue of us being one. He denies its importance but, believe me, it would have been all up with us if he had not appeared when he did.'

'He and Colonel Falconbridge were already friends, I collect.'

'Yes. They were in the same regiment and saw action together on several occasions. The last time was at Vittoria.'

'Anthony rarely speaks of it.'

'It was a bad time for him. No doubt he prefers to leave it in the past.'

Claudia hesitated. 'I should so much like to know…to understand…what happened to him. I don't just mean the physical injuries, though they were bad enough, but his state of mind at the time.'

Sabrina set down her cup. 'The physical injuries also crippled him mentally for a while. He withdrew into himself and shunned company wherever possible. Even Robert could not reach him at first.'

Claudia bit her lip. It was worse than she had imagined. 'I know that Anthony hated having to resign his commission and leave his friends.'

'Yes. It was a grievous blow on top of every-thing else, but, at the time, he felt that he had no alternative. He thought he would never regain the use of his arm, that he would be a liability in com-bat.' Sabrina sighed. 'Above all he could not bear to be pitied.'

'I can well believe it.'

'It was as though a stranger had taken the place of the man I knew. He was unfailingly courteous but he never initiated conversation any more, never once intimated at the thoughts on his mind. When one looked into his face there was nothing there, only emptiness.'

Claudia was very still, her mind trying to grap-ple with the scale of loneliness that the words im-plied.

'He did not tell anyone when he was leaving,' Sabrina went on. 'One morning he was gone. We had seen him the previous evening; he stayed a little while to take some wine with us. With hind-sight it must have been his way of saying goodbye.'

'He would have avoided any kind of fuss.'

'Yes, though we were worried about him never-theless. We assumed he would return to his family, but inquiry there drew a blank.'

Claudia's glass paused in mid-air. 'You sent to Ulverdale?'

'That's right. The Earl sent back a short reply saying that the whereabouts of his son were unknown to him.'

'I see.' The fact that her father-in-law had not even mentioned the inquiry filled her with impotent fury.

'Forgive me, but from the tone of the letter it appeared that he and the Earl were not close.'

'No, they weren't.'

'Well, it must have come as a great relief to you to have your husband back.'

'It was momentous in every way,' replied Claudia. Unwilling to pursue it further she changed the subject. 'May I come and call on you one day soon?'

Sabrina smiled. 'I should like that very much.'

The conversation stayed with Claudia long after the two women had parted again. As she had hoped at the outset, it afforded fresh insight into Anthony's past. It was evident that Vittoria had changed him irrevocably. She had never really known the man he had been before, but she did want to know the man he had become. His loneliness and pain were clearly visible to her now, and for the first time she recognised that they held those things in common. Some of the reasons for that were different, but ultimately it stemmed from the same root cause.

She was drawn from these reflections by the

men who had bespoken the next dances, but, although she smiled, they could not hold her attention. Her gaze ranged across the crowded room but could not find the one man she wanted. Then, when the next measure ended, someone announced that the fireworks were about to start and people began to move out on to the balconies and the terrace.

Feeling oddly forlorn now, Claudia followed a small group out on to a balcony overlooking the lawn. The air was blessedly cool out here, and scented with jasmine and stocks from the beds below. Above it all a million stars spangled the velvet night sky and a perfect crescent moon hung in their midst. It was impossibly beautiful, a night made for romance. All it lacked was the right man to share it with.

A blaze of light from fifty Catherine wheels announced the start of the display on the lawn in front of her. Then a shower of rockets burst with staccato pops into a constellation of red and green stars eliciting excited gasps from the audience below. Several ladies cried out as a mortar burst flung dazzling silver comets across the sky. The smell of smoke mingled with the scent of flowers. Claudia was held by the spectacle now, watching spellbound. She failed to notice the man beside her until she felt an arm around her shoulders. She looked up and felt her heart leap.

'Anthony.'

'Are you enjoying the display?'

'Very much.'

His arm tightened a fraction and drew her closer. Claudia relaxed against him, felt him drop a kiss on her hair. Then they stood together and watched. The noise intensified as volleys of rockets hurtled skywards and then burst. Almost simultaneously something whined past Anthony and hit the wall behind. Stone chips flew. He frowned and looked round, taking in the mark where the lighter colour showed through the small damaged area, and then the lead ball lodged within.

'Antony? What is it?'

'Inside, quickly.' He grasped her arm and drew her indoors, away from the open window. 'Stay here.'

He returned to the balcony, his gaze scanning the garden, but outside the ring of light created by the fireworks display, the trees and shrubs were in deep shadow. A crowd of people stood between. By the time he found a way around them the attacker would be long gone. He swore under his breath and then retraced his steps to join Claudia. Her face registered both shock and incredulity.

'Did someone just shoot at us?'

'Yes, and used the fireworks to mask the sound.'

'Why, of all the devious, cowardly.... Did you spot anything suspicious out there?'

'No. The edges of the garden provide ideal cover.'

'He would have needed it: he could scarcely have drawn a pistol in front of so many witnesses.'

'True.'

'Well, the villain is probably long gone by now.'

'And perhaps he isn't. I can't take that chance. I'm afraid we're going to have to miss the rest of the display.'

'It doesn't matter.' Now that initial indignation had worn off, she shivered a little, looking round the room, where now only a few servants were in evidence. 'Let's just be glad the attacker wasn't a better shot.'

He took her hands and squeezed gently. 'Do you want to stay for supper?'

'I don't think I could enjoy it. I'd feel as though I had to look over my shoulder the whole time.'

'Then I'll take you home. We can apologise to our hosts later.'

They returned to the hallway and, while Claudia retrieved her evening cloak, he called for the carriage. Within ten minutes they were on their way.

'Whoever took that pot shot must have known we'd be here tonight, Anthony.'

'It must have been an educated guess. Presumably he knew this ball would attract most of fashionable society.'

'It wouldn't have been hard to find out about the fireworks display; people have been talking about it for weeks. It must have suggested a good opportunity.' She pulled her cloak closer around her. 'It's bad enough knowing that one has a deadly enemy, but an invisible enemy is worse.'

'The hidden assassin is an effective tool.'

'He'll try again, won't he?'

'Almost certainly.'

She was glad he hadn't tried to lie or to offer false reassurance. 'This is connected with Paris, isn't it?'

'I'm sure of it. We may have escaped that particular net, but it's a pound to a penny that Fouché's henchmen have discovered our identities. Brussels isn't safe any longer, Claudia.'

'Will England be any better? If they know who we are they could find us just as easily there.'

'By which you mean that you don't want to leave.'

'I cannot see any point in trying to run. Besides, I'm sure the answer to all this is here in Brussels.'

'If courage were enough to defeat an enemy you'd be the certain victor,' he replied. 'But it isn't enough, Claudia. We were lucky tonight, but no-one's luck holds forever. I would not have you come to harm, my sweet.'

'Nor I you.'

He hesitated. 'Would it matter to you?'

'Of course it would matter.'

That was the absolute truth and she knew it. This latest reprieve only fuelled the desire to make the most of what they had, because it was only when she was with him that she felt truly alive.

The sincerity of her tone caused his heart to perform a sudden erratic manoeuvre. He saw her lean closer and then felt her lips brush his. Gradually the light pressure became flirtatious and teasing, seeking his response. Desire kindled instantly. He felt her arms slide around him, drawing him closer. Heat flared in his groin. He tipped back in the crook of his arm and returned the embrace hungrily.

Her mouth opened beneath his, soft, yielding, provocative. The kiss became deeper and she returned it, her tongue teasing and flirting with his, tasting him, wanting more. His free hand brushed across her breast, stroking softly, then slid deeper into the décolletage of her gown and found the nipple, caressing it to hardness. She groaned softly as pleasure turned her blood to fire.

Chapter Seventeen

The drive was not long and they arrived home a few minutes later. Since the servants had been told not to wait up, he let them both in. Then, closing the door behind them, he seized hold of her and pushed her against it, pinning her there, his mouth slanting hard across hers, searing, demanding, his hands sliding down to her buttocks, cupping them, pulling her hips against his, letting her feel the growing hardness there.

In the back of her mind a small voice whispered of possible consequences. She knew she should heed it and knew she wasn't going to. The voice was blocked out and all she could think of was the man in front of her. Letting go all restraint now, she responded with like hunger, sliding her arms around him, returning the kiss with abandon. One hand slid lower, stroking him gently. She heard the sharp indrawn breath that followed, and felt the jutting hardness stir beneath her fingers, anticipation building as she imagined its length inside her. She felt him lift her skirts and slide a hand along her thigh and thence into the cleft between her legs. The touch sent a jolt through the length of her body. Her breathing quickened; as he moved she caught the scent of cedar from his coat, and beneath it his own smell, warm and musky and erotic. The hand continued to stroke gently causing a flood of delicious sensations. Of its own volition her body quivered, responding to his touch like a finely tuned instrument.

He stepped away just long enough to pick her up and carry her to his bedchamber, heeling the door shut behind them. Then he resumed where they'd left off, his lips seeking hers and afterwards travelling lower to her throat and thence to the swell of her breasts above the neckline of her gown. Warm breath feathered against her skin. The touch caused a surge of warmth in her blood. Her fingers reached for the front of his breeches and unfastened them to close round the shaft beneath. She stroked gently, heard him catch his breath. His hands rode her waist as he guided her gently backwards until they reached the edge of the bed. Shrugging off his coat, he pushed her on to the coverlet and pulled her skirts up over her hips, before following her down. Thoroughly aroused now, she raised her knees to accommodate him, felt a shiver of excitement as he slid into her. Her fingers tore at his shirt, dragging the fabric aside, sliding the palms of her hands over the warm muscles in his back.

'Put your legs around me.'

She obeyed, felt him move deeper, felt the rhythm build and strengthen. As the thrusts grew harder she gasped, arched towards him, her nails raking his back. This time he wasn't gentle but there was no pain, only fierce need and mutual desire. The coil of tension inside her increased, taking her higher, pushing her swiftly towards the place she had visited before. Instinctively she slid her legs higher, pulling him deeper, crying out as they fell over the edge together, feeling him shudder, and then the hot rush of his seed.

For a while he remained inside her, holding her there, unwilling to lose the sensation of oneness with her. Then, slowly, he collapsed on to his elbows above her, breathing hard.

'Dear God. That was incredible.'

'Yes, it was.'

'I've wanted to do that all evening.'

She looked up at him beneath veiled lashes and then smiled. 'I've wanted you to do that all evening.'

'Unfortunately we've missed most of the evening, but we have the whole morning ahead of us.'

'You are incorrigible, and insatiable.'

'You have no idea.'

He undressed her and then himself, and took her to bed. The dawn was far advanced before they slept.

* * *

Claudia stretched lazily, her whole body suffused with a sense of well-being. Turning her head to look at the man beside her, she found him already awake and observing her closely. She saw him smile.

'Good morning.'

'Have you been watching me?'

'Yes, for quite a while now.' He leaned across and kissed her, reviving delicious memories of the previous night's love-making.

'Did you not sleep well?'

'I slept exceeding well, but a few hours suffice for me.'

'Then you must have wanted to start the day long since.'

'Not so,' he said. 'I was more agreeably engaged.'

'Indeed?'

'Oh, yes.'

'Doing what exactly?'

'Looking at you by daylight.'

Claudia surveyed him suspiciously. 'Looking at what?'

The smile became a grin. 'Did you know that you have the most delightful…'

'What?' Her eyes glinted dangerously.

'Lips.'

She sat up, regarding him with suspicion. 'Lips?'

'Yes…and breasts, of course, and waist and

hips and butt…' He broke off, throwing up an arm
to deflect the pillow aimed at his head. Claudia
launched a second blow. Choking back laughter
he grabbed hold of her and confiscated the pillow.
There followed a brief, unequal struggle before she
was pulled much closer for a deep and lingering
kiss. She stopped struggling and relaxed, letting
her body mould itself to his, giving herself up to
the embrace.

When at length it ended she drew back a little, looking into his face. She smiled and lifted a
hand to his cheek, then checked as he flinched a
little. The movement triggered another memory
and along with it a sudden and disturbing insight.

'Anthony, the night you came back from Ulverdale…when you walked away?' She held his
gaze. 'It was after I'd touched your face, wasn't
it? That's what you meant before when you said
you'd over-reacted.'

He nodded. 'As I said, personal devils.'

'Then, what happened in Paris really had no
bearing on the matter.'

'Except that I've wanted you every day since,
more than I've ever wanted anything in my life.
But the feeling had to be mutual.' He took a deep
breath. 'It seemed…it seemed as though you could
only tolerate my attentions in darkness, that by
daylight my appearance repelled you.'

Claudia stared at him, appalled. 'I have never
felt repelled by you. Paris awoke something in me

that I never imagined existed, but I was so ashamed of the circumstances that the only possible way forward was to try and blot it out. It wasn't you that disgusted me, Anthony, it was myself. The more the attraction increased, the worse I felt.'

He swallowed hard. 'Then you did not find my kisses repulsive?'

'No, I never did. On the contrary.'

'Can a mask attract a woman then?'

'Not the mask, the man beneath it.'

His jaw tightened. 'You do not know the man beneath it.'

'I think I do.'

'He is no figure of high romance, I assure you.'

'May not I be the judge of that?' She lifted her hand slowly towards the slender cord that held the leather patch. It was arrested as a hand like a vice closed round her wrist.

'Claudia, I…'

'Don't be afraid.'

His throat tightened and he knew in that moment that he was terribly afraid, that he would rather face the guns at Vittoria again than do what she was asking now. Their love-making had been beyond wonderful, and, in the forgiving darkness, she had yielded herself to him completely. The cold light of day filled him with dread for now only a thin leather shield stood between her and the truth. His gut knotted in sickened anticipation of her reaction, his mind torn between the instinctive urge to protect himself and the wish to let her see exactly who he was. And if he did that, would not the truth repel her? Would she not turn from him? He took a deep breath. Perhaps it was time to find out.

Gradually the grip slackened on her wrist and, with thumping heart, he released his hold. Her hand stole towards the cord and slipped it free, drawing the leather shield aside. He steeled himself, waiting grimly for the sharp indrawn breath, the expression of disgust and loathing.

Her steady gaze surveyed the ravaged side of his face from the jagged tear on his forehead, to the cleft eyebrow and the empty socket beneath, sewn closed. The blade had cut him to the bone, laying open his cheek almost to the jaw. A legacy of puckered skin revealed where heavy stitching had once held the severed flesh together. She realised then that the scars on his arm and shoulder were the result of other blows. Two; three, perhaps? Her mind could not begin to grasp the intensity of the pain he must have felt, then and afterwards, and the dawning horror as the reality of his injuries became apparent. Injuries that she knew were not only physical. The mental and emotional scars were every bit as deep, like his vulnerability at this moment and the anguish in his silence. In opening himself to her scrutiny he had taken a terrible risk and it must have taken every ounce of courage he possessed.

She reached out to him and with infinite gentleness traced the line of the scar down his cheek. 'Do these still hurt?'

Somehow he found his voice. 'No, but they make shaving a confounded nuisance.'

She kissed him softly on the mouth. 'Even more of a nuisance than I am?'

'Oh, no, not nearly as much as that.'

Her lips quivered. 'Would you be rid of me then, if you had the chance?'

'Certainly not; without you I would die of boredom within a week.'

'I would not have that on my conscience so I really think I must remain.'

'You're quite right about that,' he replied. 'Besides, I'm not giving you a choice.'

He pulled her towards him for a gentle and lingering kiss. And then, slowly, he lowered himself back on to the bed and drew her with him, gathering her close, curving his body around hers, breathing her subtle erotic scent, his entire being alive to the warmth and the nearness of her. He lay quite still, listening to her soft breathing, feeling the slow steady beat of her heart beneath his arm and, by degrees, his own heartbeat quietened and steadied in response until it became synchronous with hers. Gradually his taut muscles relaxed and tension was replaced by deep contentment and a sense of rightness and belonging, as though something lost had been found. Now there was no pain or dread. He let out a long breath and watched as the shadow of his fear began to shrink and fade until at last it dissolved among the brilliant rays of sunlight slanting through the curtains.

Later they walked in the park, strolling together among the flowering beds and thence in the sun-dappled grass beneath the trees. Recent events compelled Anthony to take the precaution of having Matthew with them, albeit at a discreet distance. Other company would have been intolerable just then. Having wasted so much time before, the Earl wanted to spend as much as he could now with Claudia. It was as though the world had shrunk to the two of them, and, today at least, nothing else mattered.

For some time they walked in companionable silence, just content to be with each other. Intimacy had not bred complacency, only a strengthening desire to discover more. Every look, every touch became charged with significance, enhancing the growing realisation that neither of them had spoken aloud.

She had no idea when she had begun to love him, only that she did. Somehow the feeling had crept up on her, taking her completely unawares. It filled her being with a joy so intense it was terrifying. Its shadow crossed her face. He saw it at once.

'What is it, Claudia.'

'I was just thinking about how many years we have lost.' She hesitated. 'Why did you go away, Anthony? Why did you leave Ulverdale all those years ago?'

He hesitated, then looked up and met her eye. 'Because I would not bed a fourteen-year-old girl.'

A rosy blush dyed her cheeks. 'But part of the original agreement was that our marriage should not be consummated for another two years.'

'My father was of a different opinion. He feared that, if the marriage was not consummated, it might later be annulled, in which case he stood to lose a lot of money.'

Claudia heard him in stunned silence.

'We quarrelled,' he went on, 'but when my mother joined in to lend me her support, my father backed down.'

'Your mother supported you?'

'With unusual vigour. By then I think she despised my father as much as I did. She also knew as well as I what the consequences might be if I were to get you with child.'

Claudia paled. Had he done so then, the chances were she would not have survived the birth. He had behaved honourably towards the child she was then. However, she wasn't a child any more, and the spectres of pregnancy and childbed were much closer now. The knowledge revived old fears. With an effort she pushed them down, unwilling to spoil the day.

'I had no idea.'

'It was hardly a suitable subject to discuss with an innocent young girl.' He sighed. 'That was the last quarrel I ever had with my father, and afterwards I wanted only to get out of his presence.'

'I can understand that.'

'I already had my commission by then; all that remained was for me to take it up. I threw myself into my career and, as time went by, the breach with Ulverdale widened. I imagined, wrongly, that you would be enjoying the London Season, making your own circle of friends, living your own life. I could not think that you would welcome my return.'

'If only you knew how many times I hoped for it.'

'After Vittoria I thought the way back was closed for good, that you could never regard me with anything other than loathing.'

'Oh, Anthony, how much time has been wasted.'

'I know it. We cannot recapture those lost years but we can look forward to all the ones we're going to share.' He looked into her face. 'Shall you be able to bear a husband's authority?'

Her eyes sparkled. 'Tolerably well, I think. Shall you be able to bear a wilful jade?'

'I'm quietly confident,' he replied.

That evening they ignored an engagement to attend the theatre and shared a leisurely dinner together instead, lingering over the wine to talk and share experiences. By the time they had finished summer dusk was drawing in.

Anthony glanced towards the window. 'It's a fine evening. Would you care to take a turn around the garden?'

'Why not?'

He opened the French doors and stood back to let her pass. Claudia paused on the narrow pathway, waiting for him to join her. Then they strolled together across the lawn.

It was peaceful out here, the stillness balmy with residual warmth, while, in the deepening blue vault, a setting sun dyed the high cloud orange and gold. The quiet air was redolent of summer scents; of earth and leaves and grass, overlain with rose and honeysuckle and carnation. Beyond the flowering beds shadows lengthened beneath the trees. Somewhere a blackbird sang, its liquid notes filling the deep green shade.

Claudia listened and smiled, feeling more content in that moment than she could ever remember. It was not just the beauty of the evening that filled her heart with joy, but being in the company she would most have sought. Every fibre of her being was aware of the man beside her, every nerve alive to him, but more than that he inspired in her a strong sense of belonging. Being with him was like coming home after a long and difficult journey, and never wanting to leave again.

They strolled in silence for a while until at length he paused to break a red rose from off the trellis at the edge of the arbour. Then he turned and offered it to her.

'One rose for another.'

The quiet intensity of the accompanying look made her feel unwontedly self-conscious. Rather shyly she took it from him, feeling his fingers brush hers, feeling her skin tingle in response. To cover that momentary confusion she lifted the flower and breathed its perfume.

'It's beautiful.'

'So are you; the most beautiful lady of my acquaintance.' He possessed himself of her free hand and raised it to his lips.

The touch turned her blood to flame. Involuntarily she moved a little closer and, standing on tiptoe, kissed him gently on the lips. For a brief moment she drew back a little, then her arms stole around his neck and she kissed him again, a tender and warming embrace that offered a glimpse of something beyond his wildest imagination. It also set every sense alight. His arms closed about her waist and shoulders and the kiss was returned, gently at first, and, as her mouth yielded to his, with answering passion. And afterwards, she laid her head against his breast and he held her close while the scented dusk gathered around them.

Chapter Eighteen

⁓⊷⊶⊷⊷⊶⊷⊶⊷⊶⊷⊷⊷⊶

A few days later Claudia returned from a visit to Sabrina's house to find a note waiting for her. She took it and glanced at the direction, but the hand-writing was unfamiliar. Curious now she unfolded the paper. It contained but one line: 'I'll be at the park gates at six this evening.' It was signed, MF.

Claudia's heart leapt. Madeleine Fournier must have changed her mind. A swift glance at the clock showed a quarter to six. It wasn't far to the park; if she hurried there would just be time. However, she wasn't going unarmed or unescorted. Apart from anything else, she had given her word to Anthony, so she ran upstairs and retrieved the small pistol, slipping it into her reticule. She paused for a moment then, wondering if he might be angry. At the same time, this was important.

Leaving a message to say that she had gone out again, she summoned Lucy and a footman. When they reached the door, she took a swift glance up and down the street. It revealed only a few pedestrians, certainly nothing to occasion any alarm, so they set off.

Madeleine Fournier was waiting at the appointed place when they arrived. 'I did not know if you would come,' she said.

Claudia smiled at her. 'I was glad to get your message.'

Madeleine eyed the servants warily. 'I would prefer us to speak alone.'

Telling Lucy and the footman to stay where they were, Claudia drew the other woman aside a little way, though taking care to remain in clear view.

'Now, tell me why you have come.'

'I thought about what you said, about wanting to find out who betrayed Alain. Was that true?'

'Yes. I was a colleague of his; but for good fortune I might have shared his fate. If you know anything, I beg you will tell me.'

'I was not entirely truthful when I said that Alain did not speak about his work. Of course he never told me much, but enough for me to know that it was highly sensitive. Had it not been, Fouché's men would not have shown such interest.'

'You are right.'

Madeleine nodded. 'I can tell you very little and what I know probably won't be of much use.'

Claudia resisted the urge to prompt her and waited quietly instead.

'One evening, about a week before Alain was arrested, we received a visitor, a man. He and Alain talked together for a few minutes out in the hall-way. I could not hear the conversation for they spoke low, but I did see the man's face for a few moments.'

'Would you know it again?'

'Assuredly. I have a good memory for faces.'

'Can you recall anything else about him?'

'He was a little above average height, of medium build, and he had light brown hair.'

Claudia concealed disappointment. That description might fit half the male population of France.

'I thought no more of it,' Madeleine went on, 'until, a few days later, I saw the same man again. I was on my way to the market when I saw him on the opposite corner of the street. He didn't see me. He was talking to someone else, a man whom I recognised as a member of the Paris police.'

'How did you know that?'

'He'd been among the officers who raided a gaming den where I used to work, before I met Alain.'

'I see.'

'I smelled a rat and warned Alain. He seemed much disturbed and told me he'd have to go away for a while. However, first he had to get a message to someone, to warn him. He asked me to take it.'

'Who was the message for?'

'A man called Antoine Duval.'

Claudia's stomach lurched. 'I am glad you did.'

'Was it important then?'

'It saved two lives.'

'That's something at least,' said Madeleine.

'What happened after that?'

'I was barely gone twenty minutes but by the time I returned the police were already at the house. I saw them take Alain away. For a while I was so scared I didn't know what to do. I walked around the streets for hours until I was sure the coast was clear, and then went back. The place was a mess. It looked like there had been a thorough search.'

'What did they hope to find?'

'I'm not sure.' Madeleine hesitated. 'Maybe the papers that Alain burned before they arrived.'

'Papers?'

'The fire had been unlit when I left. When I returned there was a pile of ashes in the hearth. When I looked more closely I found this. It had fallen behind the firebox and the police must have missed it.' She reached into the pocket of her skirt and drew out a small and grubby piece of paper, charred at the edges. 'It doesn't look like much but it may be significant.'

Claudia took it, scrutinising it closely. One side was blank the other held a few words of handwriting, hurriedly written and hard to read. She made out *él*, then a squiggle for the middle of the word followed with looked like *ir*. The paper had been torn part way through what appeared to be a name:

Willi. She frowned. At first sight it didn't seem to make a lot of sense. On the other hand, it was all they had to go on.

'Thank you for this, Mademoiselle Fournier.'

'As I said, it may not be of any use.'

'That remains to be seen.'

'There was one more thing. The man who came to the house was wearing a ring. It was gold and square in shape like a signet ring, but it was set with a flat black stone.' Madeleine sketched a vague, deprecating gesture. 'It's not a shining beacon of hope, is it?'

'Better than nothing at all,' replied Claudia. 'You did a brave thing coming here. I'm grateful.'

'I'd better go. I don't know if I'm being watched or not, but, if you found me, then others might.'

Thinking of recent events, Claudia knew that the concern was not misplaced. 'You know where to come if you think of anything else, or if you need help.' She handed over a handkerchief containing coin. 'In the meantime, please take this for your trouble.'

Her companion nodded and returned a wan smile before pocketing the money. Then she turned and hurried away. Claudia watched her go for a moment or two, then, summoning her attendants, retraced her steps to the house.

After dinner that evening, when they had retired to the salon, she told Anthony what had taken place. Although he had initially felt concerned when he discovered her earlier absence, it pleased him to discover that she was well-attended. Clearly, former lessons hadn't been lost on her. Besides, as she rightly said, the matter was important. So he listened intently and without interruption until she had done.

'I'm glad the Fournier girl decided to come forward,' he said. 'You must have made a very positive impression.'

'I feel so sorry for her, Anthony. She seems so alone, so frightened.'

'Independence has its disadvantages, doesn't it?'

'I'm beginning to think it does.' She sighed. 'I don't suppose there's much chance of finding the man Alain spoke to that night.'

'No, probably not. That description could apply to thousands of Frenchmen.'

It was an exact echo of her thought. 'There is still the ring.'

'Even so.' Then he smiled. 'Still, it's more than we knew a few hours ago, isn't it? You've done well.'

The words and the accompanying expression created a glow of warmth deep inside.

'May I take a look at the paper you spoke of?' he went on.

'Of course. I'll go and get it.'

She hurried off to her room and returned a few

minutes later with the relevant scrap. He took it from her, studying it carefully.

'The last word has to be part of a name,' she said, 'but what is the longer one before it?'

'Let's see; *él..im..inir*. No, wait, I believe the last vowel is an *e*, though very ill written. That would make it *éliminer.*'

She stared at him. 'Eliminate Willi?'

'Or eliminate William perhaps.'

'Not much help there. There must be thousands of Williams in the world.'

'In England, yes,' he replied, 'but not here. How many important Coalition figures can you think of with that name on this side of the Channel?'

'Prince William of Orange?'

'Just so.'

Her gaze met his. 'I don't know, Anthony. It's a long shot, isn't it?'

'You're right. It is. On the other hand, consider the implications if he were to be assassinated and his death apparently implicated one or more parties in the Coalition.'

'It would jeopardise Dutch support.'

He nodded. 'To the tune of 17,000 men, or thereabouts.'

'Enough to sway the course of a battle.'

'Enough to lose us a battle, a war, and most of Europe into the bargain.'

'What are you going to do?' she asked.

'Pass this information on. As I said, forewarned

is forearmed. Security around the Prince can be tightened until we know more. On the other hand, if we're wrong, no harm has been done.'

'Will the threat be taken seriously?'

'It has to be,' he replied. 'There's too much at stake to ignore it.'

All of that was pushed into the background when, some days afterwards, Claudia realised that her courses were late. Ordinarily it wouldn't have troubled her overmuch; a few days' variation in her cycle wasn't unusual. However, given the change in her relationship with Anthony, it now achieved a very different significance. At first she tried not to dwell on it telling herself it was probably nothing, that the tenderness in her breasts was coincidental. Then, one morning, as she was dressing, an unexpected bout of queasiness sent her rushing for the basin.

When the spasm passed she lay down on the bed again, forced now to acknowledge the truth. The shock of that realisation created conflicting sensations: while dread of childbed was very much to the fore, it was underlain by the faint hope that she and the baby might come through it. And if they did…She tried to imagine what motherhood would be like, and experienced a moment of panic. How did one care for a baby? All the mothers she had ever met looked serene and confident, two qualities she most certainly didn't share just then. Of course, they all employed nursemaids but, surely, there was more to it than that. Or ought to be…

She swallowed hard. Her own upbringing was not what she would want for any child. Anthony's had been no better, in fact it was arguably worse. That being so, how was he going to react to fatherhood? Any man might sire an heir, but it took a special kind of man to be a father. Would he take his cue from his own parent or would he rise above that? Would he be able to love a child? He had never actually said that he loved her. She had thought…hoped…that he might come to love her. If so, that might have been the point to consider a family. However, choice didn't enter into it.

When at last the queasiness abated she got up and dressed. The thought of breakfast was unappealing so she went into the salon and applied herself to the pile of correspondence waiting there. However, the gilt edged invitations held no allure that morning, not even the one to the Duchess of Richmond's ball. Balls and parties were only a temporary distraction; they weren't going to change anything. The Season would be over before her pregnancy began to show but all the time she would be aware of the child growing inside her. In the meantime, she was going to have to find the right moment to break the news to Anthony.

Chapter Nineteen

~~~~~~~~~~~

A round of social engagements in the next few evenings precluded the chance of private conversation and, during the day, when she was at home he was out. Since it wasn't the kind of news that she wanted to impart in a brief, hurried conversation, she bided her time. Then, she was further distracted when, on returning from a visit to Lady Harrington, she was informed that a visitor had called in her absence.

'A woman came to the house and asked for you, milady,' said the butler. 'A most impertinent creature, and of disreputable appearance. The presumptuous piece insisted that she knew you; said she had to speak with you. She was most persistent. In the end I had to take a message in order to get rid of her.'

'What message?'

'She said to tell you that she had discovered the truth. She mentioned a name; Alain Poiret.'

Claudia's heart lurched. 'When was this?'

'About two and a half hours ago.'

'Send Lucy to me directly.'

'You gave Lucy the afternoon off, milady.'

'I had forgotten. Is my husband at home?'

'No, milady.'

Claudia bit her lip. This couldn't wait. She had to speak to Madeleine now. Anthony would not approve of her visiting that area of town unescorted, but it couldn't be helped. All the same, she would not go unarmed. Her fingers closed over her reticule and the comforting shape of the pistol within. These days she never left the house without it.

A few minutes later she was climbing into the fiacre and giving instructions to the driver.

'Rue Hermès, and hurry.'

Then, under the bemused gaze of the footman, the vehicle pulled away.

When the Earl arrived home some twenty minutes later he inquired whether his wife had returned. On learning from the butler that she had gone out again, he frowned. They were due at the theatre in an hour and a half, a small enough margin in which to change and eat, and Claudia was invariably punctual.

'Gone out where?' he asked.

'I do not know, milord.'

The footman took a step forward and coughed discreetly. The Earl turned round.

'Well? What is it, man?'

'Milady has gone to the Rue Hermès, milord.'

'How do you know this?'

'I heard her give directions to the driver of the fiacre, milord.'

'Who has gone with her?'

'No-one, milord. She went alone.'

'Alone!'

For a moment the Earl was dumbfounded, trying to credit what he'd just heard. After all that happened it was madness to go off like that, and to an area of town that she knew to be unsafe. He'd thought she had more sense. Mingled with anger was a growing feeling of unease.

'She seemed to be in a great hurry, milord.'

'Did she give any reason for going there?'

The butler swallowed hard. 'I think it may have been concerned with the woman who was here earlier.'

'What woman?'

The man swiftly recounted what he knew. The Earl's frown deepened.

'Have Matthew saddle my horse, and one for himself as well.'

With that he hurried off to change into his riding clothes. Having done that, he slid a pistol into his waistband and another into the pocket of his coat. Ten minutes later he was on his way.

When Claudia arrived the house was quiet. She paused in the hallway, listening, but could hear no sound from any of the apartments above. Slowly she climbed the stair and, locating the right door, knocked gently. The door gave a little. It was already open. Claudia knocked again. Receiving no answer she pushed it wide and went in.

'Mademoiselle Fournier?'

She stopped on the threshold, her gaze sweeping the sparsely furnished room beyond; a wooden washstand, a chair, a narrow bed and the woman lying there. Madeleine Fournier might have been sleeping, save that her eyes were open, staring sightlessly at the ceiling. The ligature round her neck testified to the manner of her death. Claudia froze, shocked to the core of her being. Then, taking a deep breath, she advanced toward the bed.

A wooden board creaked behind her and the skin prickled on the back of her neck. She spun round to find herself staring at the muzzle of a pistol. Her startled gaze registered the man behind it and then alarm mingled with surprise.

'Monsieur Viaud.'

'Lady Claudia!' For a moment or two the pistol remained levelled, then it was slowly lowered. 'Forgive me,' he said. 'I thought perhaps the killer had returned. Did you meet anyone on the way in, my lady?'

Relieved now and striving to regain her composure, Claudia took a deep breath. 'No.'

He glanced at the bed and then sighed. 'If only I had got here sooner.'

'Why did you come?'

'I had hoped to speak to Mademoiselle Fournier.'

'I see.'

'May I ask what you are doing here, my lady?'

'I came for the same reason. She sent me a message.'

'Oh?' The pale blue eyes regarded her intently. 'What message?'

'Just that she wished to speak to me.'

'Did she give any indication why?'

'The message said that she had discovered the truth, but gave no details.'

'This is most unfortunate.'

Viaud sighed and then slid the pistol into his belt. As he did so Claudia saw the ring on his hand. It was gold and set with a flat black stone. Her mouth dried and she looked away quickly, mind racing. Somehow she had to get out of this room. However, he was still between her and the door.

'Are you all right, my lady?'

'It's just the shock…' She sniffed, lifting a hand to wipe the corner of her eye. 'Forgive me.' She fumbled for her reticule.

'It has been a shock,' he agreed. 'The question is what's to be done now?'

Claudia's fingers closed on the butt of her pistol

and she drew it in one smooth movement, pointing it at his chest. 'You can start by raising your hands where I can see them.'

His gaze hardened. 'What are you doing?'

'What does it look like I'm doing?'

'You don't think that I…'

'I said get your hands in the air.'

He shrugged but obeyed, slowly. 'You're making a mistake.'

'Now toss that pistol aside. Left hand. Two fingers only.'

She saw him ease the weapon from his belt. A moment later it clattered to the floor.

'Kick it over there towards the window.' When it was done she nodded. 'Move away from the door.'

As he edged aside Claudia moved too, keeping the same distance between them.

'I didn't kill her. I found her like this.'

'I don't believe you.'

'It's the truth.'

'Tell that to the authorities.'

'You're making a big mistake.'

'I don't think so. You were the man who visited Alain Poiret just before his arrest in Paris. Mademoiselle Fournier was there. She described you, and that ring you're wearing.'

'Yes, I visited Poiret. We met quite often. What of it?'

'She also saw you speaking to a member of the police force a few days after that. She recognised the officer from a previous raid on the establishment she worked in. I think you are the one who betrayed Poiret and the others.'

'You're wrong. The police officer I spoke to is one of ours.'

'What?'

'The man is working for us.'

'You're lying, Viaud.'

'No, my dear, he's telling the truth,' said a voice from the doorway.

She looked round in startled surprise to see Anthony standing there with Matthew at his shoulder.

'The officer in question is David Roux. He's one of Genet's best. Unfortunately he didn't have any knowledge of the planned arrests until the very last minute. He managed to tip Poiret off in the hope that he'd be able to spread the word in time.'

Claudia stared at him dumbfounded. Then Viaud cut in.

'Mademoiselle Fournier has been dead for a little while. At least an hour I'd say to judge from the temperature of the body. If I were the killer I wouldn't have stayed around to be discovered.'

Anthony moved across to the bed and laid a hand on the dead woman's face. Then he nodded. 'He's right.'

'Then who did kill her?' asked Claudia.

'Someone who didn't want her to reveal what she'd discovered.'

Claudia slowly lowered her pistol. 'It looks as if I owe you an apology, Monsieur Viaud.'

He shrugged. 'No harm done, my lady. In your place I'd have been suspicious too.'

She looked at Anthony. 'What happens now?'

'We all make a report, and we arrange for the disposal of the body.'

Claudia laid a hand on his sleeve. 'Mademoiselle Fournier must be decently buried, Anthony. She does not deserve a pauper's grave.'

'She shall have a proper funeral,' he said. 'We owe her that at least.'

'We owe it to Alain Poiret too. He cared for her once.'

Anthony nodded. 'It will be attended to. Matthew, perhaps you would lend Monsieur Viaud any assistance he might require.'

'I will, my lord.'

'In the meantime, go and find a fiacre. I'm taking Her Ladyship home.'

The Earl looked pointedly at his wife and for the first time Claudia experienced deep misgivings. Suddenly, for all sorts of reasons, she wasn't looking forward to being alone with him.

Unfortunately, from her point of view, Matthew obtained a cab quite quickly and, having received instructions to lead his master's horse home, stepped back and the small carriage set off. Claudia shivered inwardly for now she had the Earl's undivided attention. Nor was there now the slightest doubt about his present mood.

'Were you out of your mind to come here alone?' he demanded.

'I had to. There was no-one else at home and the message was urgent. If I'd received it earlier I might have been in time to save Madeleine.'

'No, you little fool, you'd have died with her.'

'I brought a pistol.'

'Do you seriously imagine that popgun would have saved you?' he growled. 'These people are ruthless, Claudia. Good God, how much more convincing do you require?'

'I…I wasn't thinking clearly.'

'No, you damned well weren't. A moment's reflection would have shown you the folly of this enterprise.'

His anger was almost palpable and the knowledge that it was justified didn't help. Moreover, the memory of Madeleine was all too sharp. Had she cried out, struggled? Claudia's stomach churned.

'I didn't mean to be foolish. I thought I could help.'

'By getting yourself killed? Have you taken leave of your senses?'

'I'm sorry.'

'So you should be.'

The churning sensation increased and was followed by alarm as she recognised what it meant. 'Stop the carriage.'

He was about to demand the reason but then saw the greenish tinge in her cheeks. As soon as the vehicle stopped he climbed out quickly and helped her down. Then she leaned on the rear wheel and vomited until her stomach was empty.

Anthony waited at a discreet distance, silently appalled. When he'd seen Madeleine's fate it was but a small step to imagine that it might have been Claudia lying there. Yet she had seemed quite oblivious to the danger. His relief on finding her unharmed had turned immediately to anger. He'd been so focused on his own feelings that he'd failed to consider how the scene in the Rue Hermès might have affected her.

When she stopped retching he handed her a handkerchief and then put an arm around her shoulders.

'Better now?'

She nodded. 'A little.'

'Come then, my sweet. Let's get you home.'

He helped her back into the fiacre. She leaned back in the corner and closed her eyes. Although the green tinge had gone her face was alarmingly pale. Guilt vied with concern now and all he wanted was to get back to the Rue de Namur.

Fortunately another ten minutes brought them to the front door. Anthony paid off the driver and carried Claudia indoors. He fired off orders to the startled servants and then took her straight to her room. Having laid her on the bed he removed her bonnet and shoes and then covered her with a blanket. A few minutes later Lucy arrived with smelling salts and tea. Between them they made their patient comfortable.

Anthony drew up a chair, watching anxiously until by slow degrees some of the colour returned to her face. Then he dismissed the servant. For a little while neither he nor Claudia spoke. There were so many things he wanted to say but he knew they'd have to keep for a bit longer.

'How are you feeling now?'

'A little better.' She hesitated. 'Anthony, I'm sorry for…'

He put a finger to her lips. 'Hush. It's all right. You're unharmed and that's what matters. We'll talk later. Right now you need to rest.'

'I do feel rather tired.'

He smiled gently. 'Sleep then, sweet.'

She managed a wan smile in return. She had never felt as debilitated in her life. In contrast his presence seemed so solid and reassuring, his strength comforting. She was glad that he didn't sound angry any more although, with hindsight, he had every right to be. It had been foolish to go off alone like that. Moreover, she realised now that his anger was rooted in concern. She might have ended up like Madeleine.

'Will you stay with me until I sleep?'

'Of course,' he replied, 'if you want me to.'

'Please.' She reached for his hand. Strong warm

fingers closed over hers. At his touch much of the tension flowed out of her and she shut her eyes, feeling safe now.

In a very short time she was asleep but he remained and watched for some time, his heart full.

Chapter Twenty

Claudia slept until the following morning and woke to find herself still dressed. Then she began to recall the events of the previous day. Madeleine was dead. What was it that she had been about to impart? What was sufficiently important for someone to want to silence her for good? The brutal deed only served to underline the ruthless determination of the enemy. It was sickening to think of a man using his strength in such a way. With hindsight it had been madness to go to the apartment alone. If she had been thinking clearly she wouldn't have done it, but for days her brain had been like scrambled egg. It wasn't only herself she had put at risk. Guilt mingled with regret. The child was not to blame for its making. Involuntarily she put a hand on her belly.

'I'm so sorry,' she murmured.

As yet there was no sign of the baby she was carrying, but she was going to have to tell Anthony soon. No doubt he would be pleased to learn of a potential heir, but the worry persisted as to how he would respond to the idea of fatherhood? Just for a moment the image of the old Earl impinged on her consciousness. Although there was a certain facial resemblance, Anthony was nothing like him, either in temperament or behaviour. He could be arrogant, even downright infuriating at times, but he wasn't cruel. Would he enjoy having a child? Would he make time to be a father? Would he still find her desirable with a swollen belly? Would he want her afterwards? What if there was no afterwards? What if she died in childbed?

She swallowed hard and, with an effort, tried to force her mind down other paths. By the time she had undressed and washed and then dressed again in a fresh gown she felt a little better. Then, taking a deep breath, she braced herself for the inevitable interview with Anthony.

He was sitting by the window in the salon but, when she came in, rose to meet her, sweeping her with a critical gaze.

'You look better,' he said then.

'Thank you, I feel better.'

'I'm glad to hear it. You had me worried for a while yesterday.'

She sighed. 'What I did was foolish in the extreme, and I'm sorry for it.'

'And I am sorry for losing my temper like that.'

'You had good reason.'

He surveyed her in silence for a moment. Then

he took hold of her hands and drew her closer. 'Promise me never to do anything like that again.'

'I promise.' She looked up at him. 'Who is he, Anthony? What kind of man would murder a woman in cold blood like that?'

'A very ruthless one, my sweet. His kind doesn't care what they have to do to achieve their ends.'

'I feel badly about accusing Viaud like that.'

'He'll get over it.'

Then another thought occurred to her. 'You don't think Lebrun or Saunière had anything to with this, do you?'

'I don't know. It'll bear investigation.'

'Has security been increased around Prince William?'

'It has.' His lips quirked. 'What concerns me much more is your security. I seem to be doing a damned poor job of keeping you out of harm's way.'

'I will be more careful in future. That poor young woman; she didn't deserve to meet such an end.'

'No, she didn't. I'm not surprised it should have upset you so badly. It was enough to sicken anyone.'

'It did upset me,' she replied, 'but that's not why I was sick—or not entirely.'

His brow creased a little. 'You were feeling ill before? My dearest girl, you should have told me.'

'It's not an illness, Anthony.' She took a deep breath. 'I...I'm with child.'

For the space of a few heartbeats he was rooted to the spot. Then astonishment was replaced by a slow smile.

'Good Lord! That's marvellous.'

'Is it?'

'Of course it is. It's the most amazing thing I ever heard.'

Her throat tightened. 'I wasn't sure if you wanted...I mean, fatherhood doesn't suit all men, does it?'

He surveyed her steadily. 'By that you mean my late father.'

'And mine.'

'They were the losers by it.' His hold tightened on her hands. 'Besides, I don't share their views.'

'You don't?'

'By no means. I promise you that our children will not be treated as we were. Quite apart from anything else they will be loved.'

Relief brought tears to her eyes. 'I am glad of it. If anything should happen to me...'

'Darling, nothing is going to happen to you. I mean to keep you safe.'

'You cannot.'

'I beg your pardon?'

''Tis I must bear this baby, not you. But if I die you will care for it, won't you?'

'You're not going to die, my sweet. Why should you think so?'

Claudia burst into tears. Horrified and bemused, he was at a total loss for a moment or two. Then, from the back of his mind, echoes of a former conversation returned: *Husbands expect their wives to bear children...it's the most dangerous thing a woman can do.* With that came sudden insight.

'Darling, you're not frightened?'

Claudia vouchsafed no answer but the tears flowed faster. He sighed and put his arms round her, holding her close. Wisely, he made attempt to stop the flow but let the emotion pour out. Then, when the sobs began to abate a little, he sat her down on the couch beside him and handed her a handkerchief.

'Dry your eyes and blow your nose like a good girl.' When she had obeyed he nodded. 'Now, tell me.'

Slowly and somewhat disjointedly she told him about the conversation with Mrs Failsworth. He listened with mounting incredulity and anger, and suddenly a lot of things became appallingly clear. He could cheerfully have shot the governess. To frighten a young girl in that way was both cruel and stupid. It had also done untold damage and he wondered if he was going to be able to undo it.

'Claudia, you mustn't think in such a way.'

'That's easy for you to say.'

'Sweetheart, such events might happen but they

are rare. We will be home soon. You will have the best medical care available. There is no reason to suppose anything other than a safe delivery and a healthy child.'

She gulped. 'Do you really think so?'

'Yes, I do think so.'

'I w..want to have a healthy child. I w..want to g..give you an heir.'

A muscle jumped in his jaw. 'This isn't about giving me an heir. This is about a child, our child. It doesn't matter whether it's a boy or a girl.'

'You wouldn't mind if it were a girl?'

'I'd be thrilled either way.'

'My father had no use for girls. Nor did yours.'

'Forget about them.' He put his arms around her and dropped a kiss on her hair. 'We're talking about us now. We'll shape our own future.'

She swallowed hard, wanting to believe it but unable to banish the spectres from her mind.

Later, when she had gone to lie down, Anthony took himself off to the Falconbridge house. Sabrina greeted him with a surprised smile.

'This is an unexpected pleasure, but I'm afraid that Robert is from home at the moment.'

'I didn't come to see Robert,' he replied.

She looked somewhat taken aback. 'Oh.'

'I need your help, Sabrina.'

'My help? How?'

'It concerns my wife.'

'Lady Claudia is not ill?'

'Not ill…with child.'

Sabrina beamed. 'Congratulations, Anthony. You must be thrilled.'

'I am. Claudia is not.'

Her smile faded a little. 'I don't quite understand.'

As he summarised the essential parts of the earlier conversation, she listened in shocked disbelief.

'Her governess told her that?'

'Yes.'

'Good heavens! The woman should have been shot.'

'My sentiments exactly. However, the damage has been done now and I don't know how best to deal with it. I've tried to reassure Claudia but, coming from a man, the words must sound hollow.'

'Would you like me to talk to her?'

'Would you?'

'Of course I will, if you think it would help.'

'I think it might.'

'We've arranged to have tea together the day after tomorrow. We can talk then.'

'Thank you, Sabrina. I can't tell you how much I appreciate this. In truth I didn't know where else to turn.'

She laid a hand lightly on his sleeve. 'Don't worry. It will all be well. You'll see.'

He took a deep breath, hoping against hope that it might be true.

* * *

When Claudia arrived at her friends' house two days later it was to find Sabrina in the garden. She greeted her visitor with a smile.

'It's such a glorious afternoon it seems a shame to waste it indoors so I thought we could have our tea out here.'

'A very good idea.'

A table had been laid in the shade of an old apple tree. A little further off a small child was sitting on a rug playing with a toy horse, under the watchful eye of his nurse. Claudia smiled.

'What a lovely little boy.'

'You mightn't think so if you could see some of the things he gets up to,' replied Sabrina.

'Colonel Falconbridge must be a very proud father.'

'Yes, he is. When John was born you'd have thought there had never been a baby in the world before. Robert was positively foolish. He spends all the time he can with the child. In fact he spoils the pair of us.'

Her happiness was almost palpable, and while Claudia was glad for her, she was also envious. That she might one day have such a relationship with her own husband seemed a distant dream. She hadn't realised till then how much she wanted it. Unwilling to go further down that road, she kept her attention on the child.

'John looks so much like his father.'

Sabrina grinned. 'Oh, he's Robert's son in every way. A perfect little scamp.'

'But you wouldn't be without him?'

'Gracious, no. I'm hoping he'll have brothers and sisters, in time.'

'Are you?'

'Yes, I should like to have a large family.'

Claudia took a deep breath. 'I'm with child.'

'Congratulations! That's wonderful news.'

'Anthony thinks so, and I suppose it is…only I…'

Sabrina regarded her sympathetically. 'You have mixed feelings?'

'Yes.'

'That's perfectly natural.'

'Is it? I don't know. I should be pleased, and part of me is, but…'

'Another part is dreading the event too?'

'Why, yes. That's it exactly.'

Sabrina smiled gently. 'Let's sit down and have some tea. Then we'll talk.'

The visit lasted so long that Claudia only just had time to get home and change for dinner, but her spirits felt lighter. While she could not entirely rid herself of fear, Sabrina's quiet good sense had allayed it somewhat, and given her another perspective. Afterwards she had held the baby for a while and then played a little game with him. For the first time Claudia had imagined playing with her own child and found the idea strangely appealing. If only it were possible to have babies without all the business of giving birth. She sighed. Since that part was inevitable she was going to have to face it, but at least now there was someone she could talk to, someone who really understood. Anthony had been kind, but a man could never truly understand these things. While kindness was good, what she wanted even more was his love.

Dinner that evening went well enough. Feeling guilty for her earlier emotional outburst, Claudia exerted herself to be pleasant, keeping up a light flow of conversation. Anthony played his part in that, and then asked casually about her day.

'Did you enjoy your visit with Sabrina this afternoon?'

'Very much. She is such easy company.'

'I'm glad you two are friends.'

Claudia selected some grapes from the fruit bowl. 'She and Robert are to attend the Duchess of Richmond's ball next month so we shall see them there. It promises to be a great occasion.'

He smiled. 'Since it is only about two weeks away I imagine the subject of dress material came up.'

'Amongst other things. Did you know that Wellington has promised to be there?'

'So I believe.'

'The guest list contains some of the greatest

names in Europe. It will be the most sparkling event of the Season.'

'I'm sure.'

As Claudia chatted on he realised she wasn't going to be drawn on the details of her meeting with Sabrina, and also that he had no right to ask or to try and force her confidence. While she looked better than she had before, he sensed so much that was still unspoken beneath the flow of words. She was making an effort and for that very reason the former easiness between them was missing. He found himself longing for some of the light banter they used to share, or even an argument where she would challenge his views about anything from politics to music. However, he kept up his part in the conversation until the meal ended and they retired to the salon. Unable to bear the thought of more polite conversation he went across to the pianoforte.

'Will you play something for me?'

'Yes, of course. What would you like to hear?'

He riffled through the sheets of music and then drew one out, placing it on the stand while she sat down. Claudia settled herself to play, focusing on the music but aware of the man beside her to the last fibre of her being. It was a relief not to have to talk any more, to let the music do it instead.

She followed it with several more pieces so that the next hour passed agreeably enough, and the hands of the clock crept round to ten. At length she stopped and rose from the piano stool.

'That was lovely,' he said. 'You play well.'

'Not so very well. You must have heard me fudging my way through the difficult bits.'

'I heard nothing of the kind and my hearing is good.'

'You are generous.'

'Not in the least.'

He took her hand in a gentle clasp and raised it to his lips. The touch burned. How much she wished that physical attraction might lead to something much stronger, to the kind of relationship that Sabrina had with Robert. Perhaps it might happen, one day. In the meantime she must rest content with kindness. She summoned a smile.

'If you don't mind, I'm going to retire. I…I feel a little tired.'

He surveyed her in concern. 'Forgive me. I was enjoying your company so much that I have been selfish.'

'Never that, I think.'

'Who is being generous now?'

There was so much more he wanted to say but, if she was tired, now was not the right time. He escorted her to the foot of the stairs and then took her in his arms for a gentle kiss.

'Goodnight then, Claudia. Sleep well.'

'I believe I shall.'

He watched until she was out of sight and then

returned to the salon. Having poured himself a large measure of brandy from the decanter, he sipped it thoughtfully. Since in youth he had never been encouraged to divulge his feelings, he found it difficult to speak of what was in his heart. The revelation of her pregnancy filled him with unaccustomed sensations; joy, pride, anticipation and, if he were honest, nervousness too. Fatherhood was a huge responsibility and he wanted to do it well. No child of his would have the kind of upbringing that he'd endured. He also wanted to support Claudia in any way he could. He hoped that her talk with Sabrina might have done some good. Childbed was hard even when the woman was a willing participant in the event. The thought of Claudia in pain was bad enough, but frightened as well…His fingers tightened on the stem of the glass.

Chapter Twenty-One

Claudia lay awake and stared into the darkness. However, it wasn't blackness she saw but Anthony's face when he bade her goodnight. Tenderness and concern were writ large there, and yet she had not said anything to reassure him. She should have shared the gist of her conversation with Sabrina, let him know that it had helped. After all, it had taken two to make a child in the first place; did he not deserve some measure of her confidence? She sighed. It was difficult to change the habit of years. She hadn't confided openly to anyone apart from Henry. If he were here, what advice would he give?

It didn't take long for the answer to come back. Unable to leave things as they were, she climbed out of bed and padded across to the door. Opening it quietly she looked towards Anthony's room. She hadn't heard him come to bed and there was no light showing beneath the door. For several seconds she hesitated, then taking courage in both hands, walked along the corridor and knocked.

'Anthony?'

No sound issued from the room. Either he was asleep or else he didn't want to talk just then. She turned away but had scarcely gone half a dozen paces before she saw the soft glow of candlelight at the end of the passageway. Her heartbeat accelerated dangerously.

'Anthony.'

He stopped a few feet away, his expression registering momentary surprise. 'Claudia, what are you doing out here? It's late.'

She saw that he had removed his coat which was now slung casually across one shoulder. His neck cloth was undone too revealing part of his chest through the open shirt. The effect was unsettling.

'I couldn't sleep.' She took a deep breath. 'I wanted to talk to you.'

'About what, sweetheart?'

'I wanted to say that I'm sorry.'

'For what?'

'I talked to Sabrina today about babies and… well, the things that have been bothering me.'

'Why should you be sorry for that?'

'I'm not. It really helped to speak to someone who understood, and it made me feel better about everything. The reason I'm sorry is that I didn't share it with you.' She hesitated. 'I knew that you were worried and I should have said something before.'

The blue gaze never left her. 'It doesn't matter. Forget it.'

'I can't forget it. I didn't mean to shut you out, and if it hurt you I'm sorry.'

Seconds passed in which he neither moved nor spoke. She knew then that the apology was too little late and, heartsick, turned away towards her room.

'Good night then, Anthony.'

She had a swift impression of movement and then his arms were around her, pressing her gently to his breast. She shut her eyes and surrendered to the embrace, craving his strength and his warmth. For a little while, neither of them spoke. Then, when she thought her voice might be steady enough, she asked the question uppermost in her mind.

'Can you forgive me?'

'There's nothing to forgive, and if your talk with Sabrina has helped then I'm glad of it.' He looked into her face. 'I never want you to be afraid.'

'I think if you are with me that I won't be.'

'I'll always be with you, darling. Never doubt it.'

With that he bent and scooped her up, carrying her back into the bedroom. He put her back into bed and drew the covers over her. Then he undressed. She felt the mattress shift beneath his weight and his body, lean and hard, against hers, a solid and reassuring presence.

'There's no reason to be afraid, Claudia. Whatever comes, we'll face it together.' He smoothed the hair off her cheek. 'In the meantime, it's late and you need some rest.'

'Anthony, I don't mind…if you want…'

'Hush. It's all right. Go to sleep, darling.'

He felt her turn on her side and moved with her, curling his body protectively round hers. Gradually he felt her relax, felt her snuggle closer with a little sigh of contentment and then, eventually, the slow steady rhythm of her breathing. He kissed her shoulder and closed his eyes. Then, at length, he slept too.

The Duchess of Richmond's ball was one of the great events of the Season and the ballroom in the Rue de la Blanchisserie was crowded. As Claudia had predicted, everyone of note was there. She cast an eye over the assembled throng of handsome young men and pretty girls whose soft pastel dresses were a gentle contrast with the brilliant array of military uniforms, resplendent with gold lace and a multitude of orders and honours.

Not content with having so exalted a guest list, their hostess had also arranged for some of the sergeants and men of the Gordon Highlanders to dance reels and strathspeys to their own pipe music. The spectacle drew a considerable crowd. Like her neighbours, Claudia was riveted.

'It's a stirring sight, isn't it?' said Lady Anne. 'There's something about the sight of handsome men in highland dress that sets the heart to beating a little faster.'

'Yes, you're right. They look magnificent.' Claudia replied, thinking that these men also exuded an aura of hidden danger, as though the warrior was never completely concealed by the elegant costume he wore.

'Did you know that Wellington had intended to hold a ball on the 15th as well?' Lady Anne continued. 'Only the Duchess sent off her invitations first.'

Claudia grinned. 'He cannot have been too offended since he has promised to be here.'

'They are old friends and he took it in good part. He said it was his own fault for allowing her to steal a march on him.'

'She should feel very proud. It's not often that anyone manages to do that.'

'No, indeed.'

'Is the Duke here yet?' asked Claudia.

'No, he is not expected until later.'

'I should so like to have the honour of meeting him, but I don't suppose I shall. There will be a hundred others wanting to monopolise his attention.'

Her friend sighed. 'Yes, I fear there will. There have been so many rumours flying about that people will want the facts from him now.'

As the Gordon Highlanders finished the guests drifted back through the anteroom to the ballroom.

Originally it had been a coach house though no trace of that was evident now. Once plain walls were adorned with paper in a rose-trellis pattern, and banks of flowers filled the air with their scent, mingling with beeswax from hundreds of candles. The heat was considerable so the windows had been opened down the side of the room. The orchestra struck up a waltz.

'I believe this dance is mine,' said a voice at her shoulder.

The sound of that voice thrilled through her and she turned to see Anthony there. She smiled up at him and wordlessly placed her fingers in his. And then his arms were around her and she gave herself up to the music and the moment, freeing her mind of everything except the two of them.

'You look rapt in thought,' he observed with a smile. 'Dare I hope that any of those were about me?'

'Fishing for compliments again, Anthony?'

He laughed. 'I should know better by now, shouldn't I?'

'Indeed.'

Her expression just then was so reminiscent of the old Claudia that it gladdened his heart.

'Am I to take it that they were not about me then?' he asked.

'By no means, but you cannot expect me to tell you what they were.'

'If I had you alone I should find out soon enough.'

'Oh? And how would you go about that?'

'You do not imagine that I am about to divulge my methods?'

Her lips quivered. 'No, perhaps it is best you do not.'

He realised how much he had missed this over the last few days; not only her smile and the mischievous gleam in her eyes, but also the light flirtatious banter that hinted at so much more. What he felt wasn't just about physical attraction, but something far deeper and far more powerful, something he had been too afraid to admit to himself even though, with hindsight, it had been there since Paris.

When the dance ended he kept her with him for two more, ignoring the reproving looks that came their way. Claudia regarded him with mock severity.

'I warned you before about this sort of behaviour.'

'What sort of behaviour?'

'You have already danced with me three times in succession.'

'It's about to become four,' he replied. 'I've missed too many dances with you. I'm making up for lost time.'

Claudia shook her head but forbore to argue. In the first place it was a waste of breath and in the second any other partner would have been a flat disappointment after being with him.

* * *

It was gone midnight when the Duke arrived. His entrance caused a ripple of excitement that spread through the room, drawing all eyes his way. Claudia was no exception. She surveyed him with frank curiosity. Though he wasn't a particularly tall man, he had a presence that was at once commanding and a little intimidating, and he carried himself with the cool assurance of a born leader. He wasn't handsome but the aquiline nose and piercing blue eyes lent his face distinction. Once seen it was never forgotten.

'I can see why men would follow him,' she observed, as a small crowd gathered about the Duke.

Anthony nodded. 'He inspires that kind of trust, if not liking. Our allies respect him too.'

'How could they not? His reputation goes before him. Follow Wellington and men know they march onto the pages of history.'

He laughed. 'I'm sure the Duke would be delighted by such a sentiment.'

'Everyone is delighted with him. The room is positively buzzing with excitement.'

Claudia looked around her at the knots of people whose animated expressions and lively conversation proclaimed the accuracy of the statement. Even the liveried servants went about their tasks with heads held higher and smiles on their faces.

Thus it was the very stillness of the figure by the far wall that attracted her attention. His livery identified him as a servant, though at present he carried no tray. Her gaze took in a stocky frame of average height, and short brown hair, the same shade as the neatly trimmed beard and moustache. For some reason he looked familiar, though she couldn't place him. She frowned, trying to remember. Like everyone else, the man was looking at the Duke, but unlike them he wasn't smiling. Something about that intent stare caused the first stirring of unease. As she watched him, a snatch of earlier conversation came to mind: *...él....iminir... no, wait. The last vowel is an e...hastily written...* Her heartbeat quickened. *Eliminate Willi...*Suddenly, and with awful clarity, she understood.

'Dear God,' she murmured. 'It wasn't an *i* it was an *e*...'

Across the room the man reached into the left side of his coat as though to touch something there, or reassure himself of its presence. Then he began to walk towards the group surrounding the Duke. With pounding heart Claudia began to push her way through the throng to intercept the advancing figure. She had no idea what she was going to do only that she had to stop him somehow.

The Earl looked round and then stared at his wife's retreating figure in silent bemusement. Then he followed the line of retreat and saw the liveried figure ahead. Just for a moment the man looked over his shoulder. Anthony frowned, experiencing a vague sense of recognition. As he watched, the man disappeared from view into the anteroom and shortly afterwards, Claudia reached the door. Then she disappeared from view as well. Curiosity gave way to a sudden sense of unease. He had no clear idea why, only gut instinct. His expression became intent as he began to move after them.

Claudia never took her eyes off her quarry. Then, as though sensing himself observed, he paused and darted a swift look around. As he did so his gaze met hers for a moment and with a jarring sense of shock she knew who he was. The hair was a different colour and he had grown the beard, but it was the same man. The implications hit her like a punch in the stomach. She had no time for reflection because in the same instant he recognised her too and turning abruptly, retraced his steps. With pounding heart Claudia hurried after him, threading her way through the other guests who continued to laugh and talk unawares. Her quarry slipped out of the ballroom and into the anteroom that joined it to the main house. For a moment she lost him among the guests gathered there, craning her neck to see over uniformed shoulders. Then she spotted the figure again, turning aside through an open doorway into one of the downstairs rooms at the far end of the passageway.

Claudia made her way through the groups of people in the anteroom and entered the main house, reaching the corridor a few moments later. It was quiet here and the sound of voices faded as she reached the room in question. The door was open and the room beyond dimly lit. It was also unnaturally quiet after the noise of the ballroom. Glancing through the crack between the door and the jamb she took in a book case, cabinet, couch, and several chairs. It appeared to be a small sitting room. It also appeared to be empty. She hesitated. Had she mistaken the door after all? Tiptoeing across the threshold she stopped and looked around. Then her gaze fell on the open casement opposite and she swore under her breath.

She ran to the window and looked out, left and right, but the small side street beyond was deserted. She sighed. Behind her the door closed softly and all the hairs prickled on the back of her neck. She spun round to find herself staring down the barrel of a pistol. Her startled gaze moved past the weapon to the man who held it.

'Alain Poiret. I knew I was right.'

'I was really hoping we wouldn't meet again, Claudine. As it is, I'm going to have to make this short.'

'Shoot me and your plot dies as well. You'll have every man on the premises after your blood.'

'I don't intend to shoot you,' he replied.

In heart-pounding silence she saw him pocket the pistol. Instinctively she edged sideways, hoping to dart past him and reach the door. He followed the movement. Claudia turned to flee but not quite fast enough. He launched himself after her and seized hold of her, flinging her sideways across a couch. Half crushed by his weight and fighting for breath, she clawed at his face, raking her nails down his cheek. He swore and hit her. Her cheek burned like fire. Then a large hand closed round her throat and squeezed. Claudia tried to scream but all that emerged was a faint croaking sound. Scrabbling fingers tried to pry his hand loose but they made no impression. Her face suffused with blood. Sparks of coloured light danced before her eyes and her eyes widened in silent horror as she fought unsuccessfully to draw breath. She knew that was going to die.

From somewhere behind them the door was flung open and light from the corridor slashed across the room. The Earl took in the scene at a glance and then rage became incandescent. He strode in. Poiret looked round just too late to avoid the kick aimed at his ribs. It landed hard, eliciting a painful grunt and throwing him off balance. His hold slackened. A second kick forced him to let go. Seconds later a large hand hauled him upright and a clenched fist hit him in the face, flinging him backwards. He slammed into the wall, blood pouring from his nose and lip. Claudia gasped and rolled aside, heart pounding, drawing ragged gulps of air. Groggily, Poiret shook his head and then launched himself at his assailant. The two men flew backwards, reducing a chair to firewood as they crashed to the floor. Claudia scrambled to her feet and leapt out of the way.

Anthony grunted as Poiret landed on top of him. Moments later large hands closed on his throat. Half throttled, he groped for Poiret's face, and found it, gouging for the eyes. His opponent's grip slackened and he rolled aside, grabbing a broken chair leg. Coming up on his knees he swung it hard. Anthony blocked it with his arm, then threw himself sideways as Poiret thrust the jagged splintered wood towards his face. The other man came after him, landing a blow across his back. Anthony swore, grabbed the nearest piece of wood and flung it. It missed, but distracted his opponent long enough to let the Earl find his feet. He seized hold of the chair leg and wrested it from Poiret's grasp; then hit him with it. As his opponent staggered Anthony's foot connected with his groin. Poiret cried out and doubled over, sinking to his knees. As he went down Anthony hit him again. His opponent slumped and lay still.

Claudia staggered across the room and was caught in a strong pair of arms. He held her close, feeling the shuddering sobs that shook her entire body.

'My darling girl. I thought I had lost you.'

She shook her head, for the moment unable to speak.

'How badly has he hurt you?'

Drawing another ragged breath she tried again. 'M..my throat h..hurts a bit.'

'Oh, my love.' He drew back a little to examine the livid marks there and his brows drew together. 'I wish I'd killed the scum.'

She blinked. 'C..could you repeat that p..please?'

'I wished I'd killed...'

'N..not that p..part. The b..bit before it.'

His gaze met hers. 'My love.'

'Yes. It's j..just you n..never s..said it before, you s..see.'

Suddenly he did see, all too clearly. 'I should have. I should have told you often. If I hadn't been such a damned fool I would have. I love you, Claudia.'

Her aching throat was accompanied by a sudden sensation of giddiness that had nothing to do with the recent assault. 'I'm g..glad you do, b..because I l..love you very m..much.'

He enfolded her in his arms and held her until she stopped shaking. Relief mingled with terror at the thought of what he had almost lost.

'Darling, why didn't you tell me you'd recognised him?'

'There was no time. When I realised the truth he was already on his way across the room to kill the Duke. I had to intercept him somehow.'

'To kill the Duke?'

'Yes. We were wrong about the words on that scrap of paper. Something you said came back to me. The name wasn't William. The first vowel was not an *i*, it was a badly-written *e*. Not *Willi* at all, but the first part of Wellington. I didn't realise it until I saw who Poiret was looking at tonight.'

'Dear God. If he had succeeded it would have thrown the Allied forces into total disarray, to say nothing of the demoralising effect of such a deed. We have some good men but none of them compare to Old Hookey for military strategy.'

'I believe so.'

'My love, you have averted a disaster.'

'I'm glad.'

Poiret let out a groan and stirred a little. The Earl eyed him with contempt. 'So help me I'm mighty tempted to mete out the same punishment that the brute gave you.'

'No, let the law deal with him.'

He nodded. 'I'd best tie him up then before he comes round.'

He left her long enough to grab the curtain cords and use them to bind Poiret's hands and feet. Claudia surveyed the process quietly.

'There's a pistol in his pocket, Anthony.'

He retrieved it and checked for other weapons. Having done that, the Earl straightened and then reordered his own dishevelled clothing as best he could.

'I need to find Viaud and let him know what's happened. Can you stay here and guard Poiret till I get back? I'll be as quick as I can.'

She nodded. 'All right.'

'My brave girl.' He kissed her gently on the cheek and then handed her the pistol. 'If he tries anything, Claudia, shoot to kill.'

He left her then and she sank wearily into a chair, trembling with reaction now, scarcely able to believe yet that the whole episode hadn't ended in disaster. Had it not been for Anthony she'd be dead now. The knowledge sent a shiver down her back.

Poiret groaned and then opened his eyes. He tried unsuccessfully to move his arms and legs and then realising they were bound, muttered a curse. Lifting his head a little he looked around and then his gaze met Claudia's. For a second or two neither one spoke. However, in spite of her loathing for the man, there were things she wanted to know.

'Why did you kill Madeleine?'

For a moment he remained silent and she thought he wasn't going to answer. Then he said, 'By sheer ill chance she saw me in the street and recognised me. I couldn't risk letting her tell anyone.'

'I see.' She regarded him with disgust. 'And what about the whole charade in Paris?'

'My superiors needed me to disappear and the best way was to make it look as though I'd been arrested. It was also an ideal opportunity to smash the British spy ring.'

'But you tipped off Duval. Why?'

'To add to my credibility. It looked better if I helped one or two to escape.'

'Why me?'

'I always had a soft spot for you, Claudine.'

'Is that why you tried to kill me just now? Why you've tried twice before?'

'Regrettably, it was necessary. Nothing personal, you understand.'

'Oh, I understand all right. Everyone else was expendable too, weren't they?'

'That's the way it is in this business.' He smiled faintly. 'Once everyone believed I was dead it meant I could be reincarnated for a far more important mission.'

'The dyed hair and beard had me fooled for a little while.'

'If you hadn't been here tonight I might have succeeded.'

'You'd never have got out in one piece.'

'Perhaps not, but Wellington would have been dead.'

'Wellington isn't dead though, and soon he's going to put paid to Napoleon's ambitions once and for all.'

He grinned. 'We'll soon see, won't we?'

A few minutes later Anthony returned. Viaud was with him, along with two others whom she did not know. He looked at Claudia, taking in her rumpled dress and disordered curls and the livid marks on her neck.

'Good heavens. Are you all right, my lady?'

'Yes, just about.'

'What on earth happened?'

Anthony summarised, then looked at Poiret. 'We need to get him out of here as discreetly as possible. We don't need a panic on our hands. The fewer people who know about this the better.'

Viaud nodded. 'We'll take him out the back way.' He looked at his companions. 'Junot, go and arrange to have a carriage brought down the side street here, and do it as unobtrusively as possible.' As the man departed to do his bidding, Viaud glanced at Poiret. 'It'll be interesting to discover what this swine knows.'

'He may decide not to talk,' said Claudia.

Viaud's smile was cold. 'Oh, he'll talk, my lady. I guarantee it.'

Poiret surveyed her keenly. 'Who are you, Claudine? Why does he address you in that way?'

'That need not concern you,' she replied. 'Nothing personal, of course.'

After the carriage arrived to take Poiret away, Anthony took his wife in his arms again. 'Come on, we'll say goodnight to our hosts and then I'm taking you home.'

She nodded. 'I'd better do something about my appearance first or we really will become the subject of scandal.'

He grinned. 'I fear you're right.'

She straightened her gown and he helped her

brush off the dust. Then with his help she re-pinned her hair as best she could. There was nothing to be done about the marks on her neck but it couldn't be helped.

'Ready to face the world, my love?' he asked.

'As ready as I'll ever be.'

He offered her his arm and then they walked together along the corridor towards the anteroom. Long before they reached it a babble of voices greeted them. A surge of people poured from the ballroom doorway. On the stairs and in the hallway, a crowd had gathered, seemingly to take their leave.

Claudia stared at them in astonishment. 'Surely the ball cannot already be over.'

Anthony waylaid a captain of dragoons. 'What's happening here?'

'Why, have you not heard? Napoleon has crossed the frontier. Every officer is to report for duty by three this morning.' He made them a polite bow. 'If you'll excuse me I must go.'

They watched him walk away.

'It has come then,' said Claudia.

As the officers prepared to depart the air became charged with tension and excitement. There were handshakes and swift smiling farewells. The mothers and wives and sweethearts to whom they spoke smiled too, at first, but then the polite society masks began to slip and reveal the fear beneath. As she watched the men go, Claudia knew it was the last she would see of some of them. Anthony met her gaze with perfect understanding.

'Come, my sweet. Let's go home.'

Claudia went upstairs to retrieve her wrap, hardly aware of the chaos around her. She knew that she wouldn't sleep this night; that most of the city wouldn't sleep. The coming battle would be on a scale she could scarcely comprehend. The Allies had their Duke, thank goodness. He would not let the French prevail. For a moment she heard Poiret's voice. *We'll soon see, won't we?* It was estimated that Napoleon would field over a hundred thousand men. The Coalition forces numbered almost as many. The number of casualties would be huge. How many of these dynamic young officers would be among their number? Determinedly she put the thought aside.

Having found her wrap she returned to find Anthony with Robert and Sabrina. As the other woman's gaze met hers Claudia read in it both courage and dread. Her heart went out to her.

'Sabrina, won't you come and stay with us tonight? Your company would be more than welcome.'

'No, I thank you. Not tonight. However, I'll see you tomorrow.'

'As you will.'

Falconbridge smiled and held out his hand. Anthony shook it warmly.

'Good luck, Robert.'

Claudia gave her friend a quick hug and murmured, 'You know where I am if you change your mind.'

Sabrina squeezed her gently in acknowledgement. Robert turned to Claudia.

'Look after Sabrina and my son while I'm gone.'

She summoned a brittle smile. 'I will.'

The Colonel laid a hand lightly on his wife's arm. 'Come then, my dear.'

Together they walked away. Claudia watched them go, wondering if she would ever see them together again.

She and Anthony made their way to the hall, now a hub of activity as carriages were called for and people hastily took their leave of each other. The normally quiet street was thronged with vehicles and the air reverberating to the clatter of hoofs and rumbling wheels and the din of many voices. It took a while for the carriage to thread its way through the traffic. Neither she nor Anthony spoke, each rapt in private thought.

By the time they reached the house they could hear the distant sound of bugles and drums announcing the gathering of regiments. They stood together on the balcony looking down on the scene below, watching the troops march by, a seemingly endless line of men heading towards the Namur Gate. Above the rooftops the first grey light of dawn began to dissipate the darkness.

They watched until the last regiment had left. By then it was close on eight o'clock and the now quiet street bathed in early sunshine. The Earl turned towards his wife.

'There will not be any news for a while, my dear. Let's try to snatch a few hours of sleep.'

Claudia nodded, recognising the good sense of this. She was weary now, although her thoughts were still in chaos. Somehow she was going to have to try and empty her mind for a while. When news did arrive she wanted to be alert enough to assimilate it.

When she woke it was midday and Lucy informed her that the Earl was already gone out. He returned an hour later. Claudia hurried to meet him. He bent to kiss her and they retired to the salon.

'What news?' she asked.

'Ney's force is advancing on Quatre Bras.'

'Quatre Bras? Isn't that being held by Dutch troops?'

'Yes, but there aren't enough of them. If they are to hold the crossroads they need reinforcements.'

'Will the Duke take personal command?'

'It looks like it. He can't allow the French to drive a wedge between his forces.'

'Sabrina told me it's a favourite tactic of theirs.'

'That's right. Divide the force, then attack one group and defeat it before moving on to rout the rest.' The Earl paused. 'Many people are already leaving Brussels. Do you wish to join them, my love?'

'Certainly not.'

He grinned. 'I rather thought you would say that.'

'How could I leave when Sabrina is still here?'

'She will not go anywhere without her husband, and if the French are foolish enough to take her on they'll regret it. She can handle a sword and pistol along with the best of them.'

'So I believe,' said Claudia.

'In the meantime, the Inspector-General of Health is ordering that tents be set up for the wounded outside the city gates. I have no doubt that he will soon be requesting equipment as well; pillows, blankets, bandages and so forth.'

'I'll look to see what spare blankets and pillows we have,' she said. 'If extra hands are required to scrape lint and roll bandages I would be glad to…' She broke off as a sound like the rumble of distant thunder rolled across the city. 'What on earth was that?'

The Earl listened intently and then, as another rumble sounded, said, 'It is the sound of a cannonade. It must be from Quatre Bras.'

They were interrupted by the sound of the doorbell. A few moments later the butler entered.

'A messenger has arrived from Headquarters, my lord. He wishes to speak with you.'

The Earl went out into the hallway. Claudia heard voices but couldn't make out the words. A few minutes later her husband returned, his face sombre.

'I've got to go out, my love.'

'Anthony, what is it? What's happened?'

'Under interrogation Alain Poiret has revealed that the French have been deliberately feeding the Coalition forces with misinformation.'

'Is it serious?'

'Potentially, yes. It seems their spies have infiltrated our courier service. Viaud has asked for me. I don't know how long I'm going to be.'

'Of course. Just be careful, that's all.'

He drew her to him for a kiss and then he was gone.

The rest of the afternoon and evening passed without any sign of him. When the clock struck eleven she reluctantly resigned herself to his absence that night. No doubt he didn't want to undertake the journey back in the dark. Forcing down her uneasiness she retired to bed.

Chapter Twenty-Two

Gradually the wagons came in bearing the wounded and soon the tents that Dr Brügmans had organised were full to overflowing. Some of the larger town houses began to take in some of the injured, Lady Harrington's among them. Rather than sit at home and worry, Claudia and Sabrina, like many other ladies, volunteered their services to help with nursing duties and take some of the pressure off the hard-pressed medical orderlies.

It was hard and dirty work but Claudia preferred it to doing nothing. In the back of her mind was the dread that Anthony might somehow end up among the wounded. As her hands bathed away dirt and blood her mind tried not to think of the implications; tried to hold on to the last image she had of him alive and well.

As the day wore on, news filtered in of a Prussian defeat at Ligny. Sabrina had the news from a courier.

'Wellington has fallen back to the escarpment

north of Quatre Bras, but his control of the cross-roads means that the Prussians have been able to fall back parallel to his line of retreat.'

'Is that good?' asked Claudia.

'Yes, because it prevents the French from driving a wedge through the Allied forces. Usually an army retreats along its supply lines. Had they done that in this instance Napoleon would have split the two forces north and south.'

'Where are the Prussians now?'

'At Wavre. General Blücher is with them. It seems he fell under his horse while leading a counter attack at Ligny, and was ridden over by the French cavalry—twice!'

Claudia's eyes widened. 'Twice and lived? The man must be indestructible.'

'He's a man whom other men will follow, that's for sure. Goodness knows we need them.'

It was the truth and they both knew it. Claudia found herself silently praying that they should come through it somehow. If only Anthony and Robert might return unscathed, then nothing else mattered.

They left Lady Harrington's house some eight hours later, both of them unutterably weary. After the stench of blood and filth the clean air was more than welcome even though the lowering clouds threatened rain. When they reached the street corner the two women embraced and then continued on their separate ways. Claudia had scarcely reached the next corner before the rain began, first in slow, fat drops and then more quickly. The drops became a shower. Fortunately it was not far to go and she ran the last hundred yards. As she reached the door the shower became a downpour. An astonished butler let her in.

'In good time, milady.'

'Is my husband back yet?'

'No, not yet.'

Her heart sank. Where on earth could he be?

The butler regarded her in concern. 'You are wet. Shall I bring you some tea, my lady?'

'Later perhaps,' she replied. 'I'll ring when I need you.'

He bowed and withdrew. She listened to the sound of his retreating footsteps. The house was very quiet. Yet, after the bustle at Lady Harrington's, the silence came as a blessed relief. This house was the place she had shared with Anthony. Every room bore a reminder of his presence and just then she needed that more than anything.

Claudia took off her damp bonnet and pelisse and went upstairs, her footsteps sounding unnaturally loud in the silence. Streaming rain muted the light from the windows and rendered it yellowish grey. Ignoring her own room she continued on along the corridor until she reached Anthony's chamber. It still bore the signs of his presence; a book on the bedside table, closets and drawers full of clothes. She caught the faint scent of cedar and her throat tightened. Carefully lifting a coat from the press she held it to her and closed her eyes. Immediately his image returned with force. The effect was to create an almost overpowering sense of loss and loneliness. She shivered a little. The air was cooler now and her own clothing slightly damp, so she put the coat around her shoulders. It swamped her, but its warmth and scent were comforting. Then she sat down on the edge of the bed. Outside the rain drummed on rooftops and bounced off the cobbles and rushed along the gutters, but, here, in this room, she was in a place apart; a place that had belonged just to the two of them. She knew now that what really mattered *was* the two of them, and the new life they had created. For too long she had let the past shadow everything; had let fear come between her and the chance of future happiness. It was all so clear now, but perhaps the knowledge had come too late. Anthony was gone and she might never see him again. The terror of that realisation rendered all other fears insignificant.

She had no idea how long she remained there, only that when she came to herself again the light was fading and it was still raining. The initial cloudburst had given way to a steady downpour. The streets were deserted and the usual sounds absent. With a sigh, Claudia took off the coat and folded it carefully before returning it to the press.

Then she left the room and closed the door behind her.

She was halfway downstairs when she heard the sound of horses' hooves and then men's voices. Checking mid-stride, she listened carefully. The voices were replaced by the sound of booted feet and then the front door opened to reveal a familiar figure. Claudia's heart turned over. Then she was flying down the stairs and across the hallway.

'Anthony!'

He seized hold of her, lifting her off the floor, kissing her hard. Claudia's arms fastened round his neck as she pressed closer for a very damp embrace and for some time speech was impossible. Then she drew back a little, looking into his face.

'Thank goodness you're back. I've been so worried.'

'No need, my love.'

'Did I not hear someone with you?'

'Matthew. He's gone to take care of the horses.'

'I'm so glad to see you. I've missed you so much.'

'And I you.'

'Are you hungry? Goodness knows what there is in the house but I'm sure that the cook can find you something.'

'That would be wonderful. It doesn't matter what it is. Food supplies are scant at the moment and most of our fellows haven't eaten. The road is littered with abandoned supply wagons. The drivers ran away when they heard we'd pulled back from Quatre Bras.'

'The wounded are still coming in,' she replied. 'Was it very bad?'

'Bad enough, but it was only the precursor to the main action. Wellington is assembling his troops near the village of Waterloo. We'll engage the French there tomorrow.'

Something about the determinedly cheerful tone struck a false note, though she could not pinpoint the reason. She paused, surveying him closely. 'You need to get out of those wet things.'

'It's filthy weather out there and no mistake. Just pity all the poor souls who are still out in it.'

Having given instructions about food and candles, Claudia accompanied him upstairs. She helped him off with his jacket and hung it on the back of a chair. He sat down to pull off his boots.

'What have you been doing in my absence?'

'Helping with the nursing mostly.'

'Mostly?'

'And missing you.'

His hand stopped in the act of unlacing his shirt front. 'And I you.'

Claudia's gaze met his. 'There's something amiss, isn't there? What is it that you're not telling me?'

He returned a wry smile. 'You know me too well.'

'But not as well as I wish to.'

'I am going to fight, Claudia.'

Suddenly it was as if all the air had been driven from her lungs and she could only stare at him.

'Ever since the ball I have been turning it over in my mind,' he went on. 'I cannot sit safe here while Robert and my other friends risk their lives tomorrow. The future of Europe hangs in the balance; perhaps the future of England too.'

Claudia paled. 'I want to say what about our future, I want to beg you not to go, but I know you have not made this decision lightly.'

'It's the hardest I have ever had to make. I love you more than my life, and the thought of leaving you is more painful by far than what happened at Vittoria. I want a future with you, but not one that has been secured in cowardly safety at the expense of others. If I do not go with them tomorrow and fight for all I hold dear, I forfeit all honour and all self-respect. How could you love such a man?'

Claudia's eyes filled with tears. 'I will love you all the days of my life, but if this decision means all that you have said, I will not try to prevent you from going, though it will be the hardest thing I have ever done.'

In another moment he was across the room and drawing her close to him. His hand stroked her hair. 'My darling girl. You have given me strength and hope; you have given me back my life. I won't throw it away. There's too much to lose.'

She didn't want to think about how much that

was. Nor did she want to be a clinging vine. He would have enough to think about now without worrying about her too.

She dashed her tears away. 'I'm sorry. I didn't mean to be so feeble.'

'That is the very last word I would use to describe you.'

'I was never so afraid in my life.'

'You are the bravest woman I have ever met, and the most independent.'

'To the devil with my independence.'

He tilted her chin towards him. 'You are a free spirit, my love, and I would not have you change for anything.'

A discreet knock on the door announced the arrival of Lucy bearing a tray of cold leftovers. She set it on the table and then turned to her mistress. 'I've taken the liberty of giving Matthew a meal in the kitchen, my lady.'

Claudia summoned a smile. 'Good girl.' Then she paused as another thought occurred to her. 'Where are the other *filles de chambres*?'

'Run off, my lady, because they heard a rumour that the French were coming. They haven't any more wit than chickens, the lot of them. There's just the cook and the butler now, and one footman.'

'We'll just have to manage.'

'That we shall, my lady. I'll fetch some candles and then get that fire lit.' With that Lucy bobbed a curtsey and was gone.

* * *

In relatively short time the room was bathed in the soft glow of candlelight and a cheerful fire burned in the hearth. Having ascertained that they had all they needed, Lucy departed, closing the door behind her. The Earl stripped off his damp shirt and towelled his hair dry. Then he sat down and attacked the cold meat and bread with enthusiasm. Claudia poured him a glass of wine.

'Will you not join me in a glass?' he asked.

'Why not?'

The ruby liquid was strong and, since she had not yet dined, its effect was to make her feel pleasantly light-headed. Her earlier tension dissipated to be replaced with a warm inner glow. He surveyed her over the rim of his glass.

'I had forgotten just how beautiful you are.'

Under the power of that gaze the warm glow intensified. She glanced ruefully at her limp muslin frock. 'If I'd known you were coming I'd have changed into something more alluring.'

'You have some alluring gowns,' he allowed, 'but you look even better without them.'

'Do I really?'

'Yes, really, as I think you know very well.'

Claudia set the glass down and rose from her chair. Then, unhurriedly, she began to unfasten the front of her gown. The Earl's expression registered increasing interest. He leaned back in his chair, stretching his long legs in front of him, watching the buttons come undone. The dress slid down off her shoulders and she drew her arms from the sleeves and let the gown fall. Stepping out of the heaped folds of fabric she bent to retrieve it, affording him an uninterrupted view of her breasts. It was greeted with a sharp intake of breath.

'You're playing with fire, Claudia,' he said softly.

She tossed the dress over a chair. 'Is that dangerous then?'

'Very.'

The petticoat followed the gown in the same leisurely manner. A minute or two later her stays joined it. Resting one foot on the chair, she lifted the hem of her chemise and unfastened her garter. The Earl's expression became intent. Slowly she rolled the stocking down a length of slender leg.

'You are now in extreme peril, my girl.'

She drew the stocking off. 'Indeed?'

'Indeed.'

Apparently unconcerned, she repeated the exercise. Without taking her eyes off him, she reached up to unpin her hair. Unruly curls tumbled across her shoulders. Finally she reached for her chemise and untied it. The sheer fabric slid down over her shoulders and kept going. He drew another sharp breath as his gaze travelled the length of her naked body and back. Claudia sauntered across to the bed and stretched out on the coverlet, propping herself on one elbow, surveying him steadily. The Earl's gaze locked with hers.

He rose from the chair and peeled off his breeches. 'You do realise that there is going to be serious retribution for the kind of provocation that you have just offered?'

Claudia's eyes widened at little. 'What manner of retribution, my lord?'

For the next two hours the Earl proceeded to show her.

It was ten o'clock before he took his leave and Claudia reluctantly bade him farewell. They said relatively little then for words were not necessary. He had shown very clearly what he felt by returning to spend a few brief hours with her, knowing it might well be the last time he would ever do so. He had been tender and considerate; he had shared his love and his passion and given her all of himself. And then he had gone out into the darkness for the long, wet ride back.

Claudia did not go to her own room that night. Instead she returned to the bed she had just shared with Anthony. It still retained the scent of him, of their love-making, and a residual trace of his warmth. Her body throbbed with it, her lips still swollen from his kisses. Her hand rested a moment on her belly. More than anything in the world she wanted to see him walk back through the door safe and sound but, if God forbid, the worst happened, something of him would remain. His line would continue. She swallowed hard and pushed the thought away. Anthony wasn't going to be killed. He was going to live. He must live. They had a future to build; a family to bring up.

Suddenly she had a vision of all the families who would be torn apart on the morrow, of mothers and sisters and wives and fiancées who would never see their menfolk again. The bleakness of such a future filled her with terror. It would be as though a part of her had died also. Drawing the covers round her, she curled up in the place where Anthony had but recently lain and then she prayed.

Chapter Twenty-Three

By morning the rain had passed leaving the air clean and fresh and smelling of damp earth and grass. Grey light filtered through the trees and across the fields of ripening crops where mist lay in the folds and hollows of the land.

At nine the Duke, mounted on the redoubtable Copenhagen, rode the two-mile length of the Allied position, checking the disposition of his troops, making final adjustments, moving a brigade here or a platoon there, pausing occasionally to survey the lie of the land through his glass. The men followed his progress as he passed.

'They may not love him,' murmured Falconbridge, as the party approached, 'but they do trust him.'

'Quite rightly,' replied the Earl. 'There isn't a more able commander alive.'

Catching sight of them, the Duke reined in. 'Ah, Colonel Falconbridge, good morning. Fine day for it, what?'

'Indeed, Your Grace.'

The Duke's piercing blue gaze came to rest on the Earl. 'Good to see you, Major Brudenell. I understand that you and your wife have lately done me a great service. I'm much obliged to you both. When occasion permits, pray convey my deepest respects to Her Ladyship.'

'I will, Your Grace, I thank you.'

'I'd give a great deal for just a dozen more of my Peninsular veterans. Fine men the lot of 'em. I'm glad to have you with me.'

'I wouldn't have missed it, Your Grace.'

'I thought Vittoria had done for you. Deuced glad I was wrong.'

'So am I, Your Grace.'

The Duke gave a short bark of laughter. 'Just see to it that you don't get your head blown off, man. I need it on your shoulders.'

The Earl saluted. 'I'll do my best, Your Grace.'

Just then a Prussian *galopin* arrived with a dispatch arrived from Wavre. Wellington opened it, scanning the contents swiftly. Then he looked at Uxbridge. 'It's from Blucher.' He read aloud, '...assure the Duke of Wellington from me, that, ill as I am, I shall place myself at the head of my troops, and attack the right of the French, in case they undertake anything against him.'

General Müffling, who was attached to Wellington's party, heard the news with satisfaction.

'If the Marshal says he and his force will be here, then you may take it as fact.'

'Just as well,' replied the Duke. 'We're going to need every man jack of them. I have an infamous army; very weak and ill-equipped, and an inexperienced Staff.'

'They will do their duty, Your Grace,' said Uxbridge.

Falconbridge looked at the Earl. 'That we shall,' he murmured.

For those left behind in Brussels the day seemed endless. Claudia and Sabrina went to Lady Harrington's house to help with the injured. This time they could not hear the sound of the guns because the wind was in the wrong quarter. The women worked in silence for the most part, tight-lipped, each trying not to think of the carnage taking place just a few miles away, carnage whose results they could see before them in the ghastly wounds they cleaned and dressed.

Claudia knew that far worse was happening in the military hospital on the outskirts of town. Some of those brought alive off the battlefield would die in agony under the surgeon's knife. Many who lived would be horribly maimed. She shivered inwardly, knowing that destitution awaited those whose missing limbs meant that they could no longer earn their living. England only valued her soldiers while they were fit enough to fight; after that they must make shift as best they could.

Her hands had become adept at changing bandages, her eye quick to distinguish between healthy and infected tissue. The smell of blood had become a given now, one that she scarcely noticed. Beneath it were other, more noisome, odours. Determinedly she ignored them, moving from one patient to the next with a smile here, a word there to try and keep her spirits up as much as theirs. She thought that, if she stopped working, the terror so firmly repressed might escape, and if it did she would go to pieces.

It was almost five o'clock before she and Sabrina took their leave. Although the scorching heat of the day had passed, the air was still very warm. Claudia could feel her gown sticking to her. Every part of her felt grubby. As soon as they got back to the house she would bathe and change.

When they got outside it was to find the streets thronged with people for many of the Bruxellois had opened their homes to the wounded. Others, with minor injuries, lay propped against the walls of the houses, and young boys and girls offered them water while their mothers hastened to fetch food and bandages. They paused briefly to ask for news from an old veteran whose arm reposed in a bloodied makeshift sling. Another blood-stained rag adorned his head. His torn and dirty uniform bore witness to the fact that he had been in the thick of the action.

'This was the hottest battle I was ever in, and I've been in a few.' He shook his head. 'The dead were piled high around La Haye Sainte and Hougoumont.'

The two women paled and exchanged glances.

'Are the Allies winning?' asked Claudia.

'That's more than I know, ma'am.'

'Do you know Major Brudenell or Colonel Falconbridge? Can you tell us anything of them?'

'I do not know the former, but I know of Colonel Falconbridge,' he replied. 'He's a fine officer by all accounts, but how he's fared today I cannot say.'

They thanked him and bade him farewell, continuing on their way. Neither one spoke, being entirely lost in private thought, and the lack of news seemed only to add to the burden of weariness. In spite of her best efforts, Claudia could not shake off the image of the dead piled high. Was Anthony among them? Was Robert?

A few more minutes brought them back to Sabrina's house. While she went to check on her child, Claudia retired to the guest room and stripped off her soiled garments. Having done that, she poured a basin full of water and washed herself down thoroughly before dressing again in the clean clothes that Lucy had brought for her. Then, feeling marginally better, she went downstairs.

She had barely reached the salon when she heard a chaise pull up outside. One glance through the window had her hurrying out to the hall. The butler opened the door to admit Matthew. The two exchanged a few hurried words. Then Matthew looked up and saw Claudia.

'It's Colonel Falconbridge, my lady. He's been injured.'

The news was like being punched in the solar plexus. With an effort, she collected herself. 'Bring him in at once.'

Leaving the two men to deal with that she hurried away to find Sabrina. Within minutes the Colonel had been carried up to bed. He was unconscious and deathly pale and presently wrapped in a cloak. His coat and shirt had been cut off and his upper torso was swathed in blood-stained bandages.

'He took a ball in the left shoulder, ma'am,' said Matthew. 'The field surgeon dug it out, but the Colonel has lost a lot of blood. There was no more room in the hospital tents and I didn't want him carted off to Lord knows where to wake among strangers, so I decided to bring him here.'

Sabrina was very pale too but she smiled at him gratefully. 'Bless you, Matthew. Can you help me get his boots off?'

Between the three of them they got the wounded man undressed and into bed. When they'd made him as comfortable as possible, Claudia looked at Matthew.

'Have you any news of my husband?'

'Yes, my lady. He was well last time I heard.'

Claudia experienced a brief surge of relief. 'When was that?'

'Mid-afternoon, my lady.' Matthew smiled faintly. 'I had it from the men who brought Colonel Falconbridge back to the field hospital. It took them a while because the action had been particularly heavy in that part of the battlefield and there were numerous casualties. When the Colonel fell, Major Brudenell went back for him even though the troop was under threat from enemy cavalry. He got him into the protection of the square while the men provided covering fire. The troop took a battering but they repulsed the French in the end. I'd been lending a hand in the hospital, and I heard the name Falconbridge when they brought him in. I thought I'd keep an eye on him.'

'Thank heaven,' murmured Sabrina. 'I am in your debt, Matthew, and in Major Brudenell's.'

She sat down by the bedside and took hold of her husband's hand. Claudia and Matthew withdrew to the corridor.

'What news of the rest of the battle?' she asked.

'A victory for the Allies, my lady. The French have been completely routed.'

'What!'

'It's true. For a while it was a close-run thing by all accounts, but then General Blücher arrived with the Prussians, and those reinforcements turned the tide of the battle against Boney. He's been forced to retreat.'

The sensation of relief intensified. 'It's over then?'

'Not quite over, my lady. They have to find Boney first.'

'I pray they do, and this time lock him up somewhere he'll never escape.'

'Trust them for that.' Matthew smiled grimly. 'Boney's just lost his last throw of the dice. They won't let him have another.'

'You must be tired and hungry,' she said. 'Why don't you go downstairs and ask the cook to give you something to eat?'

'Thank you kindly, my lady, but I have to get back. I'll not be easy until I've seen my lord alive and well.'

She managed a tremulous smile. 'I pray you may.'

After Matthew had left, Claudia returned to her friend. 'Do you want me to stay with you?'

'No, I'll sit with Robert awhile if you don't mind.'

'Of course. I won't be far if you need me.'

As the evening wore on and the light started to fade, Claudia began to experience serious misgivings. What if Anthony had survived the main action only to have been caught up in one of the final skirmishes? The thought of him lying injured somewhere, and unable to call for help, preyed on her mind. Then she told herself there could be all manner of reasons why he had not come back yet; he had his men to consider, senior officers to report to, quite apart from the long ride itself. However, that didn't stop her from rushing to the window every time she heard hoof beats on the cobbles outside. Several times she went to the door and looked out down the street.

It was just as she was about to go back indoors on the last occasion that she saw the two horsemen approaching. For a while they were too far off to make out details but as they drew closer her heart turned over. Then, regardless of all propriety, she was running down the road towards them. As they saw her coming, one of the riders dismounted and flung the reins to his companion. Then he opened his arms to the running figure and swept her off her feet in a passionate hug. Claudia's voice caught on a sob.

'Thank God. Thank God. I've been so worried.'

The Earl smiled down at her. 'No cause, my love.'

She drew back a little, her gaze scanning him. 'Are you all right? You're not hurt?'

'No, just filthy dirty and rather tired.'

'I thought I'd lost you.'

'No chance of that. I want the future we talked about.'

'So do I, more than anything, but I know how much the army means to you. If you ever wanted to…'

'The army doesn't mean a damn thing now. I've just fought in my last battle.' He drew her close. 'I have my arms around all that I want.'

'Are you quite certain?'

The answer was a long and passionate kiss that removed every last trace of doubt.

Epilogue

England: April 1816.

As the carriage turned in through the great wrought iron gates the Earl surveyed his wife steadily.

'Are you sure you want to do this, Claudia? If you've changed your mind I'll have Matthew turn the coach around right now.'

She shook her head. 'I'm quite sure. It's time to lay the ghosts of the past.'

'All the same, I know how you feel about Ulverdale.'

'Felt,' she corrected gently. 'So much has changed since then, and all for the better.'

His hand squeezed hers. 'I have never been as happy in my life as I am now, but I don't ever want you to be unhappy for my sake. This place…'

'The place is not to blame,' she replied. 'You told me that once, and you were right. It is people who cause unhappiness, and those who were responsible for so much of it are gone. It's up to us now, Anthony. We have a chance to create something better.'

'I want that too.'

'Besides, Ulverdale is your ancestral home. Your roots are here.'

'Yes, I suppose they are,' he said, 'although I tried to deny it for long enough.'

'You cannot deny who you are; none of us can, or not for very long.'

'You're right, of course, although it took eight years of warfare and madness to make me realise it.'

'We have been so very lucky. There are thousands and thousands who will never have this chance.'

'I know, and I can never be complacent about that.'

'No-one could who lived through Waterloo,' she replied. 'I know that Sabrina and Robert feel the same.'

'Their last letter said he was fit again. We must invite them to come and visit.'

'I'd like that very much. I have missed them both.'

'So have I.' He hesitated. 'I used to envy them their happy marriage. Now there is no need; we've found what they have.'

She smiled wryly. 'It took us long enough, didn't it?'

'Too long. I don't want to waste another second of our married lives.'

* * *

A few minutes later the carriage, followed by a chaise, drew to a halt at the foot of the steps that led to the great front doors. As the Earl helped her to alight, Claudia glanced at the imposing, grey stone frontage of the mansion and the light reflecting from a thousand leaded panes in the mullioned windows. She had not known quite how she would feel on seeing it again, but, oddly, the old resentment was conspicuous by its absence. It was just a house. All the negative associations it had once held had faded to a distant echo.

The Earl looked at her in quiet concern. 'Ready?'

She smiled at him. 'Ready.'

Together they went in to the hall, followed by the occupants of the chaise. The Dowager Countess was standing at the foot of the stairs, a slender, regal figure whose expression registered both hope and fear. For a moment none of them spoke. Claudia surveyed the other woman steadily but now with understanding and compassion. Married to a selfish brute and estranged from her son, she had known her share of bitterness too. It was time to change that.

Then Anthony stepped forward. 'Mamma.'

She saluted him warmly and then looked over his shoulder to where Claudia was standing. The older woman smiled tremulously.

'Claudia, I am so very pleased to see you.'

'And I to see you, ma'am.' She came forward and

took the outstretched hands in her own, squeezing them gently. 'It has been a long time, has it not?'

'Too long.' The Dowager Countess' eyes met hers. 'Welcome home, my dear.'

'We thought you might like to meet your grandson,' said Anthony. He took the child from the nurse who had accompanied them, and brought him closer. 'This is Henry.'

The older woman took him carefully and smiled through tears. 'He's beautiful, and he looks just like you.'

Anthony grinned. 'Yes, but I'm hoping he'll take after his mother in everything else.'

When her visitors had taken some refreshment and talked awhile, the Dowager Countess left them to themselves until dinnertime.

'We will have plenty of time to talk later,' she said. 'At the moment you must be tired after your journey. Perhaps you might like to rest, or to get some fresh air after being shut up so long in a carriage.'

The latter suggestion was readily accepted.

For a while they strolled in companionable silence, enjoying each other's company and the warm spring sunshine. Newly-opened daffodils filled the air with their scent. Claudia breathed it contentedly, her gaze taking in the colourful beds and green lawns stretching away towards the lake and the wood.

'I had forgotten how beautiful it is,' she said.

'And I.' He sighed. 'But, you were right; it is a part of me.'

'Ulverdale doesn't release its hold easily, does it?'

'No. Perhaps it wants a future too.'

'Well, now it has its wish. I want our son to grow up knowing his ancestral home. Besides, this place needs children.'

For a moment he wasn't sure he'd heard correctly. 'Children?'

'I'd rather our son wasn't alone, you see.' She paused. 'I was hoping you might help me there.'

'You may take it as read but...well, are you sure, Claudia? I mean, after Henry's birth you might not want...'

'I'm not going to pretend I wasn't afraid, but he is worth every bit of the effort it took to bring him into the world.'

'You weren't the only one who was afraid,' he replied. 'It was the longest night of my life.'

'But we came through it.'

'What you did was the bravest thing I've ever known anyone do.'

'I won't be afraid next time.'

He took her gently by the shoulders. 'You're absolutely sure it's what you want?'

'I was never more certain of anything.'

'You may be certain of my love for you.' He drew her closer. 'It's only fair to warn you that you're about to be kissed, and that it's likely to go on for some time.'

Claudia's eyes sparkled. 'Do I have any say in the matter?'

'No,' he replied. 'None at all.'

* * * * *

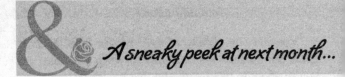

011

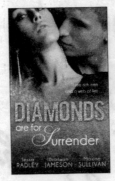
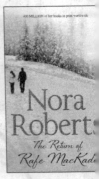

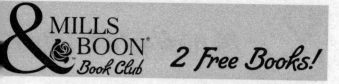

The World of Mills & Boon®

There's a Mills & Boon® series that's perfect for you. We publish ten series and, with new titles every month, you never have to wait long for your favourite to come along.

Blaze.
Scorching hot, sexy reads
4 new stories every month

By Request
Relive the romance with the best of the best
9 new stories every month

Cherish™
Romance to melt the heart every time
12 new stories every month

Desire™
Passionate and dramatic love stories
8 new stories every month

∫A℞